THE BIG REVEAL

The Big Reveal

JEN LARSEN

HENRY HOLT AND COMPANY
NEW YORK

Henry Holt and Company, *Publishers since 1866*
Henry Holt® is a registered trademark of Macmillan Publishing Group, LLC
120 Broadway, New York, NY 10271 • fiercereads.com

Our books may be purchased in bulk for promotional, educational,
or business use. Please contact your local bookseller or the Macmillan Corporate
and Premium Sales Department at (800) 221-7945 ext. 5442 or by email at
MacmillanSpecialMarkets@macmillan.com.

Library of Congress Control Number: 2021906547

First edition, 2021 / Designed by Liz Dresner
Printed in the United States of America

ISBN 978-1-250-25217-3

10 9 8 7 6 5 4 3 2 1

For Meagan, my eye in the hurricane,

and

all the beautiful fat girls and femmes
who shape the world to fit them

1

The street is dark, and the sidewalk is ice, and the headline of my obituary is going to read "Dancer's Bright Future Cut Short by Frostbitten Butt, Embarrassment."

But I keep slip-sliding along, hood up and shoulders hunched inside my raggedy parka, because I'm so close now. So close to warmth and friends, the two-story brick house glowing like an ember in front of me, the faint thump of bass already reaching my frozen ears.

And when the front door blows out of my iced-over fingers on the downbeat, music and warm light pouring into the cold and sweeping around me, it's like coming alive. The bass is so much louder than all the half excuses in my head—too wiped from rehearsing, too tired to see Gavin, too worried about Monday and what it means for my entire future—

I let the anxiety rush out of me in a gust of breath. I'm already grinning as I step inside.

"Oh my gosh! Addie!" Katherine screams, appearing in the crowded entryway like magic to fling her arms around me, squeezing all the bulk of my coat, knocking my hood back and dragging me into the house in a flurry of love and long limbs, flushed-pink skin, blond ponytail. "You made it!"

"I didn't die from frostbite!" I shout, delighted and maybe a little surprised, as always. I've still got the Florida-girl constitution, despite three and a half years of boarding school in the frozen wasteland of Michigan.

She grabs my hand and we plunge into the crowd, the house packed, voices and hip-hop music echoing off the high ceilings. "I *told* them you would make it!" she yells back over her shoulder.

Katherine is happiness and cotton candy spiked with righteous anger, hugs and warm sweaters, a finely tuned sense of justice, a piece of pure sunshine that's sometimes blinding. She knows me, knows that as much as I like to spend every second I can snatch in the studio, even if it means skipping homework (maybe especially if it means skipping homework), I can't resist the call of this dance floor when day-student Shannon and her older sister throw a party.

Katherine whirls down the hallway, towing me through the crowd of warm, half-naked bodies. I'm leaving wet footprints and I want to protest, but I am swept up and swept along, the energy in the house enough to blast out the walls. Lakeshore Academy is one of the toughest prep schools in the US. Our arts program is a feeder for Juilliard, RISD, Tisch—all the top arts colleges— and the academic-track kids end up at Ivies and similar. After an endless school week of classwork and homework and rehearsal and then more rehearsal and, hey, maybe more rehearsal, even those of us who can handle the pressure need places to explode.

We're slipping around the flailing limbs of theater kids and gliding past the sudden smiles and shouts of glee when I'm spotted. Pausing to hug Halim, my partner in last semester's pas de deux, I accept quick kisses on my icy-cold cheeks from the girls in ensemble and that cute girl Grace I bonded with in repertory (the only other full-scholarship arts kid at Lakeshore, as far as I know). My freshmen girls, the clever, quick, intense dancers I mentor, squeal my name as I pass, and I'm waving at them and blowing kisses as Katherine tugs me on, and we dance through the great room and the kitchen and into the den, where the hard-core dancing happens with the chairs pushed against the walls, and the music floods the room, crashes into your chest, and sinks under your skin until you can't tell the difference between the beat and your body. The feeling is good in rehearsal, and the best onstage. But when it's all yours and you can do anything you want with it, that's when the adrenaline fizzes like champagne.

My hips are already moving, and the urge is building to strip off all my winter gear and just *dance*, no choreography, no counting time, just my body pounding with the boom of the bass and everything falling into place.

I go up on my toes, searching the den for Nevaeh and Taylor. The chandelier overhead is dimmed all the way down, the dark wood paneling on the walls gleaming and the crowd a great pulsing mass of joy. Everyone's in dancewear or less, which always feels defiant—students aren't allowed to show up at academic classes with bare shoulders or collarbones or scandalous leggings—too distracting, we're told. Spaghetti straps once got me sent back to my room to change, feeling vaguely ashamed and angry, the way everyone turned to stare at me. Saturday detention because of my shoulders, as if girls' bodies are against the rules and our skin is a sex crime, and cracking down on that is more important than our actual education. (And no one ever mentions that our performance costumes show *way* more than shoulders.)

But we're free of that, all of us together here. The room is swaying, hopping, spinning, twirling, all of us hot and alive, and no one's caring if our skin is distracting or if our behavior is appropriate. And is it possible to smile even harder than this? Because there are my sweethearts, Nevaeh and Taylor.

Nevaeh—she's serenity, ribbon-curling grace, heartbreaking precision, Instagram eyebrows, volcano heart. She's your nuclear safe house. She has tampons. And she's vulnerable, sentimental. Tenderhearted, if she loves you, if she trusts you. Now she's glowing, a sheen of sweat and sparkle on her dark shoulders and neck and cheekbones, glittering lips, a mass of tiny braids threaded with gold and blue wrapped up like a bow on her head. She's spinning pale, freckled, blushing Zoe, my first-year mentee who has a crush on her, in swooping circles.

Taylor is close to the center of the floor, surrounded by his usual selection of swooners and admirers.

He's take-no-bullshit, take-no-prisoners, leave-no-heart-unturned, rule-the-world. Popping out to crush your enemies and steal their significant others, no big. Weight lifting, red lipstick, outrageous flirting, and burning across the stage. First-generation Korean American, a dancer like his mom was. Making me laugh always and right now when he gleams at me.

And then I glance behind him, and my own smile teeters right on the edge of fizzling out.

Gavin.

Crap.

Dark curls, dimples, beautiful face against the long, slim neck of a tall, elegant girl, copper skin against her gold. His lips moving up to her jaw; his hand tracing down her spine. She spins away, her black hair flying out like a flag, then moves back against him. His fingers grip her hips tight. His eyes close, but she catches my gaze. She smiles that cat smile of hers. Ellory. Of course Ellory. Of course my audition competition. Of course they're a couple now. I mean, they've both already dated everyone else in this tiny-ass school. Nevaeh and Ellory were even a thing sophomore year.

I wonder—for only a second, the tiniest wallow of self-pity—why did he date me first? She's got that it-factor and the kind of body I keep hearing that dancers are supposed to have, slim and ethereal, while my body is considered exactly the opposite of that. I can move. I am graceful. I am a powerhouse. Fat and fierce. Delicate, I am not.

All that jumbled in the longest split second in the world, before I remember to wrench my eyes away.

I keep up my performer's smile, the one I've got a lock on, my bulletproof shield that says *I've got nothing to prove to you.* I'm trying hard to be nonchalant, but I fumble with the zipper of my coat, old and always sticking.

Katherine leans into my shoulder, because she can always tell when I'm faking it. "Right?" she says, rolling her eyes. "Nevaeh was like *Oh my gosh, just get a* room *already.*"

I snerk at that and then murmur in Katherine's ear. "Is 'man slut' a thing? Because if it isn't, that's sexist."

She laughs, the big braying cackle that carries, and that is maybe the only not-dignified thing about her. Taylor's and Nevaeh's heads both whip around, and when they see us, their faces are the best thing in the world, knocking Gavin and Ellory and that tiny bit of self-doubt out, out, out of my head.

I wave at them and then give up on my coat with a huff of disgust to kick off my clunky, stiff boots and yank off my itchy, woolly socks. I stuff it all into a pile near the couch and sigh, flexing toes that are red and aching. My focus is contemporary dance, but classical ballet is my first love, and it's the foundation of my ensemble piece this term. I've been *en pointe* since after dinner, because the winter showcase is less than a month away. But there's no taking a break, because Taylor is skidding up to me, taking me by the shoulders.

"Oh my god, it's *you*!" he shouts, ridiculous, so good at making a scene. "It's really you! You made it!" I love the drama of his face, impossible to ignore. The broad cheekbones and the thick, swept-back black hair, his shoulders wide in his white tank. He likes boys more than girls, and he's got a superhot Damien back home in Queens, but he knows that smile tempts everyone.

"I did!" I shout back. "I made it! Everyone keeps telling me that!" I press my cheek against his and breathe in his good, comforting, so familiar clean-sweat smell.

Then the music stops for a split second, just a breath—and it comes back with a *boom* that makes him whoop, grab my hand, and yank me through the crowd. I'm laughing, protesting, when he slides across the floor on his socks, clearing a space around us in the mass of bodies. I don't recognize this song—lush, weird midtempo, heavy bass, irresistible—but I realize that my body is so ready to play, aching for it, sinking into the music as my muscles respond to the beat. We've already got an audience circling up, because performing-arts kids, they have an instinct for drama.

"Let me take off my coat, for god's sake, Taylor!" I shout, fumbling again with the half-undone zipper, feeling it finally give. But I still my hand. Because Taylor's dropped bang to his knees with the most wicked smile.

"Take it *all* off, girl!" he calls. He is just *daring* me.

A long breath where I'm motionless, staring right back at him.

Inside I feel a waiting all around us. A curtain's-just-gone-up kind of moment, an indrawn breath, the rich thumping beat and the croon of that song saying *do it, do it, do it.*

I lift my eyebrow. His smile is so good and so dangerous and so full of pure, delighted confidence in me—and suddenly, I let myself go. I'm drunk on *yes, let's do this thing.*

On the beat, I cock my hand on my hip, whip off my scarf, and swing it above my head to the sudden shouts and cheers around me. My heart zings, sharp and clear like a bell, with that glorious adrenaline I'm addicted to.

Taylor leans all the way back, cups his hands around his mouth, and howls.

"Aaaaaa-DEEE!"

Katherine is cracking up, and Nevaeh is going to tease me about this for weeks, and the crowd is mine, and I love it.

To the *boom*, I snap the scarf over my shoulder, and to the downbeat I trail it down the front of my body, over the ridiculous puffy coat, let my knees bend and my hips sway and my shoulders roll as I trace my hand slowly up the curve of my thigh. With a flourish I fling the scarf at Taylor, who catches it against his chest, laughing. I hear my name, over and over, a heartbeat under the music, and it's inside me now, in that breathless moment when everything in the world stops when you step onstage. My body is singing, and I'm about to perform an aria.

That sublime place where I'm not locked in my head. Not worried about perfect. Pure joy. All eyes on me.

Arching my back and moving like I'm the beat and the bass, delighted by the ridiculousness of the puffy coat and the sexy dance, I tug the zipper of my coat down the rest of the way and shrug it off my shoulders. Let it slide down my back and arms until it drapes over my elbows, slides off my fingertips until I catch it, swing it in a graceful arc around my head, and toss it into the laughing, jostling, cheering crowd.

A hand goes up, and—and it's Gavin, snatching the coat out of the air, but he doesn't matter. I just blow him a kiss, swing my hips around, and rip off my wool hat to absolute shrieks of glee that reach a fever pitch as I slip my fingers down my neck, down my sides, my hips, then dip to the ground, toss my mass of dark curls, and glide back up in a perfect S-curve, flawless.

Sometimes it's a slog to push away what other people think my body should look like, but dancing like this—no binder around my chest, no taming my "too big" boobs, just *me*—I take fierce pride in the strength and size of my body and in the way I can move.

I make a kissy face at Nevaeh when I see her taking a video, grinning at her phone screen, and she blows a huge kiss back.

My dance skirt flutters around my thighs as I stalk toward my still-kneeling Taylor, one bare foot in front of the other, feeling like a panther. He's grinning like a dope, and I can't stop grinning back.

With a single fingertip on the top of Taylor's head, I prowl around to his broad back, sliding my hands down his shoulders and chest, tossing my mass of hair into his lap and flinging it back. I press my lips to his cheek, and when I straighten, he slaps a hand over that lipstick print, pretending he is swooning.

Gavin is watching as I slither back to the center of the circle, and now I want to know if he's remembering us. I ruthlessly crush the flare of anxiety. I *want* him to. Catching his gaze again for a long, slow moment, I smooth my hand across my waist, bite my bottom lip, and tug at the wrap tie of my sweater. Another toss of my hair and I strip the wrap off in one silky movement, sending it fluttering into Zoe's hands, and I laugh. It feels so good. The crowd is cheering the appearance of naked shoulders in a leotard. I roll them, along with my hips, a slow circle. Stretch my arms above my head, throw my head back, admire the arched curve of my naked arms. No more naked than I'd be performing, but it's different. There's a flutter in my stomach.

A senior boy shoves his way forward, waving a twenty at me, hooting. Christopher, pale-and-splotchy pink with a red-cheeked face, captain of the soccer team, in the academic program. The type that doesn't hang out with the arts-program kids. Owner of a bright blue Tesla convertible. Twenty bucks doesn't mean anything to him, but it's plenty to me.

With graceful hands and a graceful neck, I sweep my finger-tips along the curve of my leotard's neckline. *(Is it too low?)* He takes the hint, his grin getting even wider. But then I spin away when he reaches for me, not letting his hands touch my body, even for his twenty. I hear his shout, but not what he says, and shrug it off.

I catch Taylor's eye and slide my palms down the arc of my body to loosen the tie of my wrap skirt, let it slip down my thighs, down to the floor, and then I'm done, when this song slips into the next. I kick the skirt up with one toe, catch it, and take a long, flourishing bow, breathless in my leotard and tights and leg warmers, and my heart is pounding and I am flushed and swarmed by hoots and cheers and my people.

The adrenaline is wild, like lightning. Different from performing onstage. An audience gathered not to admire my talent, my dancing, but to admire me. It's a strange kind of head rush, and I feel a little too warm.

I get a big smacking kiss from Zoe and monster squeezes from Taylor and Katherine, and I nestle into Nevaeh's arms, laughing into her shoulder. Around us the dancing is already heating up again, and they melt back into it.

I duck my head, searching for my sweater, and snatch it up off the floor. Then I feel a hand on my arm, tugging insistently. I turn—Christopher and his smirk, too close to me. I don't want to talk to him, but he follows me to the edge of the dance floor, and I can hear his friends calling and hooting behind him.

"You like to be a tease!" he shouts, too loud. "I can get into that."

His eyes are pale blue, and he's squinting down at my cleavage, standing so close.

"Yeah, not interested," I tell him. I shrug into my sweater and tug it closed over my chest, but he's still looking at my boobs, leaning closer.

"You know," he says, pitching his voice under the music. I hate sentences that start with the words *you know* . . . and I'm right, because he finishes with "You're pretty hot for a big girl."

I stop for a second. It doesn't matter if I don't care. There's always that split second where you're just startled, when someone just makes a remark like that. I shake it off.

"Great!" I say, pulling my arm out of his hand, looking back at my friends on the dance floor. "Cool!" *And you're an ass*, I don't say out loud, because you're not supposed to say that kind of thing out loud. I swear I could have invented the cure for cancer if I didn't have to spend so much energy being grossed out by dudes fetishizing fat bodies, reminding me how hard I have worked to stop caring what people are thinking about mine.

"That doesn't mean you're hot enough to jerk me around, though," he adds.

"I have a boyfriend," I say, interrupting him. I try to move around him, back into the crowd, but he doesn't want to let me go. His hand snakes out to catch mine, and his voice cuts through the music.

"I thought fat girls didn't like to play hard to—"

I lunge forward when I see Taylor slipping out of the room, but Christopher is right behind me still.

"This is my boyfriend," I announce abruptly, flinging my arms around Taylor's waist. Christopher looks back and forth between us. I hate myself for resorting to this, but I need to make him stop. *Fat* isn't a dirty word, and I proudly claim it—still, it's shitty to hear it used like a weapon.

Taylor rests his arm around my shoulders.

"Oh yeah," he says, raising his voice over the music. "We're a thing."

Christopher pauses, and then he says, "I thought you were a—" to Taylor. He waves his hand in a vague circle.

"A what?" Taylor says, tilting his head. His voice bright and curious.

Christopher sputters before he says, "Into dudes. Or whatever." Hand wave again.

"Nah, man," Taylor says very solemnly. "It's a spectrum."

I turn my laugh into a cough.

"Cool," Christopher says. "Right." A glance for each of us, and then an extra glance for my boobs. Up and down my body, and I get the skeeves. "See ya," he says. He bumps Taylor's shoulder when he pushes past us.

"Nice," Taylor says, and then looks down at me. "What was that?"

"I'm sorry," I say, collapsing against Taylor's side. "I needed him to leave me alone."

It feels terrible to hide from one guy behind another, like I can't just speak for myself. It feels terrible, the way Christopher talked about my body as if he's allowed to. I feel like I have ants crawling all over my skin.

"He has a crappy reputation," Taylor says. He rests his cheek on the top of my head, and I sigh. "I'm sorry, Addiebear," he says.

"Me too."

"If we're eloping, I have to tell Damien first."

I laugh, straightening up.

"Dance now," he says. "Okay?"

I nod and let him tug me down the hall, back into the crowd, and I stomp Christopher off like snow from my boots.

2

Hours later, the four of us head to the great room to collapse. It's close to senior curfew and we should be hustling, heading back to our real lives in the dorms and leftover homework and snacks we hide under our beds and whatever sleep we can get. But with the music lower and slower now and the lights turned down even lower than that, being all wrung out and happy makes us want to just find a place to be very, very still now, in the mostly empty house. All the younger kids have scattered back to the dorms for their earlier curfews.

"Ellory and Gavin," Katherine says when she plops down on the couch. I put my head in her lap to stretch out luxuriously flat, but groan at that. *Oh, them.*

Nevaeh is sprawled in a straddle split on the floor, uncoiling her bun so that her braids spill over her cheeks. Her long toes are pointed gracefully. She wrinkles her brow.

"Oh, those two," she says.

"You okay, Nevvie?" I ask. I will knock heads if this has upset her.

"It's been a minute since we dated," she says. "It's whatever."

Holding a handful of braids in one fist, head cocked to the side, she adds, "How about you, boo?"

Gavin and I spent time together during our summer intensives last year. First just flirting, and then making out, and then I decided to get naked with him, the night of the final showcase. I was amped up by my performance, the adrenaline, the applause, my head still ringing. It was my first time, and it was an adventure, except for the part where I got unexpectedly shy when he touched me and I panicked, wondering what he was thinking when he squeezed my hips, skimmed my belly. Hard work to put it aside and just kiss him. But I did, and I slept with him two more times because I liked it and I thought I maybe, possibly really liked him. Then summer ended and other students came back to campus, and he started avoiding me. He ditched me with a text: *sorry, didn't know you thought we were a thing.*

I stared at that text, and I realized: He was embarrassed of me.

And I was so mad at myself, because I should have known better, should've seen through him, should've remembered how so many hot guys actually believe that fat girls are desperate and that I should be grateful for their charm. Like Christopher, trying to ruin my night.

But the thing with Gavin was months ago.

Now I'm looking at Nevaeh for maybe a second too long, but finally just shrug. "I'm fine," I say. I think that's true. Maybe. I mostly try to avoid him. He's friendly, like he doesn't know he crushed the juice out of my heart with one fist, and, because I've got pride, I am fake-friendly back. Only my mentor, Carly, and these three know what a wreck I was for a bunch of the fall semester, under the big stage smile, armor engaged.

"I don't even remember what I saw in him," I say.

"Well, those shoulders, for one," Taylor says.

"Taylor!" Katherine says.

I laugh and kick at him but miss, and he catches my foot and holds it. "Watch with the deadly weapons," he protests.

"*Finely tuned instruments*," I say.

"Of destruction," he says.

"Of magic," I say cheerfully. I am fine. I am just trying to be here in the moment and all the other things they say at the end of our yoga class.

Taylor squeezes my ankle. "Beloved pretend girlfriend, you *know* he's utterly, utterly worthless," he says to me in a very matter-of-fact way. "And he never deserved you."

"Let him wallow in his regrets," Nevaeh says. She grabs and kisses my palm quick, leaving behind glitter, and smiles one of those rare sunny, whole-face smiles that fills my heart.

Taylor bops Nevaeh on the head with a pillow. "Oh, hey, you and little Zoe tonight," he says, and I am so glad to let Ellory and Gavin go.

Nevaeh groans and covers her face. "We were just dancing!"

"She's so cute," I say. "She has such a crush on you." Half the freshman girls, gay and straight, have a crush on her.

"And it's all your fault!" Taylor says gleefully, poking at Nevaeh while she whacks his hand.

"It is not!" Katherine says. "Quit it." Katherine always squirms when we joke about Nevaeh's heart-slaying. And Taylor's long line of wannabe lovers, or my daydreams about artistic boys with melancholy eyes and lion hearts. Katherine doesn't date. She says she's never been interested in anyone. *Never?* Taylor asked once. She shook her head and shrugged. So we never bug her about it. I worry she feels left out sometimes when we talk about our own crushes, but I don't know how I would even ask her about it.

"Thank you!" Nevaeh says, throwing up her hands. "At least

Katy-Kitten remembers I will never in this life hit on a straight girl."

"That's not what I meant," Katherine protests.

Nevaeh grins at her and goes back to her phone, scrolling through the photos she took tonight. I close my eyes and try to enjoy Katherine's hand stroking my hair, her soft, absentminded humming. Listen to Taylor and Nevaeh debate filters and face tuners. Nevaeh is a true-blue Insta celebrity, #nofilter, makeup and skin care and natural-hair tutorials and a ridiculous number of followers. She started practicing makeup to hide, I think; she used to hate how she looked in photos. It took her a long time to build her confidence, but it's grown along with her skills. Makeup is art now, never camouflage. She takes a billion photos of everyone and everything every day, but always lets me see ones of myself before she posts them, and she doesn't argue or try to talk me out of it when I say no.

When she makes an unexpected strangled noise, Katherine and I both bolt up.

"Oh, shit, you need to see this," she says, waving her phone. She spins around so we can see the screen and cranks up the sound. I recognize the song from the party with a jolt—the strip-tease—oh no, why did I do that?

"Give it," I say.

Taylor scoots over to peer at the screen, bumping me out of the way. "Well, holy hell, Ms. Adeleina."

"I know!" Nevaeh says. I lean over Taylor, and she pushes the phone into my palm. The video loops to the start, and I cradle the phone with both hands. That's me. Skin too pale (thanks, Michigan) and dark hair wild. Pouring across the floor like water. Radiating confidence.

"That's me!" I say. I hear the surprise in my voice. Of course I've watched all my onstage videos, studying every rest and breath, making sure my technique is solid. I hate photos, but video shows how I move. This, though—I've never seen myself like this before. Katherine leans against me to watch, her hand over her mouth.

"Oh, look at you," she says, in a hushed tone. "Oh my gosh."

"Look at that rack," Taylor says.

"Taylor," Katherine says, but there's a grin in her voice.

"Haven't you heard that dancers shouldn't have boobs?" I say, rolling my eyes. I wish them away sometimes, when I'm struggling into sports bras and then compression binding them for rehearsal wincing as I tape before performances, gritting my teeth as I peel it off after.

I watch the video again, letting it loop. There I am, everything unbound. It was a performance, pretending to do a sexy striptease, but the thing that gets me is the way I am radiating confidence right there, looking beautiful and powerful. It's kind of amazing.

"I love this," I say. I do.

Nevaeh snatches the phone back. "And now I am going to post it to show the world how hot you are," she says, her expression challenging me.

"Wait—" I say. It feels too vulnerable. Why does it feel too vulnerable? Her finger is poised over the screen. She lifts a perfect ombré eyebrow at me. Challenge upgraded to epic.

Pretty hot for a big girl, Christopher yells in my ear. But screw that guy.

"No. Do it," I say.

"Okay, then! Hashtag—" Her thumb moves fast over the keyboard. "Hashtag sex goddess, hashtag hotness, et cetera, et cetera et cetera," she announces.

"Nevaeh!" I say, but she waves her hand at me, still typing out hashtags, and I sigh. She's the marketing genius slash Instaceleb or whatever. She watches the screen as it uploads and makes a satisfied noise when it's in the world. We all watch it loop on her feed, and the number of hearts start to flip up almost immediately.

"You should've stripped for your Angles audition," Taylor says.

My heart does a fast, sharp wobble. "Shush!" I say, and kick at him again but miss. Angles. I've barely thought about it since walking through the door, which has to be some sort of record. And I don't want to think about it now. "Shush, shush, shush!" I repeat, kicking at him, shoving aside all thoughts of my future.

But Nevaeh's staring at me, her eyes huge. "Oh, shit, honey, I forgot," she says. "Angles results on Monday!"

The thump in my chest hurts.

I sit up and tuck my legs under me. "Oh yeah!" I say very casually, totally not hyperventilating. "I had forgotten about that!" I smile, but probably there are too many teeth in it.

"Addiebear, are you okay?" Katherine asks, her hand on my back.

"Oh yes! It's just my entire future is all! No problem. Totally good!" Voice squeaking.

Angles is this incredibly prestigious dance company in Milan, with a terrifyingly competitive summer program for aspiring professional dancers. If you're accepted, it's a couple of months studying with one of the most innovative and boundary-pushing dance companies in the world. But it's Mohadesa Rabei, the director of the program, who blows me away. She has a dance vocabulary like no one else. And she's dramatically, unapologetically fat, and perfect, and my heart stopped the first time photos of her, videos of her dancing, blazed on my laptop screen. I need to study with her. I have to.

I jump up and start to pace.

Just a handful of new dancers work with her and the company's principals, choreographers, and guest instructors from across the globe. Learning from them, dancing with them, proving what we can do. At the end, there's a chance that one of us will be invited to join the company as an apprentice.

It would change *everything* for me.

Even for the very best dancers, making it as a professional is no joke. Trying to make it as a person of color is the highest difficulty setting—I've seen the exhausting bullshit Taylor and Nevaeh have to push through every day from all directions. (We all almost collapsed and died of happiness when they both got their Tisch/NYU early acceptances.) What I deal with is trying to make it with no family money to help with bills or college, a mom whose debt has made me determined never to rack up my own, and a body nowhere close to the stereotypical dancer's. Of course, they say that contemporary dance is a little more welcoming to all types of bodies, but in the real world, fat dancers still get laughed off some audition stages, if they get up there at all.

While Angles isn't a guarantee of success, it feels like the best chance I'll ever get. To prove to my mom that the professional dance world is where I belong, not chasing a career in LA—that's her dream. Angles is the only vision I have of my future. I've already downloaded an Italian language app.

I suck in a deep breath. I know how to breathe through every moment and movement. I am the calm in the eye of the goddamn hurricane. But if I let myself think about this too much, it feels like I am being leveled.

"Addie—" Nevaeh says, and I know they're all glancing at one another.

"It's totally fine," I say to them. "I don't want to talk about it. It's just—it's that—it's fine."

I've made it through three intimidating auditions on campus—and so has Ellory. She and I are the two final senior contenders, out of all the schools in the country, because that is how irony works, I guess. The decision is supposed to come Monday, 9 a.m. Milan time, 2 a.m. central time. Which is just two days away. I put my face in my hands, demanding that my heart slow. I breathe in, and out.

"Addie?" Katherine asks.

I don't want this to be my only chance. I'm afraid it's my only chance. But more than anything, I just want it. I want to go. I want to meet Madame Rabei. I kind of want to make her love me. I have to get in.

"If you don't get it—" Taylor says, like he's reading my mind, and I look up.

"Taylor!" Katherine says sharply.

He glares at her and looks back at me. "*If* you don't get it, as I was saying before I was so rudely interrupted because no one has any faith in me . . ." He pauses to glare at all of us in turn, and we each roll our eyes. "Then there's something wrong in the world," he finishes with a flourish. "It's yours."

I swoop down and kiss the top of his head, feeling grateful for him. All of them.

We four found one another the first week of our first year here, me and Taylor and Nevaeh and Katherine—our meeting the surest sign that magic exists. We kind of grew up together. Fourteen years old when we met and eighteen now. Three and a half years of classes and lunches and rehearsals and off-campus adventures, and we've got one another's backs no matter what. We make one another better, and we shove one another toward extraordinary in the studio, onstage. We all know what it's like to work so hard and want something so much.

Now the end of our senior year is just a few months away. The three of them are moving to New York City, Taylor and Nevaeh to Tisch and Katherine to Julliard. They'll be in prestigious schools, maybe all getting an apartment together, and me . . . ?

"Group hug!" Katherine cries, and Taylor groans "Noooooo," but Nevaeh has climbed into Katherine's arms on the couch. They press their cheeks together, and I heave Taylor up onto the couch, and he yanks me down across his lap and half of Nevaeh's and Katherine's, and I fit my arms around all of them as best I can and close my eyes and wish everything were this easy and that nothing bad would ever happen to any of us.

I spare a wish for myself too.

There are many, many things wrong in the world, of course—but please, please, *please* don't let the Angles decision be one of them.

3

Monday, late morning, our pointe shoes boom as we thunder across the floor in technique. It's a minor miracle I feel this alive and invigorated after a sleepless night spent waiting for a text from Angles that never came.

But it's allegro, my favorite part of class, when we're cut loose from the barre and spun into motion, sent crisscrossing across the studio in packs, leaping up like we'll never come back down, soaring like eagles. And the sound when we do land becomes a heartbeat louder than my own, and every leap is another release that my hip muscles howl at like a war cry, and every return vibrates through my perfectly extended foot and calf and thigh. My arms catch fire, but I stay flawlessly precise in every turn of my wrist and tilt of my head and lift of my rib cage.

We're in the air once again when *clap, clap, clap,* Madame George signals with three short slaps that time's up.

"Fine for now," she says crisply.

I'm stretching long and slow over my lifted, extended leg when Ellory takes a spot next to me at the barre instead of at the end, where she usually cools down.

"Any news?" she says, her voice too casual, locking eyes with me in the mirror.

I shrug. "I haven't checked," I say, and wipe my forehead with the back of my wrist. I can't help but glance at my folded warm-up, where I've hidden my phone.

"Right," she snorts, and then pauses. "So . . . you and Gavin had a thing?"

"Sort of," I say cautiously. "Last summer."

"That's nice," she says. She glides down to the floor, leaning forward over one outstretched leg, clearly dismissing me.

"What do you mean, *'That's nice'*?" I blurt.

She glances up and shrugs. "Nothing," she says, then adds after a beat, "Good luck with Angles."

"You too," I respond automatically, but she doesn't look up again. I don't know whether to move away to stretch or just pretend she's not there.

But then the door of the studio opens in a rush of air, and my head snaps around when Madame George barks, "Ms. Valentine!" and my adviser, Carly, says, "May I borrow Addie?" They look at me along with everyone else in the room, halted midstretch.

Carly's face is serious, too serious. Madame George nods and waves me away. I grab my warm-up and make my way to the door, keep my neck long and my expression neutral, and don't even glance back at Ellory. The door swings shut behind us. I can hear the muffled sound of classical music from the studio down the hall, and my teeth are gritted for the bad news I am now convinced is coming, a panicked plan B already surging up: moving back in with my mother, maybe convincing her to let me go to the dance program at Florida State; *it's not bad, I can get state grants, maybe I can make this work*, I tell myself, even as rebellion is boiling up in me. Carly grabs my hands, squeezing them hard.

"Look," I say, clearing my throat. "I don't cry over spilled—"

But she interrupts me. Her eyes are a pale, clear ice blue, and now she's grinning.

"You got it, Addie."

I stare at her. I don't understand what she's trying to tell me. I'm sitting at the top of a roller coaster for an endless, timeless instant.

"Addie?" Carly says. "You *got it*." Every word is very firm and very clear, and I am still frozen, now because it's too huge. It's too much. It's everything.

My scream echoes down the hall, bounces off the ceiling, and should be shattering windows, and my heart is a firework, and oh my god, the relief, the complete, sheer relief. The hollow, grateful feeling that's left behind when the terror vanishes.

Carly squeezes my hands even harder, and we're jumping up and down in tandem. She has been 100 percent behind me from the moment I ran into her office with the flyer crunched up in my fist with that glorious photo of Mohadesa Rabei, swearing this was mine, because it had to be. She kept me going through all those hours of rehearsal before my dance block, after dinner, through dreaming my audition piece, rehearsing it in my head in class, in line for coffee, everywhere.

When she lets go, I slide down the wall to the floor. "Is it real?"

"It's real," she says, smiling. "I couldn't wait to tell you—I should have had you drop by my office." She helps me up.

Dancers are beginning to fill the hallway, headed down to the changing room before they're off to the boring parts of the day, arts block now over. My friends will be here any minute, and I cannot wait to tell them. But it's Ellory I see first, emerging from the studio. Carly's attention has been grabbed by Halim, passing by. Ellory stops in front of me as I'm undoing my pointe shoes.

"Was that you?" she says. She's frowning. She must know already.

"Angles," I say. I'm still out of breath. "I got the senior spot." I try to keep my voice even, not gloating. One senior spot between the two of us. Should I feel guilty for winning? Screw that. I earned it. I owe her respect, not regret.

The briefest flicker of emotion sparks in her eyes. "Good for you," she says, and then adds, "I'll let Gavin know." My heart stutters at the dig. She glides past me and down the hall without a backward glance.

"What's wrong?" Carly asks, attention back on me. I shake my head, hating that my face is giving anything away.

"Just excited," I say. Angles is better than a boy. A boy who rejected me because I wasn't enough, or I was too much or—no. Forget him. *I got Angles.*

"Do you have time to talk? I'll make you a cup of tea," Carly says. "We have a couple things to discuss, okay?" She slips her arm through mine to guide me to the double doors at the end of the hall. I'm still kind of dazed. I want to tell my friends, and I crane my neck, but they still haven't appeared from their different studios yet. Then, all of a sudden, Carly's words and new tone of voice register and stop me.

"Talk about what?" I say as the hall doors swing shut behind us.

"We can talk in private," she says, but I am not moving. Maybe it's ridiculous; maybe I worry too much, expecting something bad. Still, dread's curling around my heart.

"Please tell me right now." I try to lighten my tone. "You know, if this is a joke, I am going to be just a little bit upset."

She looks at me for a long moment. Other dance students sweep by us, their voices a blur.

"Funding," she says, her voice serious. "We can talk about it when we go upstairs."

Funding? There's a scholarship, full funding for the summer. Full funding that's supposed to come along with the spot—a scholarship for the winner. I *know* I read that. I wouldn't have applied if there wasn't.

"A position and a scholarship," I say. "The website said that."

Carly shakes her head, hesitates. "Addie—there's just one scholarship." Her face is so sympathetic. "It's need-based, not talent-based—"

"And I didn't need it?"

She purses her lips at me. I know I sound ungrateful—someone else needed it more. It's just that without it, the expanse between here and there is six thousand dollars wide, and impossible.

"There's got to be other ways to fund you," Carly says, her hand on my sleeve. Not *there definitely are.* Not *everything's fine; don't worry.* My heart disappears into a sinkhole. "I can ask around . . . ," she says, her voice trailing off.

"For six thousand dollars?" I say numbly.

"Loans, maybe . . . ," Carly continues, and then stops. She's probably remembered I'm a little too young to apply for a bank loan and my mother wouldn't be approved even if she agreed to put herself on the hook. Six thousand bucks is like six thousand unicorns riding six thousand rockets over Candy Mountain.

"We'll figure something out," she says after a moment.

I don't let her take my hand. I'm breathing too fast. I press my hand to my chest. It's all out of control. I can't catch it. Shaking my head. Why didn't I know this could happen? How could I have not known this? What am I going to do?

"I can give you a few days to get back to me," Carly says. "Maybe we can—"

"I'm sorry," I gasp. Still breathless. "I have to—" I back away. Can't talk about this anymore.

"Addie, please," she says. "Don't go."

"I have to!" I snap, too loud, too harsh.

Without another word, I turn and thunder down the stairs.

4

Nevaeh's and Katherine's coats are still hanging up in the locker room. I hesitate, but I can't wait for them. I grab my things, stuff my arms into my coat, and hurry out into the quad. The sky is too bright, the frustration too hot, the guilt too sharp. I can't believe I just ran away from Carly like that. Carly, of all people.

She's been my adviser since my first semester, back when I thought getting *into* Lakeshore would be the hard part. When I got here, *everything* was hard: academic classes that made me feel lost; dance classes ten times tougher than those at home; being surrounded by dancers just as dedicated as me, just as good as me. Smaller than me, and not shy about pointing that out.

But from the start, Carly didn't give a shit about what anyone said to me, or what I was saying to myself. She'd seen my audition. She knew what I could do. After I skipped lunch the whole first week, she pulled me into her office.

She said: *Don't shape yourself to fit the world. Make the world shape itself to fit you.*

I wrote that all over my notebooks the first year. Have always thought maybe I'll get it tattooed on me one day. It's already knitted into my bones.

I take a deep breath that hurts my lungs, it's so cold, and another. I've been rushing across campus with my head down, not sure where I'm going. At the fountain in front of the theater, the statue of the school's founder still wears the knit hat Taylor crowned him with months ago. There's a wall of notifications on my phone screen from Katherine, Nevaeh, and Taylor. They've been messaging me all morning, asking if I've gotten news yet, even though they shouldn't have been using their phones in the studio. They care as much as I do. And now I don't know what to tell them. I don't even know what I'm thinking.

The last text from Katherine has so many question marks that the actual message has scrolled off the screen, and I get that little surge of gratitude for her, as always.

I pull off my mitten and stand there with my thumb poised over the on-screen keyboard.

I'll fix this. Somehow.

Meet at the coffee shop? I type, and they tell me they're already halfway there; didn't I read my messages?

My nose is cold and the sky's a flat gray and out of nowhere I'm homesick for Mom, how she smells like coconut sunblock and sun. I don't know what I'm going to tell her about Angles either. She didn't even want me to come to Lakeshore. She wanted to take me out of high school and move to LA, where she thought I'd become a big star. But I knew what I really wanted. To be an artist, not an entertainer. And Angles is the next step to that. I've made that clear to her. So now what do I say?

More to not think about.

I sign out at the side gate, flash my ID, scribble my name, and rush down the driveway, leaving Lakeshore behind.

The town surrounds campus on three sides, residential streets giving way to the tree-lined blocks with shops and cafés and chiropractors. It's like the set of a Hallmark Christmas special, or what you'd build if you asked for the exact opposite of where I grew up.

Java the Hutt, halfway down the second block, is usually empty. It smells like flavored coffees and cinnamony baked goods and wet newspaper and homey familiarity from all the times we've been here. Bright, filled with plants, and everything they sell, including the coffee, is truly terrible. We love it.

They're already here when I arrive. Katherine's wiping down the table with a napkin, and Nevaeh is laughing at Taylor, who is making his usual sweeping gestures as he talks animatedly, and there's a cupcake with a match stuck in it sitting in front of them. They expect it to be good news.

Katherine sees me first, her whole face bursting into light, and she goes up on her tiptoes to wave me over, as if I could miss them.

"Congratulations!" she shouts across the room at me, and something in my chest unclenches. Taylor whistles, sharp and loud and shrill, and Nevaeh is clapping like I've just won a basket of infinite kittens. The usual barista frowns at us the way the usual barista does, dragging a rag across the counter, but my friends' excitement is softening some of the ugly knots of self-pity.

"How'd you know?" I say, grinning at them and unwinding my scarf.

"Because you are amazing," Katherine says, reaching up to grab my hand, pulling me down into the booth next to her. Her blue eyes are glowing like she's snatched down pieces of a Florida beach sky. "I told you. We all told you."

"We believe in you," Nevaeh says, her voice matter-of-fact.

"Also, we're always right," Taylor says. "Do you think you're ever going to listen to us?"

"Probably not," I say to him honestly, and he laughs.

The lopsided cupcake is slumped on a chipped saucer in the middle of the table. The baked goods are terrible here, yes, but that's not the point. They got me a victory cupcake. I look up again when Nevaeh calls my name, like she's been trying to get my attention for a while.

"Maybe you should look a little less emo in your celebration photo," she says, aiming her phone at me. I cover my face, and she laughs. "I know, I know, you hate the paparazzi. Just give me a thumbs-up, you beautiful winner."

That catches me completely off guard.

They're so happy for me. I don't want to change that, and I don't want to say the words out loud to them: *I didn't get the scholarship. I can't afford to go.*

I don't remember the last time I cried, but now I'm crying. My shoulders shake and I gasp a little bit, and I hear Nev's phone clatter to the table, and Katherine's arms are around my waist and Nevaeh's around my shoulders, and Taylor is half out of his seat and across the table, patting my hand and murmuring soothingly at me.

I rub my eyes with the heels of my hands. "I'm sorry! I'm so sorry. I don't know what's wrong with me. I never do this; you know I never do this."

Taylor presses my hand in a calloused palm. "You're totally overwhelmed."

"It's huge news," Nevaeh says on one side of me.

"Of course it's emotional," Katherine says, nodding at Nevaeh. "It's wonderful."

I can't take it.

"I didn't get the scholarship," I say. There's a long silence. They're frowning at one another, like they're trying to puzzle it out among them. "I got into the program," I say, and then my breath hitches. I breathe in through my nose. "But I didn't get the scholarship. So I can't afford to go. Unless I can magic up six thousand dollars."

"Your mom—" Katherine starts to say, but I cut her off.

"You know she—there's no money." I sit up straight, trying to get myself back together. I catch myself and swallow. "I mean, if I don't figure out how to make money. Obviously I'll figure it out."

"But how?" Taylor says abruptly. He's mad.

"Taylor," Katherine warns.

"Am I wrong?" Taylor says. "It's ridiculous."

"Taylor," Nevaeh says.

"No, it's a good question, right?" I smile at him briefly, and then look at my victory cupcake, swipe my finger across the frosting. "I'll figure it out," I repeat. "Carly says we'll figure it out." I wipe the grainy frosting off on the stack of napkins in front of me. None of them respond, so I look up. Nevaeh is lifting an eyebrow, and it is such a skeptical eyebrow that I almost flinch. Her mouth is a jewel, as always, painted this afternoon a glowing emerald green and gold, the kind of colors my mentees have shown up trying to wear, but only Nevaeh can do those looks justice.

"I'm going to go get a coffee," I say to her eyebrow. Taylor drops my hand, and Katherine and Nevaeh unwind their arms from around me, let me slide out of the booth. I go and stare up at the menu for a long while, even though I've memorized everything on the list, and then just order a black coffee, a flash of my mother's voice—*the calories you save, if you just skip the cream! And the sugar!*

None of them look up when I slide back into the booth. They've got their heads bent over a spiral notebook. Katherine snatches the pen away from Taylor. "Taylor," she says sternly. "Serious suggestions."

"There's nothing frivolous about international bank robbery," Taylor says.

"It's just brainstorming," Nevaeh says to me, and flashes a smile. "So you can scuba dive for treasure, right? You're from Florida."

They've already got a list scribbled halfway down the page: *Find spare change on street. Steal from the rich. Invent viral app. Stock exchange. Kitten farm.* There's a heart drawn around *Kitten farm* in another pen color. *Sell blood. Sell kidney. Sell sibling's kidney.*

"I don't have any siblings," I say, tapping that one.

"I was suggesting mine," Katherine says. She has two sisters, one at Harvard, the other at Berkeley. "That is a lot of kidneys between us all."

"This is my problem, everyone," I say.

When no one says anything, I look up.

"She can sell their kidneys if she wants," Taylor says.

"We have a *list* already, Addie," Nevaeh says. "Don't be difficult."

And then I shake myself.

I'm in the program. I *made* it. That means something. *Which Carly was trying to say*, my guilty voice whispers. It means something to her and to these three, and I can worry about the money in private.

"Don't sell any kidneys," I say to Katherine. "That is illegal."

Taylor scratches out *Sell kidneys*. Nevaeh takes a photo of me crossing my eyes at her. "Can I?" she asks, showing it to me, and I nod. She posts it and then looks up after a moment, grinning, and shows the screen to Taylor. He whistles.

"Did you see your video? Did you see my post?" Nevaeh says.

I shake my head, and she clucks her tongue, shoves the phone across the table at me. The striptease video has scrolled down her list of posts, but it is still getting liked. Over eight hundred hearts since Saturday night; almost three hundred comments.

"And look!" She reaches over to scroll up. "Thirteen likes already on the pic I *just* posted. That's a good omen."

"Bona fide star," Taylor says. "We'll just monetize you somehow."

I shake my head at them, laughing.

Katherine leans over to look at Nevaeh's screen and makes a terrible face. "Oh my gosh, what is that?"

Quick as a flash Taylor grabs the phone, over Nevaeh's protest.

"Who in the hell is sending you uninvited penises?" He frowns. "It's not even a very good picture." He holds up the phone. "The lighting is terrible."

An uninvited dick pic feels aggressive, and ugly. "What is wrong with people?" I say indignantly.

Nevaeh snatches her phone back from Taylor. "Trolls," she says. She taps her screen with a flourish. "Deleted!" She's flicked it all away with a flash of her shining fingernails. "Because penises aren't going to get us six thousand bucks," she says, and she grins when I choke on my coffee. "What else have we got?"

Taylor suggests GoFundMe, which makes me wince and argue—that's for people with real needs. We stay at the coffee shop and pick at bad pastries and brainstorm through our lunch period. We do some actual grant research, too, and learn that application deadlines are long past and I'd need to win all of them to afford this. We still haven't figured out a moneymaking scheme by the time we have to get back for the academic block.

When I pull five singles out of my wallet, Katherine shakes her head. She snatches them out of my hand and stuffs them into my cleavage. "You should be making money, not giving it away," she says.

I look down at the bills and my boobs. "I can be a stripper," I say, plucking out a dollar and smoothing it on the table, remembering Christopher's smirky face and the look of maybe-desire on Gavin's when he watched me move. And the idea . . . doesn't sound like the worst idea I've ever had.

"Addie!" Nevaeh says, grabbing my arm. "Do you know how much a stripper makes in one night?"

"It is monetizing the male gaze!" Katherine says. "I love it."

"That doesn't seem very feminist to me," Taylor says.

"She's taking advantage of a paradigm designed to benefit men and turning it instead into an opportunity for her own wealth and well-being," Nevaeh explains.

"She's giving dudes boners!"

"And getting paid for it!"

"It still doesn't sound feminist to me," Taylor says.

"You *know* you don't get to decide what's feminist," Nevaeh says, and Taylor sighs. They've had this argument before. They both look at me.

"They are very athletic too," Katherine observes. "Strippers."

"I am athletic!" I say. "But I—" *I've let only one guy see me totally naked in my life, and it turns out he wasn't impressed.* "I don't think I could do that." Plus how do strippers manage a whole athletic act topless without hurting themselves?

My three friends, none of whom have ever been in danger of hitting themselves in the face with their own boobs when they jog, nod with understanding and a touch of disappointment.

"It's such a good idea, though," Taylor says wistfully. "Go-go girl in Vegas?"

"Burlesque dancer in Chicago?" I offer.

"Isn't that just fancy stripping?" Taylor says. Katherine is tapping at her phone.

"It's a performance," Nevaeh says. "With a cool vintage aesthetic. And nipple tassels."

"And feathers!" Katherine says, holding her phone up, her eyes wide. "Look at her! 'San Francisco School of Burlesque,'" she reads. We all lean forward to see.

The dark-skinned woman is apple-shaped, snugged into a velvet fringed corset, caught midmotion. Her leg, broad and dimpled, extends gracefully all the way up over her head, skin shining under the spotlight, her bare toes hooked into the loop of the fluffiest pink feather boa I've ever seen. Her other arm, sheathed in a pink satin opera glove, is flung triumphantly in the air.

Everything about her is goals, from the perfect arch of her back and the flex of her toes and the line of her throat to how she's gleaming from head to toe, the dark cloud of her hair a glittering galaxy, and something about her plucks a booming, bright chord in me, right in the center of my chest. She's got thighs that look like mine, thick and sturdy and tiger-striped, and, I realize with a thrill, her boobs are overflowing her corset. And that's not a performer's smile. It's real. "Oh," I murmur. It's a noise of amazement spilling out of me, and a little awe.

Nevaeh sighs at her phone. "No theaters closer than Chicago."

"Oh, Nevvie, I was joking," I say to them. "And it's not like a club would hire a high school student. Even if I'm eighteen."

"And the commute," Taylor adds. I snort.

"If only we could start our own burlesque club," I say. Katherine sighs, puts away her phone, and slips her arm around me.

"We will find a way," she says. It feels true when she says it.

We head back to campus through the quiet backstreets. It's February but there's still bunting on every streetlamp, and the holiday lights are still up on most houses. The cold smells like wood smoke, a smell I didn't know I loved until I moved here. Behind the black and bare trees, the sky is a wide, gray sheet of ice. Nevaeh and Taylor link arms and go back to arguing about the male gaze. The two of them are a matched set, tall and lean in long black puffy coats. Katherine pulls my mittens out of my pocket and hands them to me, and then keeps my gloved hand in hers. I can't stop thinking about the burlesque dancer in the photo, her shine and energy, her beautiful skin.

We sign in at the campus gates, turn toward the quad, and join the stream of kids heading toward the afternoon block of academic classes. Taylor stops so suddenly I bump into his back. Our classmates are jostling past us, but he doesn't notice; he just starts talking, his hands waving, his tawny brown eyes bright.

"Hold up now. How did we not think of this?"

"What, Taylor?" Nevaeh says patiently.

"A *pop-up* show," he says to me. He pokes Nevaeh in the shoulder. "We were *just* talking about it last week. Those kids in the eighties—"

"That fundraiser!" It's a yelp very unlike her, and her smile is broad. She hooks her arm through mine, lowering her voice. "It's brilliant. This is brilliant!"

I don't know what's brilliant, but Katherine's face has lit up.

"Oh! Wasn't it—music kids in the seventies? They needed some money in order to enter a contest!" Katherine says in a stage whisper.

"No, it was eighties dance kids who wanted money for costumes," Taylor says.

"And one of their moms was related to someone in some band?" Katherine says.

"R.E.M.," Nevaeh says. "And the whole band came."

"And they put on a secret show!" Katherine says, clapping her hands.

"Wait, what was secret? Why was it secret?" I bounce from foot to foot, starting to freeze standing here. I hate feeling lost like this.

Nevaeh prods us back into motion, down the path that splits off to the campus chapel and the roofless gazebo where students sometimes perform in summer.

Taylor leans against the railing of the gazebo's steps. "Lakeshore wouldn't go for it, obviously," he says.

"So they invited students to a one-time-only, after-curfew, top secret music club at a top secret location," Nevaeh explains. "They charged so, so much for tickets."

"*And* they raked it in," Taylor finishes triumphantly.

Of course they did. So many kids here, they have that cash to spend. I mean, the bragging about weekends in Cabo and convertibles for Christmas. And having that cash makes a lot of them act like the rules aren't a thing for them, going around paying for term papers or buying their roommate's Adderall or bribing RAs when they break curfew.

"We don't know any famous musicians," Taylor says to me, "and you don't play an instrument . . ."

I blink at each of them for a moment as the idea catches and starts to burn. "A *burlesque* club," I say slowly. "An underground, pop-up, midnight burlesque show. That's what you're saying." I can already see us. Glimmering under the spotlight. Ruffling, rippling feathers and laced-up satin corsets. Performing, dazzling, owning the room. Skin—but only as much as we want to show. After-curfew adventure and sneaking and danger. A secret burlesque club. I think again of that picture, that incredible burlesque dancer, shaped like me. My naked skin under a spotlight. In front of an audience. Could I do that?

Nevaeh is tapping her phone against her chin, a tiny smile on her face. Katherine's got her fists clasped against her chest, and her eyes are bright. At the top of the steps, Taylor's got his hands in his pockets, and he's looking kind of smug. Nevaeh gets a photo of him.

"Well," he says. "Wasn't that basically your idea?"

Could we do that? We could do that.

I laugh and speed up the steps of the gazebo, spin, and spread my arms out wide.

"Exclusive midnight access to the hottest private underground burlesque show in town, live at Lakeshore Academy," I announce.

"Dirty Little Secret!" Taylor cries, sketching out a flashing neon sign across the sky.

"Yes! Sure! Okay! We can work on the name!" I say.

"Brainstorming session!" Katherine cries. She loves to brainstorm.

"Select invite-only show," I go on. "Major buzz, because you want to be one of the ones who dare to go. You want to be there so you can say you were there!"

"You're such a fool if you miss it," Nevaeh says, watching me with bright eyes.

She's so good at igniting me. They all are. And it feels like I could go off like a firecracker.

"Oh, man," I say. "Wouldn't that be amazing?"

Nevaeh snaps a photo of me. "You are so gorgeous when you're excited," she says, leaping up the stairs to pass me her phone. I spin in a circle and then peer at the screen. In the photo, my cheeks are flushed with cold and excitement, and my eyes are shining. I could do this, right?

Nevaeh takes my hand, spins me in the snow, and dips me, her braids tumbling across her face, snow from the trees above us plopping down on our heads.

"We'd be so, so good at throwing an underground burlesque revue," Taylor says reverently, as Nevaeh sets me back on my feet.

"It would be beautiful," Katherine says.

"So why the hell not?" Nevaeh says.

All three of them are grinning. But Nevaeh's words stop me. Why the hell not? There's got to be a *why not*.

The idea still fizzes and pops and sparkles in my head with a *what if?* and a *wouldn't it be amazing?* But the sounds of the normal world—the kids crunching along the paths to class, the distant *bong* of the clock tower, the chattering and the wind— it's all so normal and ordinary and safe, the music of our days. We could get caught, and then we would risk losing it all.

It's an idea that's tricky at best and just plain ridiculous at worst. I can't let myself get worked up about fantasies, get side-tracked from doing something real, concrete. Workable. And not against school rules.

"Addie," Katherine says. "What is it?" I shake my head at her.

"It'll work," Taylor says.

"It wouldn't be a problem," Nevaeh says. She sounds so reasonable.

I love the idea. But why am I the only one of us who notices how absurd it is? I mean, Nevaeh is usually the practical, level-headed one, but if she were the kind of person who bounced around, she'd be bouncing right now.

"Okay," I say after a moment. I square my shoulders. "Pretend it's the best idea ever."

"Which it is," Taylor says.

"Fine, yes, it's pretty great. But how do we pull it off?"

"It's not like I haven't snuck around extensively after curfew," Taylor points out.

"The rest is just logistics," Nevaeh says, sounding reasonable. "I'm good at that."

"What if we get caught?" I say. "This is more than sneaking out. We'd get suspended. They'd take our pieces out of the showcases. Our parents would freak. We'd be totally screwed."

Katherine says simply, "So we won't get caught."

"You don't know that," I say.

Nevaeh starts ticking off points on her mitten. "One, it turns out you do have a genius, marketable skill. Two, you have us."

"Three, it is senior year, and we must do something wonderful," Katherine breaks in.

"Four, and here's the thing, for real: I guarantee you that we will regret it all our days if we don't even try," Taylor says.

"I am going right here on record to say I'm all in, because it's going to be legendary, no matter what happens," Nevaeh says. She's got her winner-takes-all smile on, and I have a shimmering rush of make-me-high confidence. When Nevaeh believes in something, it becomes absolutely, 100 percent real.

"Six, you will make so much money, Addie," Taylor says, dropping his hands on my shoulders and putting his forehead against mine.

"You missed five," I say.

"Five AND six, it'll be like taking money from a baby. A really rich baby who drives a Tesla," Taylor says.

"Seven, it would be the most fun way to make money ever," Katherine says.

"Eight," Nevaeh says. "We can't get jobs here. We can't borrow cash; none of us can get a loan. There are no easy after-school felonies to commit. But this idea. This is everything we're good at, and the four of us could pull it off."

"And so what if we're sitting in detention for the rest of the semester?" Taylor says. "It'll be worth it."

"It's not your responsibility to figure it out," I say.

"*Addie*. We keep telling you," Katherine starts in again, but the clock tower is bonging again.

I shake my head. "You are all wonderful, and we are late."

"Are you really saying no?" Taylor says. "That's not the Addie I know."

I snort. "That won't work either."

"What if—" Katherine starts.

"If you sneak off and start your own, I will never talk to you again," I say.

"That is not what I was going to say!" Katherine says. "I was going to say what if we *want* to do it? Not just for the money."

"You can strip in our room all you want," Nevaeh tells her, and Katherine pushes her shoulder, and I shake my head at them, point up toward the clock tower when the bell rings.

"All right, I need to go fail English now, okay?" I say.

Katherine scoffs at that, but we all plod back to the path. They break off at the science building.

"I'll see you all at dinner," I call to them, and I take off down the path with a fizz of sequins and silk and worry still stuck in my brain.

5

I don't remember anything about any of my afternoon classes, and now, before dinner, I'm trying to catch up on my reading for class tomorrow. I'm not thinking about Angles or the email Carly sent me with links to grant possibilities, all of which we had already found at lunch. I texted my sweethearts that I was sorry and turned off my phone, because I also don't want to keep looking at the pictures of burlesque costumes Taylor keeps forwarding me without commentary.

They're distracting, and I am trying to work.

And yet I'm doing less reading and more clutching Rachel, my worn-out childhood stuffed tiger, to my chest, staring at the constellation of faded stars on the ceiling of my tiny, single room, listening to Amy a couple of doors down argue with the hall supervisor about what "open flame" technically means when you get right down to it. I'm feeling mostly convinced by her argument when the Skype noise jangles on my laptop, sitting open on my desk.

I peer over the bed rail and then yank my pillow onto my face. My mom. But I've avoided too many of her calls lately, and the guilt has reached pick-up-the-phone levels. The ringing stops, but then she calls again. She must have remembered the Angles decision was coming.

I tumble over the rail and onto the floor to answer.

"There's my star!" she says as soon as her face takes over the screen.

"Hi, Mom!" I say, nudging my door shut with my toe. I smooth my hair back and smile into the camera, trying to look perky and alert. I don't want to worry her. Or get her started about whether I'm dieting or rehearsing enough. Those are the cures for everything, according to her.

She leans forward, squinting. "Oof. Look at those bags under your eyes."

"Mom!"

"Dab a little concealer, honey. You don't want to look like an old hag at eighteen," she says.

"I've been really busy—"

"Tell me about it! You know I haven't slept a wink in days either!" I can tell she's looking at the picture of herself in the corner of the screen. She tucks a wing of her hair, platinum blond, chin length, and ironed straight, behind her ear. She's got a glass of her boxed Chablis at her elbow. "I would have called sooner, but I've just had so much going on," she says. "You know me."

"It's okay," I reassure her, smiling. She's busy—the wine-tasting club she started, community association president, head of the neighborhood committee, drawing crowds and always planning things, now that she has time with me gone. "I'm glad you called," I say. "It's good news!"

"Well, how did you know already?" she says.

"What?"

"Is it on my face? Do I look radiant?" She laughs at herself. "I do feel radiant!"

I feel a little lost. "Great, but . . . why?"

"Clive just asked me to move in with him!"

"What?" I say again.

"I'm amazed too!" she says. She squints, finally realizing that I'm a little confused. "You remember Clive, honey."

I don't. She goes on anyway.

"The one with the beach condo? No? He has that kind of thing on his cheek, you remember?" She taps her own smooth cheek to illustrate and then waves her hand. "You should. But never mind. Our condo has the ocean right there at our doorstep."

"Wait, Mom—"

"I know. It's only a studio. But doesn't that make it even more romantic?" She sighs, leans back in her chair, and pats her helmet of hair. She's in the kitchen at home, sitting at the scratched-up laminate island. "He wants me to move in just as soon as possible because he says being apart from me is hard, which is sweet. And he says it's about time I get out of this dump." She waves her hand around at the old wooden cabinets and the intricate flower stencils she painstakingly painted around the top of the walls when I was little. She didn't always think it was a dump. "The girls say I shouldn't be rattling around here all alone, empty nesting since you left me," she says. "Summer on the beach sounds much better." She stops to take a long sip of her wine.

My first, immediate thought is that it'll be a summer with no place for me to go home to if I can't make Angles work. And who is this Clive guy, anyway? I don't even know where he came from. But she always tells me to trust her, so I don't want to let on I have misgivings.

"I think he's going to propose soon too," she confides, leaning closer. "I think he wanted to say something else at dinner." I hope my face says "supportive," not "alarmed." Her shoulders are white-lady pink-tan and freckled and too bony. She's on another diet, a strict one it looks like, and it worries me.

I clear my throat, coughing back things I want to say. She can get so upset when she thinks I don't understand, or thinks I don't support her.

"Wow" is what I come up with.

"Don't worry; he won't make you call him Daddy!" She laughs at her own joke.

"Ew, Mom," I say, cringing.

"I know, I know!" She puts her hands up. "Just a joke. You know how I am."

"So wait, you're moving soon?" I push around the magnets on the bulletin board above my desk, forming them into a smiley face. Someone, probably Taylor, has put together a poem from the magnetic poetry kit on top of my semester-schedule printout: *Flat dogs beef in sky / dance your but off / donuts ask why*. Also on the board, that picture of Mohadesa Rabei.

"Well, if you hadn't stolen all the suitcases, I could have," she says, shaking her finger at me playfully. "You know I can't afford to buy new ones right now."

"It sounds like he'll buy you all the suitcases you want, Mom."

"It's true!" she says, and then hesitates. "You're happy for me, Addie?"

I want her to be happy.

"It sounds like you like him," I say to her.

"Of course I do," she says. "He says he's never met anyone like me."

"That's what's important, right?" I say.

She's sipping her wine, but her eyes widen over the rim of her glass at that, and she sets it down, points at me. "Speaking of important!" she says.

"Yes!" I say, sitting up taller, ready to share the good part of my Angles news.

"I got one of those silly parental alerts from your school! The emails? I swear I told them I don't need them."

"An alert?" My stomach wallops my insides.

"Something about a grade being low? I deleted it, of course. Is there a way you could tell them I don't want to be bothered? We all know books aren't your thing."

"It's not *that* low!" I blurt, and I feel myself getting defensive. I don't even know what class it is. "I've just been—"

"Sweetheart, you're a dancer, not a student," she says. "You can't be good at everything."

"But what class is it?" I don't want to fail my classes. Where did I screw up?

She shrugs. "I don't know. Don't fail, mind you. But stay focused on what's important."

"I am," I tell her, "but—"

She glances over her shoulder. "I really do have to go, sweetie, but talk soon?" I see her finger reach out to hit END on her tablet.

"Mom!" I say, too loudly. She looks startled, and her eyes flick up to meet mine in the camera. "Angles!"

She blinks, so I repeat it. "Angles, remember? I got in. I got the senior spot this summer."

She frowns at me, cocks her head. "Oh!" she says. I can see her smoothing out her expression, because wrinkles. "Right." She brightens. "Of course I wouldn't forget. You should have reminded me." She lifts her glass, toasting me, affectionate. "You're a star! I've been telling my girlfriends that. That while their kids are working at Target or wherever this summer, you'll be dancing in Paris."

"Milan," I say, but she doesn't seem to hear me.

"My talented girl," she says.

"It's great, right?" I enthuse. I can't tell her I didn't get the scholarship. She's beaming at me, her contest winner, her star on the local dance-kids circuit.

"Oh! Clive and I get to visit and see you dance *in Paris*!"

"Milan," I say.

"I'll go up and give you a big bouquet at the end," she starts, but I interrupt.

"It costs a lot of money to go."

"Excuse me?"

Deep breath. "It costs six thousand dollars. And I—"

Her expression changes, and before I can admit I didn't get the scholarship, she's set down her wineglass, leaning forward, her voice clipped.

"What? They're asking you for money? You *won*."

I bite my lip and nod. "It's the cost of the program plus—"

"No," she says, holding up her hand. "That is ridiculous."

"But Mom—"

"You *won*," she says. Her voice is confident, stern. "They should be paying *you*."

"It's tuition," I try to explain. "It's like—it's like a summer class." But she's not listening.

"Go to that woman in your department, and explain to her that she needs to fix it. That's not the way it works."

"Carly? She can't do anything about it, Mom." I grip the edge of the laptop, leaning in.

Her lips make a knot. "Oh, really?" she snipes. "I sincerely doubt that. Does she get part of what they want you to pay?"

She's in dance-school-mom mode, raised voice until she gets what she wants.

"No, of course not—"

"If Carlin doesn't listen, I can call the dean and tell him about the kind of people he's hiring."

"No! I'll—I'll talk to Carly."

She huffs. "I can't *believe* they think they could get away with this. That's not how this works in the real world. They're not getting a *dime*."

"I'll talk to her tomorrow morning, Mom. I promise."

"Just walk away," she says. "Show them they can't do that. They're lucky you agreed to be in their little thing in the first place."

"Let me just check first, okay? She must have missed something. Or I maybe misheard her?" My voice trails off.

Mom snorts at that, her face relaxing. "Well, that wouldn't surprise me," she says. She sighs, shakes her head. She reaches for her wineglass, gestures at me with it. "You go straighten it out first thing, you hear? You don't let people take advantage of you, Adeleina. And don't give me a heart attack like that again. Good Lord."

I apologize and she sighs again.

"You know, though," she says. "It wouldn't hurt to just give it up. I know you wanted to try this thing, but we can just move straight to LA after school."

I freeze at that. I don't know what my face is doing. After all these years, she still doesn't understand the difference between my dreams and her dreams.

Does she know that LA basically means cutting me right in half? I mean, how much weight will I have to lose before anyone out there even looks me in the eye?

She doesn't notice I'm not answering her.

"Maybe this Angles thing just wasn't meant to be, Adeleina," she says.

"I'm going to figure it out."

She shrugs. "We'll talk about it." And with that, she seems to push it out of her mind, her face brightening. "I'm glad I got to tell you my news! Aren't you glad you picked up for your mother this time? Now go get some beauty sleep." She kisses her fingers at me, and I smile through her usual reminders about vegetables and skin care, her cheery, air-kissing goodbye, until she finally hangs up.

I sit there in front of my laptop with a falling feeling in my chest, pressure behind my eyes, tingling in my fingers, breath catching in my throat.

I shouldn't have opened my mouth about the money. She doesn't even want me to try to get a job in a serious dance company, let alone do a program that you have to pay for.

She wants the whole world for me, but it's not the world I want, bright lights and diets. Whittling me down to the good parts, she'd say. So they can see how wonderful I am inside and out, as if my body's hiding a secret.

That's not the kind of famous I want to be. I don't know how to explain that I want to be a groundbreaking dancer. I want to change the dance world, make a mark. Learn from the best, become one of the best. Make the world shape itself to fit me. Most of all, just dance.

Angles, not Los Angeles.

I put my head down on my desk so I don't have to look at my reflection in the screen, and then I sit up to google again, but this time instead of grants it's "how to make money fast" and "make $6,000 in three months" and then "what is a pyramid scheme," and an hour later I close my laptop and stare at the wall and try to let myself give up on Angles and my own idea of a future in dance. There are other ways to make it as a dancer; I know there are.

I push my chair in, pace my small room, shake out my hands. I can't stay still.

It's not too late to apply somewhere I could afford. It's not too late to grit my teeth and start planning auditions to dance companies. It's not too late to come up with some very practical plan. Right. So many other ways.

I stop in the middle of the room. Stuck to my bulletin board, the picture of Mohadesa Rabei, mid-*assemblé*, I tore out of a brochure.

But so many reasons why Angles is the only way for *me*.

Thundering heartbeat. Then another.

I push open the door of my room, march down the hallway.

A fire blooming in my chest, so fierce and roaring that I'm trembling.

I am talented, and I am ambitious, and I am *lucky*.

I dodge around my RA, who is tacking a flyer up on the community board, and swing around the corner.

This time, I'm lucky because I have these friends. And this brilliantly creative, perfect, ridiculous idea, whole and glittering and glamorous. A totally wonderfully absurd idea that has not stopped sparkling in my imagination, that hasn't stopped whispering possibilities and plans in my ear. That feels like a roller coaster. That could work, if we can pull it off. The idea is too bonkers for any adult to catch on to, if we do it right.

I march through the second-floor lounge.

Of course we'll do it right. Every one of us is creative, clever, crafty. And for all of us, success has always been our only option.

Not even at the worst moments, at my most exhausted, my angriest, my most frustrated, icing my knees, gritting my teeth through injuries, have I ever once considered the idea that I could fail. Never once.

I knock on their dorm room door, crack it open a bit to peer inside the dim room. I see the fluff of the fancy performance tutus Katherine and Nevaeh have hung on the walls, and then the static cloud of Katherine's hair and her sleepy face when she sits up on her elbow in the top bunk. Nevaeh is stretched out next to her. They've been napping together, snarled-up limbs and snores as usual.

"Hey," I whisper to Katherine. "So I was thinking. Do you really want to do it? Are you really sure?"

There's a long, long moment of silence while Katherine stares at me, and then a sudden flurry, shaking Nevaeh's shoulder.

Nevaeh sits up, her hair wrap askew. "What, what, what?" She reaches over to click on the light and sit up all the way.

I slip into the room and go up on my tiptoes, clutching the rail of the top bunk. Pull myself up on the lower bed, bounce a little. "I just need you to be sure. I need you to swear it."

"The burlesque show," Katherine says slowly, her voice dipping so low I can barely hear her.

"*The burlesque show*," I whisper back.

"I don't know why we're whispering," Nevaeh whispers, and pokes my shoulder. "What the hell do you think we were saying?"

"That we have terrible, wonderful ideas!"

Katherine is frowning and punching at her phone. "Darn it, Taylor, pick up," she mutters. "Ha! There. Tell him, Addie," Katherine orders, turning the screen to face me.

"We're doing it," Taylor says, leaning into the camera,

before I even open my mouth. His hair is perfect, of course. He smirks.

"Only if you're sure!" I yell over Nevaeh's and Katherine's excited voices.

"Of course I am." He's beaming. "This is the best adventure ever."

I pull in a breath. "Then let's do it," I say.

Katherine and Nevaeh tumble off the bunk, wrapping their arms around me, and my face hurts from smiling. I've dropped Katherine's phone, and Taylor's shouting from the floor, "I'm on my way! Get your asses downstairs and sign me in," and I tell Nevaeh, "No, you know I never cry," as she dabs at my cheeks with the hem of her gauzy skirt. They don't ask why I've changed my mind.

We're a whirlwind, racing down to the lobby to meet Taylor. So fast from an idea to planning. This is the way big things happen; I know it is. You leap because you know you're going to stick the landing.

We're doing it.

6

When we come back from dinner, the lobby is busy, voices echoing up to the exposed metal rafters and bouncing off the tall glass that frames either side of the front doors, which are never closed for long. We started arguing about burlesque names while we ate, and we're still arguing while we wait in line at the front desk, because a clever name is a thing you're supposed to have. It's loud, but we're keeping our voices super low, like we're spies with strange code names.

"No, I am not going to call myself 'Paris Boom Boom,'" Katherine whispers. She frowns at Taylor. "It doesn't even make sense."

Taylor points to Nevaeh's phone, and his voice rises. "The *internet* says it's a perfectly respectable burlesque name!"

Nevaeh rams him in the side with her elbow. The student in front of us turns, and my heart does a lurch—*we've been found out!*—even though I know that's ridiculous. I start giggling, and Taylor elbows me in turn, folding his lips in like he's going to start laughing too.

"Oh, hi, Katherine!" says the girl who turned around, because Katherine knows every single person on campus and they all like her.

"We're already so bad at this," Taylor whispers as we shuffle forward in the line.

"Speak for yourself," says Nevaeh, snickering as Katherine signs Taylor in.

"We're doomed," I say.

"By the way, I will quit if you don't call yourself Candie Kisses," Taylor says to Nevaeh, signing his name next to Katherine's with a flourish.

"Oh, ugh," Nevaeh says, her voice suddenly loud. She's looking over my shoulder, and I turn.

Gavin. Who has seen us, smiles, and waves. He is cute. I hate it.

"Aw, shit," I say.

Katherine grimaces. The expression always seems hilariously wrong on her face.

"Go, go, go," I say, hustling us over to the elevator, which is already almost full. We manage to cram ourselves in.

"Emergency!" Taylor says when people complain. Nevaeh stabs the CLOSE DOORS button one, two, three times, but of course Gavin is quick enough to stick his hand between the closing doors, making everyone around us groan again.

"Hey, dipshit, get out of the way," someone in the back says.

"Hey, Mark," Gavin says to him, but he's grinning at me, his eyes crinkling at the corners and his dimples deepening. Dark and wildly curly hair like a halo. Probably smelling like something warm and woodsy. Making me want to smile back at him. He's not letting go of the door.

"Are you running away?" he asks me. His mouth is a perfect

Cupid's bow, and I know that stubble he's working right now feels like the most delicious rough velvet on your skin.

"Could you let the door go?" Mark says.

I clear my throat to say something polite but devastating, but Taylor beats me.

"Hi, Gavin!" he says brightly. "We were just heading upstairs and never talking to you again."

Gavin ignores him. "Come here! Let me talk to you for a sec," he says to me.

"Oh, come on, dude," Mark says.

"I know, right?" Taylor says, twisting around.

The elevator alarm starts to ding, and I shove Gavin backward, push him through the crowd, past the sign-in desk. Taylor, Katherine, and Nevaeh swarm out of the elevator behind us.

"I'll just be a second?" I say to them. Katherine frowns but stops Taylor from following me, and Nevaeh rolls her eyes and slouches against the side of the check-in desk, looking pointedly at her wrist like she is wearing a watch.

"Hi," I say, turning back to Gavin, my hand on my hip. "So? What do you want?" I sound totally unconcerned, I hope, because, oh, he makes me feel breathless, nervous, fluttery. Which switches on my bravado, the confident smile, the hope that he can't tell how nervous he makes me, because I'd die of embarrassment.

His smile is warm fingers gliding down my spine, a hand gripping my hip, lips at my ear, teeth nipping at my earlobe, and I suck in a breath. I remind myself that chemistry like this between people, it's just chemicals. Unfortunately, chemicals don't get the memo when the rest of you is done with someone.

"Hi," he says. "I was going to text you, and here you are."

"Pretty sure I blocked you," I lie, sounding very casual.

I did delete his number. (After Nevaeh scolded me.) But I never blocked him. Because maybe he'd realize he made a terrible mistake and come beg for my forgiveness, right? It hasn't happened in the last six months, but he could have had an epiphany.

"Well, then I'm even more glad I ran into you," he says, leaning forward. Eyes still hazel, check. Eyelashes—nope, not thinking about eyelashes.

"It's a small campus," I say. And why Gavin hasn't dropped off a cliff and into the center of the earth, I do not know. It is unfair.

"Too small," Taylor calls from behind us.

"We need to go finish a thing before curfew," I say, waving toward my friends.

"Finally!" Taylor says.

"And it's rude to leave Ellory waiting," I add, because I can't resist.

"That's the thing," Gavin says. He reaches out for my hand, but I pull it back with a snap. His nothing words give me a whisper of, a hint of—something in my stomach. Which is ridiculous. "Can you give me just a minute?"

"For you? Never." Obviously I am lying, though, because I'm still standing here.

"Still beautiful, still stubborn," he says.

"Still leaving now," I say, and manage to spin, but he stops me with a touch on my arm, which ruins my flounce.

"Meet me tomorrow at the end of the arts block?" he says in a low voice, quickly. "Before lunch."

I shake my head. "Busy," I say, and I turn away, tossing my hair, ignoring him, not looking back over my shoulder as if I am cool and calm and confident and self-assured and not at all rattled just because he smiled at me, and I still really like his smile, and I still really like when he smiles at me because he's paying attention to me, because he's acting like he wants to pay attention to me, because I am, what would Katherine say? A dingbat.

"What did Gavin the Jerk want?" Nevaeh demands as we get back in the elevator. She stabs the CLOSE DOOR button. I am positive that he winks at me from across the lobby as the door glides shut.

"Ugh, he is so cheesy," Taylor says.

"That was an actual wink, wasn't it?" I say to him.

"Of course it was," Taylor says.

"At least it wasn't finger guns?"

"Was he mean to you?" Katherine demands.

Was it mean that he just waltzed up to be mysterious? To be all, *Oh, Ellory? That's the thing.* I know so much better than to get tangled up with him again, any worse than my brain is already stuck on him, wanting the kind of closure you get in romantic movies. No, wanting to win at the end, me triumphant, my foot on his back and my sword in the air and hearts in his eyes.

"Well, he was all charming at me," I start.

"He's such a louse," Nevaeh says.

"Hot cream pie on the outside and maggots inside," Taylor says.

"Taylor," Katherine says.

"Not maggots exactly," I say.

"Addie," Nevaeh says.

I blow my hair out of my face. "He claims he wants to talk," I say. "He made noises about Ellory."

They all glance at one another. The elevator dings again for the next floor, and a group of theater kids get on. I can tell by the completely smooth, completely blank white masks they're all wearing.

"Hi, creepy," Taylor says to the one standing next to him. They raise their hand.

"How's it going?" they say.

"Is this a performance?" Katherine asks.

"Life is a performance," another masked person intones. The elevator dings, and the theater kids file off at the third floor.

"I didn't think for a second he wanted to get back with me!" I blurt. Taylor snorts. "Oh, be quiet! Okay, yes, for a split second. I'm terrible."

"You're not terrible," Katherine says, petting my arm. "Just maybe—"

"I know," I say. "I have thought all those things too. But—he did say he wants to talk."

"But obviously you're not going to, right?" Nevaeh asks. She stares at me. At the fourth-floor ding, I leap out of the elevator.

"Addie!" she says, calling after me. I am already halfway down the hall, where the overhead light is flickering.

"I don't know what he wanted to talk about!" I call back. I wait for them to catch up to me.

"Nothing good!" Nevaeh says.

"Just good-looking," Taylor says.

"Taylor," Katherine says.

"I mean like a well-baited trap," he explains.

"That is actually a very good metaphor," Katherine says.

"I'm good at so many things." Taylor sighs.

"I cannot with you two," Nevaeh says.

Of course the common room isn't empty. There are kids sprawled on the big brown couches near the window, and Zoe's curly blond head pops up from one when we bump through the doors.

"Addie!" she cries, climbing over the back of the sofa and leaping toward me as if she will fly into my arms. "I nailed the *grande échappé* in—" She stops short, and her eyes get even more huge—big, bright blueberries under the heavy mass of bangs. "Hi, Nevaeh," she says, and flushes a little bit the way she always does, her face mottled pale and strawberry.

"Hi, Zoe," Nevaeh says, and Zoe gets even redder. Katherine shakes her head and drops her bag on the big, soft chair next to the watercooler.

"Can you kids clear out of here for a while?" I ask. "Do you mind?"

"Of course not!" Zoe chirps. "I'll see you tomorrow after dinner?" I blink at her. She says, "We're supposed to go over the fairy variations?"

I hesitate. I had forgotten. That is not like me. "I might be a little late," I say. "But definitely. Make sure you warm up well, okay?"

A tight hug around my waist, and Zoe and her friends are gone. I was nervous when I was asked to be a senior mentor to a group of freshmen. Being a role model and adviser felt like a big, scary responsibility. But it's turned out to be one of my favorite things ever.

"Nevvie and Zoe, sitting in a tree," Taylor is singing, and Nevaeh is whacking him on the head with a pillow in time with the beat.

"Quit it, quit it, quit it!" she sings.

"Straight-girl fever, meant to be," Taylor sings. They're both laughing.

"How do you know she's straight?" Katherine says crossly. "You don't know that!"

Nevaeh shrugs. "Gaydar? Do I have gaydar?" she asks Taylor.

"It's standard issue for the queers," he says, giving her one last bop on the head.

"But do you have a crush on Zoe?" Katherine asks Nevaeh, who looks surprised.

"No, of course not," Nevaeh says, sitting down next to Katherine and nudging her in the shoulder. "You're my platonic life partner."

"What if I had a crush on someone?" Katherine says.

"Well, we'd welcome them into our imaginary marriage," Nevaeh says, patting her hand. "Are you trying to lock the door?" she calls to Taylor.

He's rattling the handles, and then he grabs one of the heavy easy chairs in front of the double doors of the room and drags it in front of them.

"Is that excessive?" I ask.

"We are in secret planning mode," he says. "Everything is top secret!"

I drop to a cross-legged seat on the pilled gray carpet, then dig through my bag looking for a pen and notebook while listening to them talk about their burlesque names. Taylor has decided that Ella Mental is absolutely brilliant.

"Puns are the lowest form of humor!" Katherine is arguing. "Puns are so *doofy*." She's very passionate about it. Nevaeh pats her shoulder consolingly.

"But what if they were the highest form of humor?" Taylor says, sprawling on one of the easy chairs and stretching his long legs out. "*High*-larious!"

Katherine growls and throws a pillow at him.

"Aha!" I say. I hold up a pen and battered notebook triumphantly, but before we can start planning our secret scheme, the door whacks against the heavy chair with a crash.

Taylor sings out, "Occupied!"

A small, indignant face appears through the half-cracked door, red braids dangling. Elsie. One of the theater people who pace up and down hallways muttering to themselves. "You guys can't just, like, keep the whole room for yourself. It's called the *common* room," she says.

"We reserved it," Taylor calls. "There's a sign-up sheet downstairs."

"There is not," she says, scowling.

"Is too," Taylor says. I cover my mouth to keep from laughing out loud at that.

"Well—then I'm going to go look." The long, sad wail of a trombone briefly drowns her out. "Watch where you stick that thing," she yells at the musician, letting the door clunk shut behind her.

"I thought hardly anyone ever comes here!" Katherine says. "Where are they all appearing from?"

"They sense greatness is about to be born," Taylor says, sitting up.

"Okay!" I say. "Then where do we start? I know where to start when you're choreographing a piece—improv. Brainstorming."

Nevaeh finger combs and braids Katherine's hair while Taylor paces, and all the questions come pouring out: *Where do we do this? When do we do this? How do we do this? Who do we do it for? How do we get the word out? How do we not get caught getting the word out? How do we keep it secret? How do we keep out creeps? How do we not get caught setting up a burlesque club on campus? How do we find/make costumes? How do we build sets? How do we choreograph a burlesque act? How do you take your clothes off without falling down? How do we pull this off in, like, under a month? Sparkles?*

Taylor looks over my shoulder at the list. "Well, those are very good questions," he says.

"Yes, that's why we asked them," I say.

Katherine raises her hand. "The answer to the last one is 'yes.' Or 'a lot.' The sparkles question," she reminds us.

"Good point," Taylor says, and reaches down to grab the pen and circle that one.

"Okay, well, make research and choreography numbers one and two on the list," Nevaeh says. "We need those done yesterday. But item three should be 'Where do we do this?'" She pauses. "I wish I had a hair tie," she says, surveying the fishtail braid she's created in Katherine's hair.

"I think we want to keep it way small," I say. "Easier to find a spot to set up. And safer that way. More exclusive too. Not more than twenty people a night, three shows."

"A hundred bucks a ticket," Nevaeh says, nodding.

"I did the math right!" I'm pleased with myself. Six thousand bucks. "Is that too much?" I ask.

Nevaeh snorts. "Pocket change to most kids."

I grimace at that. Of course it is. And then I am struck with a thought. "No, we have to make more than that. I can't take all the money."

"That is the entire point!" Katherine says.

"We'll see," I say, and they're all groaning at me.

As for location, it needs to be somewhere we can set up fast and easy, gives us enough room for us and the audience, and is easy to sneak people into and out of.

In our heads, we're seeing a tiny trickle of students slipping out of their dorms, sneaking from building to building. Sliding silently across the campus and through basement doors or back entrances, to a darkened room full of twinkling fairy lights and shimmering cloth and gauzy veils and velvet pillows—and the smell of incense to cover up the smell of dank basement, Taylor adds.

"Gross, Taylor," Katherine says.

"Accurate," he says.

But we can spin magic up out of anything, we're pretty sure. As we brainstorm a list of possibilities, from basement common rooms to storage rooms to groundskeepers' buildings, it starts to feel real.

"That's a lot of places," Katherine says.

"We're just going to need to scout them—" I start to say, before I get overwhelmed, and then I jump when the doors bang against the chair again. The freshman-curfew warning bell rang not too long ago, which means the halls are filling up with noise and snatches of singing. The doors whap against the chairs once, twice more. Taylor arches to his feet in a cat stretch and glides over, peering out.

"There's no sign-up sheet!" someone says indignantly. It's Elsie.

"It's in the laundry room," Taylor says, leaning against the door, but she's pushing back.

"You said it was downstairs!"

"Definitely in the laundry room," he says, and bangs the door shut, then leans against it casually. Outside Elsie thumps a few times, halfheartedly.

"Come sit down," I say to Taylor. "Where were we?"

"So the problem," Nevaeh says, "is that most buildings are locked at night."

"Jack," Katherine says, so quickly and firmly it's clear that this is something she's already thought about.

"Is that a noun or a verb?" Nevaeh teases, and Katherine flushes pink but pushes on.

"Jack," she repeats. "He was in my trig class last year." She points at Nevaeh. "He was in your Shakespeare class last year, too, I think."

"The grumpy one with no friends?" Nevaeh says.

"He is just quiet!" she says. "He is *so* nice."

"You like everyone, Kitty-Kat," Nevaeh says.

"He *is*," she insists.

I glance at Taylor, who lifts an eyebrow at me.

"He's just not a joiner or whatever, but he has always been super nice to me," she adds. "I tutored him in trig last year. He's funny, when you get to know him, and sweet, and we talked about a lot of stuff, and we still do, and—"

"Katherine Mary Elizabeth James, do you have a crush?" Nevaeh says delightedly, teasingly, as Taylor sits up and claps.

"I don't!" she says.

"Are you sure?" I say.

"Yes!" she says in a very dignified way. "I am sure I do not have a crush on Jack."

Nevaeh and I trade glances. Nevaeh shrugs, the tiniest movement of her shoulders, one perfect eyebrow just the slightest bit arched. I think we both believe there's something maybe, possibly happening, but we will not push it.

"No one should," Taylor says, reaching over to take Katherine's hand. "I heard he has rabies."

"He does not!" she says, and then she laughs. "Shut up." She clears her throat. "Anyway! He also does AV things all over campus for teachers. For our performances! You have all seen him plenty of times."

I shake my head, and Taylor shrugs.

"There are a weird number of Jacks on campus," Taylor says. "And every Jack I've ever met has been grumpy. And hot."

"He is not that grumpy!" Katherine says.

"Hm, is he hot?" Taylor asks, perking up.

She flushes a little. "No! I mean, probably, I guess? I don't know! But that is not the point!"

"Is he a burlesque dancer?" Taylor says.

"He has *keys*," Katherine says. "He has security codes. He knows every building. He can get in everywhere."

Taylor waggles his eyebrows at that, and Katherine whacks him on the shoulder as Nevaeh protects her face from the mayhem.

"So," I say slowly, trying to catch up with her thought process, "you want this Jack guy to help us?" I realize I am uncomfortable with the idea of letting someone else in on this. "Katherine—" I start.

She looks at me expectantly, pleased with herself.

I amend what I'm going to say. "Aren't there other ways to get into campus buildings?"

"After dark, though?" Nevaeh says. "How are we going to get in anywhere after lights off and lockup?"

"But—" I chew on the inside of my cheek. "I worry that it could make this more unsafe for all of us."

"We can trust him," Katherine says. "I like him; I really do."

Her tiny bit of extra enthusiasm for him aside, she does have good taste in people. I know that. I'm twisting my fingers together in my lap anyway.

"We can think about—" I start to say, but Katherine interrupts.

"I mean it, though. I've been thinking about this. I think we need him."

"Maybe we don't need him," I say.

"We might need him," Nevaeh says.

I look at Taylor.

"I think we need him," he says, lifting a shoulder.

"Traitor!" I say, and sigh. "Okay. I trust you, I do. But I'm nervous." I'm terrified, actually, and I think this is the worst idea. "Can we meet him before we decide anything?"

"Of course!" Katherine says. "I would love for you all to meet him! I would love for him to meet you too."

A flash catches my eye, lighting up my phone screen. Contact not found. Message: *Did you *really* block me? ;)* I flip it over as the senior-curfew warning chimes and Katherine asks Nevaeh what's wrong. Nevaeh is looking at her own phone.

"It's just trolls," Nevaeh says. She hands the phone to Taylor.

"Another terrible one," he says. "The lighting is tragic."

"I've seen worse," Nevaeh says.

"God, Nevaeh, how many dick pics do you get?" he says, sounding serious now.

She shrugs. "A couple. A few. A bunch. Sometimes the dickstorm picks up, sometimes it dies down. You know there's nothing you can do about it."

"But could you report it somewhere—" I start.

"What would anyone do?" Nevaeh says. "They keep coming, I'll keep blocking them."

"They are udickquitous!" Katherine blurts out. We all pause. "That was a pun," she adds.

Nevaeh breaks into a guffaw like I have never heard from her, and I'm laughing so hard I can't breathe, and Taylor flops over onto his side, wheezing.

"I'm dying," he says. "This is me dead."

"Oh my god, I love you," Nevaeh says, wrapping Katherine in her arms. Katherine is very red and very pleased with herself, and my stomach hurts from laughing worse than it has ever hurt at Pilates.

The warning chimes again, and we sit up, catch our breaths, and quickly go over our plan for the week: Research burlesque acts for inspiration, for guidance. Meet Jack so he and Katherine can get scouting underway, if we approve of him. Come up with a way to invite only the people we want. Keep it all secret. Sure, sure, we can do this in a month, we agree.

I'm grinning, and my stomach feels like it's full of glitter, a little bit of nerves, a little bit of glee. Nervous glee.

"Wait," I say, as Katherine and Nevaeh stand and stretch, and Taylor shrugs into his coat. "Here's the thing." I can hear how wobbly my voice sounds, and I clear my throat. "I know you're doing this for me, and—and I'm worried it'll go wrong—"

"It will be okay," Katherine says, taking my hand.

"But it's going to be dangerous!" I blurt. "We're going to be sneaking around, lying to instructors and teachers and everyone else." I start to build up speed. "We're going to be doing this thing *and* our regular dance classes, *and* there's spring showcase rehearsals *and* all our schoolwork on top of that, and midterms are coming up too!" Nevaeh takes my other hand, and I look at her pleadingly. "If we're caught and get suspended or detention until we're dead or whatever or both and lose all that time from our lives and piss everyone off, it will be my fault."

"All of our faults," Katherine says.

Taylor catches my gaze. "Hey. You'd do anything for me, right?" he asks me. His eyes are drilling into mine.

"Of course," I say. The answer is immediate and sure.

"Well, same same," he says, and finishes putting on his parka. "So." He shrugs.

Katherine shakes my hand a little. Her face is so serious. "I am in. I have never, ever done anything like this before. Maybe I would never get a chance to ever do something as wonderful."

"I'm up for anything," Nevaeh says to me, squeezing my hand. "I wouldn't miss this for the world."

"You are all out of your minds," I say. They know that means *thank you from the bottom of my heart.*

"And I'm ready to get naked," Taylor says.

"We know," Nevaeh says.

"Well, okay, then," I say. "This is it." I let myself feel a curl of anticipation in my belly, edged with a bright gold ribbon of hope and excitement, enough fear to make me want to double down. That delicious thought again: *We're doing this.* We can pull this off.

The doors rattle again, and Elsie shouts, "There's no sign-in sheet at all! I know you're lying!"

"She's got a great sense of timing," Taylor says.

"And we're ready to go?" Katherine says.

"Full-speed ahead," Nevaeh says to her.

I raise an imaginary glass. "To—" I pause. Did we ever come up with a name?

"Dirty Little Secret," Taylor says.

I laugh. "Okay, fine. To our Dirty Little Secret!" We pretend to clink our glasses, and we pretend to down our drinks, but there's nothing pretend about the sunburst of excitement in my stomach, like nothing I've ever felt before. Could there be a better way to send off senior year? There's never been a better one.

"Do you think she's got a crush on Jack?" Nevaeh says to me in a low voice, pushing open the stairwell door to our floor. Katherine's running downstairs to sign Taylor out.

"I don't know," I say. "I've never seen her have a crush."

"I just don't want her to get hurt," Nevaeh says.

"We'll protect her with our lives," I say.

"Good point," she says, poking me.

I'm still smiling in front of the bathroom mirror in my fuzzy bathrobe, listening to the shuffle of seniors through the hallway, slamming doors, scraps of conversation: *good night* and *shut up!* and *don't forget tomorrow*—and *no, she did*—and a scrap of a song. While I brush my teeth, bubbles of anticipation are still frothing inside me as I think about this ridiculous plan we have. Where to start choreographing a number so far removed from anything else I've ever done. Fascinated already by all the ways it might be the same, and all the ways it's going to blow what I already do out of the water. A dreamy image of peeling off a long satin glove to the whoops of glee in the audience, flinging it out to the crowd, gleaming bare neck. *You may enjoy me. You're welcome.* I smile experimentally at the mirror, big and confident, then squeeze my eyes shut. Confident, powerful, fat, beautiful, proud show-off under warm spotlights, never afraid. I spit my toothpaste into the sink as the door swings open and a group of girls in camis and sleep shorts come chattering in— and I'm automatically sizing myself against them before I can cut off the knee-jerk thought, the habit that's so hard to break. I straighten up, clutching my toothbrush, and wipe my mouth with the back of my hand. I'm going to have to practice.

7

The next day I skip breakfast, because I'm too keyed up to eat, but between classes I dig out the emergency protein bar from my locker. It turns into a rock in my stomach as I go back and forth—should I go see Gavin or not? I did say no, but he didn't seem to believe I meant it, and if I went I'd be proving him right. In Pilates I decide I want to *know* what he wanted to tell me, even though I know it's not important—and the second the clock ticks over to noon, I hop up and grab my yoga mat to roll up on the way out the door. Avoiding Carly, who stopped me before class to assure me she was still looking for funding solutions while I shifted from foot to foot. "Don't worry," she told me, with her hand on my arm. "Okay," I agreed, and she shooed me into the studio.

There's no time to change if I want to see Gavin before lunch—I head straight to the rehearsal theater, clawing my bun down and combing the hair spray out with my fingers. My sweat cools in the frigid air, and my ears hurt without a hat. He'll keep badgering me to talk to him if I don't go now, I tell myself. I'm going to be cool, and poised, and witty, and he's going to look at me with those warm eyes and want more. Ha.

When I swerve to cut across the quad, out of nowhere Christopher falls into step with me, blowing all the almost-pleasant adrenaline out of me.

"Where are you running off to?" he asks, picking up the pace when I speed up.

"That way," I say, pointing the direction I'm walking. I don't want to stop to talk to him—why doesn't he notice that?

"Ha, funny," he says. "Haven't you heard guys don't like funny girls?"

"Sorry," I say. "I can't help it."

"Aw, come on," he says. "You're afraid I'm out of your league, huh?"

My face scrunches up. "Yeah, that's right," I say.

Still with the eternal crooked smile, pleased with himself. "I'll tag you in!" he says, spreading his hands wide. "Let you play in the big league! Get out there on the field with the winners."

There's a sharp edge to his voice that scrapes over my skin, makes me think of the girls in my Florida dance classes, gathering around me with glittering eyes, telling me they wanted to be my friend. But I'm not seven years old anymore.

"Not interested in playing."

"You're no fun!" He glances sideways at me, his grin wider. "Well," he says, drawing the word out, "at least send me the link to the rest of your hot videos?"

I halt. "*What?*" My heart thumps hard.

He laughs. "Like that one from the party," he says, nudging me with his shoulder. "You could make some money with videos like that. I'd subscribe. 'Big, beautiful women with big—'"

"I'll send you an invite when I launch the site," I interrupt, my voice sarcastic.

"All right," he says, pleased, and I don't hear the rest, taking a sharp turn down the sidewalk that leads to the theater. Relief when he doesn't follow. I fumble for my phone with frozen fingers and start a text to Nevaeh, my fingers moving automatically.

Hey do you think you could delete that vi—

I stop.

That video. He's such a dick. I was dancing. I was play-acting. I felt beautiful, and he tried to make it sleazy. He can't turn my sexiness into something he's taking from me, because that's backward, the opposite of burlesque entirely. Which is precisely why someone like him would never, ever get the privilege of being one of the people invited to come see our show. And, oh, it makes me smile to think of that. Sucks to be you, Christopher.

I click off my phone screen without finishing the message.

Before the door closes behind me in the foyer, I can hear Gavin. He's got a velvety baritone that fills the entire theater, no mic necessary. It's a love song I don't recognize, but the song still feels familiar as he hits a long and longing note, and I realize I've stopped in the middle of unwrapping my scarf in the lobby to listen. When I push through the theater doors to see him onstage, his hair glints red in the spotlight as he sings. He's graceful when he shrugs out of his suit jacket, swings it in one smooth move over his shoulder, and strolls across the stage.

He looks up, midnote, midstroll, and he sees me. His smile tilts up on one side. He cocks his head and steps to the edge of the stage, extending his hand to me as the music soars.

"So taunt me, and hurt me," he sings at me. I sigh, amused

and irritated. "Deceive me, desert me," he murmurs in a voice that drops low.

I shake my head at him.

"I'm yours, till I die," he continues, and he leaps into the air, off the stage, landing so lightly on his feet and way too close to me. He strolls those last few steps toward me.

"So in love, so in love," he croons, reaching out a hand, and I let him take mine because I know a good dramatic moment when I see one. And then he lifts it to his lips, and I fold my lips in so I don't start smiling at him.

"So in love with you, my love . . ." His eyes are locked on mine, silver-bright, and his voice is rich, and his acting, I remind myself, is superb. "Am I," he murmurs. The music swells to a stop, and he drops my hand to acknowledge the scattered clapping of his fellow castmates, give a thumbs-up to someone in head-phones. He turns back to me, grinning, and claps his hands together.

"We're just sound testing, but—" He shrugs. "I think I sound all right."

"You are a total, complete, cheesy show-off cheese ball," I say.

"You are so impressed!" he says. "That's your 'I'm hiding how much I secretly love it' face; I can tell."

I roll my eyes at him, and he lets out a laugh, a real one. He's always seemed to enjoy the fact that I refuse to take him seriously, or pretend to, anyway. I know how to protect my own heart. I thought I knew. *Just chemicals*, I remind myself.

"So what did you need to talk about that you couldn't just text?" I ask.

"I thought you blocked me," he says.

"Right! I mean if I hadn't blocked you," I say, fumbling.

He starts up the aisle and gestures to me. "Come here."

"That can only work on me once," I tell him, and he snorts another laugh, surprised. He remembers. It did work on me, just the once.

We met at one of the first blowoff parties during our summer intensives, him in drama and me in dance, and we just fell into flirting, the back-and-forth so easy and so fun, how he complimented me so ridiculously, how I teased him back and made him laugh, how he looked at me, how it made me feel so bright and glittery. I was smiling a lot when I thought of him.

The night of my showcase, he was waiting for me backstage. My heart was still pounding, my breath coming fast. Still exhilarated. When we locked eyes, he mouthed *come here*. I pushed through the crowd, and he caught me when I flung myself into his arms and kissed him.

When he tightened his arms around me, when he made that satisfied growl that carried through the noise and chaos around us, it was like having a shot of adrenaline punched directly into my heart.

The story always goes that boys want only one thing—but girls can want just one thing too.

And then we got out of there, running along the edge of campus, and then along the lake to the little sandbar, a couple of ancient picnic tables in the grass, the sky scattered with stars. He backed me up against one of the trees and kissed me hard, and I kissed him back, surging up against him, jerking awake from the dream when I could feel his hands roaming down my body. I pulled away, gasping for air. He buried his nose in my neck and breathed in gustily.

"I've been wanting to do that for a while," he panted, and that sent a shiver through me. Made me ask, in a whisper, if he wanted to head back to his dorm.

We kissed all the way there. I flicked off the light in his room, pulled the door shut. In the dark, I tugged the skimpy mesh of my costume top up over my head, flung it into the air. But there was a moment—his hand gripped my waist, and I sucked it all in automatically. Worried how my body felt to him.

"What's wrong?" he whispered against my neck, hesitating. I was glad he couldn't see my face.

"Nothing," I whispered back. I moved his hand to my hip and kept kissing him.

After that night, there were the other two times, and then the *didn't know you thought we were a thing* text.

And now, here we are.

"Let's see what happens this time," he says, holding his hand out and grinning when I shake my head to refuse.

He hits the theater doors with both hands and leads us over to the low benches along each window-wall of the rotunda. Of course he sits in a sunbeam, because he always knows how to find his spotlight.

He reaches out and plucks a bobby pin from my loose hair, hands it to me. "Were you looking for this?"

I blush and take it from him, comb my fingers through my hair again. He's watching with a smile, and I want to smile back. "I'm just coming from rehearsal," I say inanely.

"Do you need me to help you find them all?" he says, gesturing at me like he's going to reach out and run his fingers through my curls.

"I'll check when I get home," I say. I remind myself sternly that he flirts with *everyone*: moms and babies and baristas and the entire admin staff and dogs. But he doesn't demand anything from you, like Christopher. He actually seems to like people.

"You have so much hair," he says, still smiling.

My hand goes up automatically to pat it, but I force it back down to my lap. "That's what you wanted to talk about?"

"Of course," he says. "I thought you should know."

"Well, of course I know," I say.

"And an excellent personality."

I can't stop myself from laughing, but I roll my eyes. "Okay, Gavin, fine. And you have nice teeth."

"And about the party," he says.

"What about it?" I say, my smile fading. Oh no. *He's going to say something about my dance.*

"I felt bad when you showed up and you saw—I should have warned you that Ellory and I are kind of together."

"Oh!" I say. That. The surprise that this is what we're talking about clears my head fast.

"I didn't want to hurt you," he continues.

"Hurt me?" I am going to die. "Do you think I'm still into you?"

"Of course not!" he says sympathetically.

He absolutely does.

"I just didn't want you to think I was a dick," he continues.

I don't know if he knows it, but he's being a dick.

"Because you have a girlfriend and I don't?"

"You're gorgeous," he continues. He didn't hear me, or he's pretending he didn't. He pats my hand. "The thing about you is that you're hot because you've got such a great spirit. You don't need to look like a supermodel. You'd get a boyfriend without a problem."

"Seriously?"

"Oh yeah."

I stand up, and he does too.

"I just want you to be happy is all," he says like he means it.

"You're the sweetest."

He doesn't seem to notice my tone.

"So are we friends, then?" he says.

"Do you not hear yourself?" I say.

"What do you mean?" His frown makes a tiny V between his eyebrows. I sigh.

"It's—you know what, never mind." My blood sugar is too low for this conversation.

Just the idea of explaining it to him irritates me even more.

He takes my scarf to wind it around my neck. There's that warm, woodsy smell. "Hey! Congratulations on Angles," he says, like I could forget.

"Oh yeah, thanks," I say, tugging the scarf out of his hands.

"It's so shitty you can't go," he adds.

"What? I'm going. Why wouldn't I go?"

"Without the scholarship, though, aren't you—"

"Aren't I what?" My voice is solid ice, and now he's the one blushing, the copper skin of his cheekbones brightening into molten.

"I mean, I know that—that you're . . ."

I let him flounder for a second while I work to rein in my already irritable temper, keep my voice even. "Broke?" I ask. "*Broke* is the word you're looking for."

I'm not ashamed of it. Sometimes it was hard when I was a kid, because other kids notice when you don't have the same school clothes or lunch food as they do, when your dancewear has obviously been thrifted, mismatched and threadbare. But I learned to tune it out, and now I am so tired of other people acting like I should be embarrassed and feel small and less powerful.

Gavin looks shocked. "I meant, I know that you needed a scholarship! You had said so once!"

"I said it would be easier with the scholarship," I say. So calmly. "But I'm figuring it out."

His shoulders relax, and so does his face. "Oh! Well, that's great!"

"Yeah," I say.

He follows me to the doors, still talking.

"When Ellory was pissed you got the place, I explained it's because she's not the one who needs it." He looks like he's waiting for me to praise him.

"I'm sorry?" I manage to say.

"Ellory doesn't need the leg up," he explains, like I'm stupid. "But you do, right? So of course between the two of you, they gave you the spot. She thought that was cool."

He's smiling like he isn't telling me that I got Angles only because I fill the diversity quota for "fat" and "broke," and honestly, it kind of feels like he's just spun around and kicked me in the face.

I let this guy past my guard. For some reason. I let him see the vulnerable parts. Thought it was safe to talk to him about the scary stuff and that he'd understand—the dance world's hostility to dancers who don't have the "right" bodies, its obsession with some unreal, violently narrow aesthetic ideal, the way those of us who don't fit are sneered at so often, and mocked, and almost never given a chance to prove that we can do more than just keep up—we can conquer. I told him about my fears, how I was worried about overcoming so many obstacles in my way, that I would never get a chance to prove them all wrong, why Angles was important. Blah, blah, blah.

And he thought it was a great idea to share that all with someone else.

"I'm so proud of you," he adds.

Okay, this was all my fault for coming here.

"You're an ass, Gavin," I say to him.

"What the hell, Addie? I was standing up for you!"

I suck in sharply. No. I'm done. "Sure, you know what, thanks. Thanks, Gavin. You're the best."

"Is that supposed to be sarcasm?"

"Just—next time, try minding your own business." With that, I bang away through the glass exit door.

I don't think that went the way he hoped it would.

"I just won in a fight with Gavin," I announce to my friends, dumping my bag on the cafeteria floor and falling into the chair next to Taylor.

"So why were we talking to Gavin?" Taylor says. He puts his chin in his hand. Nevaeh pauses mid–photo shoot of Katherine in her new hat.

"Because I thought *let's make the worst decision ever* when I woke up this morning," I say.

"Mm, no. Those bangs last year were probably the worst," Taylor says. He examines his package of trail mix and fishes a raisin out with slender fingers. He has always eaten each element of trail mix separately, unmoved by the idea that it says *mix* in the name of the food.

I smooth my hair down self-consciously. "They were cute!"

"I'm sorry, honey, they were not your best look," Katherine admits, pulling the pom-pom of her hat over her face.

"They were a lot of look," Nevaeh says.

"Are you going to enlighten us, beautiful Addiekins, who we

support no matter what, even when we give you the side-eye about Gavin the Jerk, which you deserve because you didn't tell us you were going to go talk to him?" Taylor says.

"I'm sorry!" I say, both hands up like I'm warding off a curse. "He said he had something important to say!"

"That was yesterday," Nevaeh points out.

"So you agreed to meet him today?" Katherine says.

"I told him no," I say, looking down. "I went anyway, though."

"Oh, Addie," Katherine says.

"I know it was a mistake! I'm sorry I didn't say anything."

"Does the guilt burn?" Taylor says.

"Yes," I say.

"Go on," he says. "He said?"

"He was just like . . . like, *Oh, Addie, I'm a jerky butthead with a jerk face, and I say jerky things that are jerky.*"

"Direct quote, right?" Taylor says.

"Best impression of Gavin the Jerk I've ever heard," Nevaeh says. "Do it again, but make the voice even smarmier."

I flap my hand like a puppet. "Blah, blah, blah, Ellory, blah, blah, blah, penis for a head, blah, blah, blah, you're still totally in love with me, blah, blah, blah, let's be friends because I *suck rotten duck eggs*—"

"Jack!" Katherine cries. "You made it!" She jumps up, and I turn. She's doing an awkward dance with a tall boy, half hugging him while he pats her on the shoulder. And when he pulls back, I get a good look at his face. He's got the kind of tan skin that gets much darker in the summer, dramatic eyebrows, and a crooked nose. Transparent-rimmed glasses. A broad, serious face and chin. The face of someone who talks over people in class and doesn't seem to notice and thinks he's smarter than everyone else. He's looking right back at me.

"Everyone, this is Jack!" Katherine says. "Jack, you know all the everyones."

"He's not Jack," I say to them. "You're John," I tell him accusingly.

"Mr. Hoffman doesn't do nicknames," he says. "As you're aware, Adeleina."

I scowl. I already dislike it when Mr. Hoffman calls me Adeleina. But when John does? I scowl harder.

"Crushed anyone else's soul with your pedantry lately, *Jack*?" I say.

"I don't recall anything like that, no," he says. He smiles slightly. "I wonder, have you refused to accept any apologies lately, *Addie*?"

I gasp. "When did you ever apologize?!"

Nevaeh, Katherine, and Taylor are looking back and forth between us like I'm Serena Williams and he's someone at Wimbledon who sucks.

"You two know each other?" Katherine says, her eyes wide with anxiety.

"He's that guy!" I say, pointing. "The awful one! In history! Who keeps correcting me! Who *ruined* my presentation on the women's suffrage movement!" Jack looks skeptical, which makes me even madder. I turn to my friends. "He complained that I was leaving out the men who were also—what did you say, *Jack*?—'an integral piece of the historical contextualization of the immunization of the mumble, mumble, *blah, blah, blah*'?" I'm even worse at presentations than just speaking in class, and I froze when he started talking.

"Oh, *that* guy!" Taylor says.

John's dark eyes narrow. "I didn't complain! And that is not what I said! I was interested to know what you thought about the concurrent behavior of the men at the time who were both—"

"Not a part of my presentation and also not important!"

He throws his hands in the air. His hair has fallen on his forehead in an unforgivably aesthetically pleasing way. "Typical of you to take it all wrong, I'm starting to learn, I guess."

"Typical of you to be so superior and condescending!"

His eyes widen. "Well! Typical of you to be willfully ignorant of my intentions—"

"Typical of you to be a *toad*," I interrupt. Nevaeh laughs, and Katherine makes an odd squeaking noise, like she's not sure if she should laugh or cut in.

"Typical of you to—" He starts to say, and then glances at Katherine, her big eyes. He stops and looks frustrated, pushes his hair off his face.

"To what?" I challenge.

"To nothing!" He throws up his hands again.

"Clever," I sniff.

"Maybe you can sit down? And we can talk?" Katherine says to him, looking back and forth at us both.

"Or he could go fall down a well, actually," I say.

Katherine is startled into laughing, then slaps her hand over her mouth. I don't look at John—Jack! Nevaeh and Taylor are grinning at each other.

"I can go," Jack says. He's got his hand on the back of the chair.

"No," Katherine says. "I mean—" She looks at me pleadingly.

"It's fine," I say, gathering myself. "I was just surprised." I clear my throat. "I'm sorry. It's okay," I add to Katherine.

After a second, Jack pulls out the chair and settles in with quick, neat movements. I can feel him studying my face. He always makes direct eye contact, but at this close distance it feels dialed up.

"This is so interesting!" Taylor says, propping his chin in his hand and staring avidly at Jack. Nevaeh elbows him. "What?" he says.

"Addie, I'm sorry," Katherine says, leaning toward me. "I didn't know you knew him!"

"Well, to be fair, I think she's just been referring to him as Captain Knobknocker," Nevaeh says mildly.

Katherine grabs my hand. "Addie, you know I wouldn't have invited him—anyone—if we didn't need help."

"I'm glad to help," he says, serious. "It's a great idea."

"You told him!" I say, and this time my voice is strangled.

"I'm sorry!" she says. "I was excited. I didn't tell him everything straight off."

"Katherine only told me after I agreed to keep a secret," Jack says quickly. "I always keep my word."

I just shake my head. Katherine trusts him, I remind myself. Katherine likes him for some reason. It's fine that he doesn't like me and that it'll be awkward to see him in class. Totally fine.

"So, from what Katherine told us, it sounds like you really know your way around," Taylor puts in.

Nevaeh elbows Taylor, but Jack ignores that, or doesn't notice because he's boring. He tells us he's been coming for summer arts intensives since middle school, doing AV work to help instructors, and has a big old ring of keys that he offers for Taylor to admire.

Jack can help us, I admit.

"Can you and I start scouting this week?" I ask him. Much as I don't want to spend one-on-one time with Captain Knobknocker, I want to be the one who's doing things that could get us in trouble whenever possible. Sneaking into buildings counts, for sure.

"You and me?" Jack glances at Katherine.

"I thought—Jack and I would go?" she says. "I mean, especially if you two are like, um. Not best friends."

Jack and Katherine are sitting arm to arm.

I really think she has a crush on him. And it looks like he might like her back! I feel like a cockblocker when I say, "I think it needs to be me. I don't want you to get in trouble for sneaking around. Or get noticed somewhere you shouldn't be, because you're friends with everyone. Or have trouble picking because you like everything, while I am ruthless and decisive."

She slumps a little, pokes her milk carton. "Ugh, fine."

"I'd volunteer if he were cuter, maybe," Taylor says thoughtfully.

"I am sitting directly across from you," Jack says.

"And those socks, though," Nevaeh says.

"What's wrong with my socks?" Jack kicks out a leg to examine them with a furrowed brow. His burgundy corduroy pants are slim, and they stop just above the ankle. Totally inappropriate for the snow.

"Hot dogs?" Taylor says, shaking his head. "Tacky."

"Irreverent," Jack argues. "Cheeky. Humorously camp. Engagingly silly, in contrast to my serious demeanor."

"Socks are not a personality," I tell him.

"Good point," he says, and I can't tell if he's joking, but Taylor snorts.

"You're sure you want to scout?" Nevaeh asks. "I'm happy to do it with him," Nevaeh says. "Well, not do it with him. No offense."

"The socks, I know," he says, nodding.

"That too," she agrees. "Also, into girls."

"I want to be the one who takes any extra risks," I say. I glance at Jack. "Jack and I are grown-ups. Mostly."

"For a given value of 'grown-up,' yes," he agrees.

I narrow my eyes at him. "Right," I say. "So it'll be fine. If you're fine with it."

"I don't believe I ever said otherwise," he says.

"You—" No. I will not argue with him. I am growing as a person. "I guess I misunderstood," I say in a very noble way. "I appreciate your help very much. I mean, we all do."

"I'm very glad I can help you," he says very formally. And then he flashes a brief, bright smile at Katherine. The corners of his eyes crinkle when he smiles like that. She twinkles back. He says something to her in a low voice and she laughs.

Nevaeh widens her eyes at me then.

"Then we're good?" I say, a little loudly. Jack glances away from Katherine and blinks at me.

"I'm looking forward to it," he says.

"I bet," I say.

And then the cafeteria lights go dim. "Oh god," I say. I recognize drama-kid drama when it's about to happen.

A muttering rises up, and then a clear alto voice rings out. "You've got a golden ticket!"

Spotlights hit the cafeteria door. A short boy in a gold top hat and tails bursts through, with a backup crew in tiny golden leotards. No pants, because backup girls never get pants. There's a shriek from the far side of the room, and then a roar of approval rumbles through the crowd.

"Aw!" Katherine says. Her hands are clasped against her chest. Jack glances over and smiles at her obvious delight.

Under cover of the promposal, I can escape. I push away from the table, blowing a kiss at Nevaeh, who is the only one who notices I'm sneaking away, and she shakes her head at me, looking amused.

Fleeing is slow going, since everyone has crowded between the tables, trying to get a look at top hat boy and his enormous bouquet of gold roses—I am not even sure where gold roses would come from. He and his boyfriend have got their foreheads pressed together by the time I am close to the exit. Most people are applauding, but a lot of the non-arts kids are rolling their eyes at one another. *Another day, another stunt from the performing-arts kids, showing off how cool and weird they are.*

Ok? Katherine texts me. I send her a row of hearts, shouldering out the door. It's fine. If getting to Angles means trusting the most pompous dude in the world with our secret, so be it.

I'll endure the ridiculous socks for us to get this right.

8

This is the week we fall deeply, madly, inevitably in love with burlesque. We go in thinking *you know, vintage-style striptease!* and have vague ideas about nipple tassels. We come out glittery with excitement because it's so much cooler than we even realized, a parallel world of dance and performance and art and inclusivity. It's an art form all its own, and women invented it. And so many of the women we see in photos and videos look like me, or a little like me. They're rounder, lusher, built on a grander scale, soft and dangerous. Less white than she figured it'd be, Nevaeh said, with Ada Overton Walker and her Dance of the Seven Veils, Josephine Baker setting Paris on fire, the recent boom of dancers and shows and festivals all over the world. And we love it, filling up to bursting with inspiration and ideas. Even Jack challenging me in history on *both* Tuesday and Thursday when I answer a question, always turning everything into a debate, doesn't dim the spotlight shining in my heart. Even when he stops me on Thursday after class and asks me for my number.

"I was going to ask Katherine for it, but I thought it would be more seemly to get it directly from you."

"Right," I say. "Seemly."

"Mm," he agrees. "*Seemly*." He is very deadpan.

I take his phone from his hand and text myself a poop emoji, and then hand it back.

He looks at the screen, and it seems like he is about to laugh, but instead he says, "I'll text you about, uh, getting together?"

"This weekend, maybe," I throw over my shoulder, hurrying away. I have to get to ecology on time for once. I stop, though, thinking about Katherine, and about not being a jerk, and rush back. "Thank you! Again."

"You're welcome. Again." He's got his hands in his pockets, bag slung over his shoulder, rangy. Taller than me, but not by much. And it seems like he's laughing at me, just a little, maybe? I stare at him a second, shake my head, and speed away, screeching around the corner, skidding around Mr. Banerjee, my pre-calc teacher.

My phone buzzes before I hit the stairwell. Jack has sent me back an emoji—the monkey with its paws over its mouth. I shove my phone back into my pocket. Definitely laughing at me.

That night after dinner, the four of us meet in my room to try to catch up on the homework we've missed all week and talk about next steps, but Nevaeh finds the movie *Burlesque* with Cher and Christina Aguilera on a streaming service. Every burlesque and dance blogger hates this movie, we know, and by the time it's ten minutes in, we've all abandoned our homework to climb up into my bunk to watch it with our hands over our mouths.

I don't know how inaccurate it is (the bloggers say very inaccurate), but it is even more terrible, and bad, and kind of gross, than anyone said. We shriek with laughter until the hall assistant has to come and threaten to kick Taylor out.

"I got nothing done," Katherine says mournfully at curfew, flipping through her calculus workbook and then shoving it into her bag. "I'm going to have to skip my run again tomorrow."

"You are not sad about skipping a run," Nevaeh says, tapping her folders together on my desk to line them up, and Katherine makes a face at her. Taylor shoves his notebook into his messenger bag.

"Before we go," Nevaeh says, "I have a surprise."

Taylor eyes her. "Is it a good witch or a bad witch?"

"You know we can't do this without seeing a live burlesque show," she says, ignoring him. "So. We're going to Vaudezilla tomorrow night, in Chicago. An all-ages burlesque show for all ages! You all better have your off-campus permission slips signed this semester. Yes, I love you too," she says to me, patting my back. "Don't cry."

"Stop making me cry," I tell her.

Nothing could have prepared us for what it's like to be sitting in the audience of a burlesque. The theater is old-fashioned, with a red velvet curtain, dark wood, gold-painted columns on either side of the stage, and a glittering crystal chandelier overhead. Our seats are flat green velvet, creaky, narrow, and so close to the front and center.

When the emcee swaggers onstage in a bustier and kimono and welcomes us all in their deep, vibrating bass, it's a lightning strike. A spotlight bursts onto a woman in gold, slinking onto the stage to a low thrumming beat, a boa constrictor twined around her body.

"No snakes," Nevaeh whispers to Taylor, who waves her concern away, not taking his eyes off the stage.

I'm sitting right on the edge of my seat, and I can't help whooping and clapping with unbridled enthusiasm every time a piece of clothing falls to the floor, at every flourish and cartwheel and all the fairy queen's trapeze tricks, the stage bursting with flowers and glitter as she swings and blows kisses at her captivated audience, brushes flowers across the cheeks of the fans in front. All full of joy. Giving two enormous middle fingers up to the idea that we should hide our skin and our bodies are too distracting, and rejoicing in the idea that every body is beautiful, and all I want is to be a part of it.

Carmen Go is the headliner, a phoenix, bold and bright in vivid oranges and yellows and reds that look like they're burning against her inky skin, and her hair is a thundercloud around her head and as bright as her plumage. She pulls us into her orbit as she wiggles down to a glittering almost-nothing, the pieces of her costume discarded around her. Broad shoulders, lush curves, rolling hips, and wide thighs, glittering skin and a body that's taking up the whole stage and the whole theater. When she bursts into flames, a bonfire in the dark theater, we jump to our feet, our applause booming and the audience roaring her name.

Taylor leans toward me, still clapping and his grin huge, but before he opens his mouth I shout, "No, you are not going to set yourself on fire." He pretends to pout, and I can't stop laughing.

When the lights finally come up, we are dazzled, slightly dazed, a little breathless, like we've just stumbled off a roller coaster.

We're invited to mingle with the performers in the lobby. My tiny *oh my god* is involuntary when Carmen Go sashays over to us, that soft burst of ruby-red hair glowing in the dim golden light of the lobby. She's wrapped in an enormous gold feather boa, smothered from neck to knees. When she smiles so kindly at me, I tremble all over, feeling unexpectedly shy. I grip Katherine's hand. Taylor starts flirting with her immediately, unsurprisingly, and Nevaeh is making her laugh, a sound like bubbles in champagne.

Then she turns to me and I freeze.

I blurt, "I love you." Oh my god, my face is so hot it's going to melt off my skull.

She throws back her head and laughs again. "You're darling." She touches my shoulder, just a brush of satin-gloved fingers, but it tingles. "Did you like the show?" It's a purr.

"I want to know how to do that!" I say in an unexpected rush. I want to ask her, *How do you make it seem so easy?*

"Here's the secret," she says, capturing my hands in hers. "You think about the thing you like best about yourself," she says. "And then you brag all about it."

She spreads my hands wide when she steps back from me, wiggles me a little bit. "I mean, look at those tits!"

Taylor, Nevaeh, and Katherine are howling as Carmen presses a soft kiss on each of my flaming cheeks, and then she spins away to greet another fan who is rushing at her, a heart-eye emoji in action. I cover my face, and Nevaeh, still laughing, has to shake me awake and drag me away, laughing at my dazed grin, my flapping hands.

"Carmen Go likes my boobs!" I hiss. "She said I can do burlesque!"

"No shit, Sherlock," Nevaeh says, shaking her head, spinning me around and poking me out of the lobby, into the fresh, dark air. "Where have you heard that one before?"

"You!" I yell, and wrap an arm around her. She smells like peppermint, and she squeezes me with an arm around my waist. Taylor distributes the coats we checked and then hoists Katherine up onto his back and bursts ahead of us, shooting over the salted sidewalk and darting around tourists and people handing out flyers all the way down the neon-lit strip of theaters and ticket booths.

In Nevaeh's car, we crank down the windows because we're all still feeling flushed, and we shout all the way back to her parents' house in Oak Park, the car jerking too often through the backstreets because Nevaeh is looking at us more than the road.

"And then she touched me—did you see—"

"Oh, no, me too, no idea what to say—"

"But those feather fans—"

"Right, but did you see the fire-eater's corset—"

"No, the best part was when she threw the knife right at that—"

"Okay, but maybe if I set just a little bit of the costume on fire—"

"Taylor, you are not setting yourself—"

"And then she leaped from the top of that ladder! How do you—"

"Right, okay, then what about roller skates?"

"Okay, everyone, hush it; you're going to wake up the parents," Nevaeh says as we tumble out of the car onto the paved stone driveway of her house, set at the top of a snow-covered lawn. I know this is what people call "upper middle-class," but it seems *rich* to me when I visit, and it makes me feel a little awkward.

We follow Nevaeh through the gate at the end of the drive-way and around the side of the house, with its big windows and french doors and fancy garden, to the little guesthouse, where we always stay overnight. Once inside, we throw off our coats and turn on the music, and none of us can sit down.

"I love burlesque! This was such a great idea!" I say, grabbing Nevaeh by the shoulders and joggling her. "Thank you so much."

"I know," Nevaeh says excitedly. "I'm so inspired."

She whirls around to grab Taylor's sport coat off the back of the couch and spins to the beat of the drums, slinks across the room toward Katherine, hips twitching in time with the music, drops down low, and then slithers back up along Katherine's body. Katherine blushes. Nevvie struts away, poses with her hands in her pockets, makes finger guns, winks, and swaggers to the middle of the room. A pause, and then she spins and slouches out of the sport jacket, shimmying it to her elbows, watching us over her shoulder as she rolls it to the music. She kicks back, lets the coat fall, and catches it on her toes, then whips forward into a graceful handstand, jacket still draped over her pointed toes. We're startled into shouting, and Taylor's clapping like he has lost his mind, and I am whooping, and the bass is pounding. Nevaeh grins at us upside down, twirls her leg to fling off the coat, and then rolls sideways into a split.

"That is *amazing*," Katherine says. "You are *amazing*."

We change into pajamas and bounce ideas off one another like we're in improv and comp, starting to sketch the shapes of acts and the beginning shadows of choreography. Taylor's shoulders make every roll look a little raunchy. Nevaeh pretends to bite my cheek until I pose for a selfie. Katherine stops in the center of the room.

"I'm going to hula-hoop," she says decisively.

"How are you going to remove your clothes and hula-hoop?" Taylor says, with very skeptical eyebrows.

"I can do anything and hula-hoop," Katherine says, and then demands that we stop making dirty jokes.

I strut down the center of our very small imaginary runway and pose, one hand behind my head, one hand on my bumped-out hip. And pose, hand on my butt, and pose, flicking open the buttons of my pajama shirt. And pose, throwing it open to my soft sports bra and cleavage and also immediate goose bumps, unexpected nerves, unexpectedly shy; what the hell? I've gone onstage in essentially sports bras and shorts without even blinking, and now I'm balking at taking my shirt off in front of my friends, getting wobbly at the idea of taking my clothes off in front of a bunch of people.

"Addie!" Nevaeh cheers, and Taylor whistles, and I let my top fall shut again, instead of off my arms and to the floor. I play it off, bounce onto the couch, and tease Katherine about her hula-hooping.

Nevvie, her dark skin brilliant against her ivory camisole, points at Taylor's jacket, declaring she's going to start in a three-piece suit and a hat and strip down to lingerie. Taylor is going to go from super femme to drop-dead bodybuilder, and all the genders in between, he decides.

"What about you, Addie?" Nevaeh says, cracking open a bottle of water. She drinks and hands it to me. "What's your act?"

I shrug, realizing I'm mimicking her casual one-shoulder thing.

"I am still waiting for a bolt of inspiration," I say.

Nothing feels quite right to me yet, my vision of myself onstage still fuzzy. I can picture myself step-by-step through the shapes of every one of my moves in the showcase—but a burlesque costume, and confident, naked skin, me front and center, I falter. Lots of people have felt free to tell me they don't like my body, because fat personally offends them. Shrugging off unsolicited comments is easy. Mostly. But when I invite their opinion?

"I'll be right back," I tell them, and slip into the little white bathroom. I lean against the door, check my phone, and scroll through the voice mails.

I hear Nevaeh in the other room—"kind of like role-playing and kind of like being totally open"—and then my mother's recorded voice is loud in my ear.

Her voice is cross in the message. "Why aren't you picking up? I tried you on Skype and—"

I sit on the lid of the toilet and delete and skip to the next message, tapping ahead through it. "So I sent you a package. Did you get the package? You never check your mail—" I flinch, remembering her last care package, with a book about fasting diets and three packs of tights three sizes too small for me. I should have given the tights to Nevaeh or Katherine, but I pushed the whole box down into the bottom of the trash can outside the mail office and power walked away. *I love them*, I told her. *They're my favorite color.*

Delete that message, skip to the last one. She sounds drunk. "Please call me, hon. I don't know why you never answer. Call tonight. I'll be up."

She picks up on the first ring, and her voice is sharp.

"Oh, there you are," she says. "Nice of you to check in on your mother."

"I'm sorry, Mom, I didn't see that you had called—"

"Well, I did," she says. "Have you been out drinking?"

"I was at a performance—"

She interrupts again. "Drinking makes you fat, Adeleina. Your friends can drink all they want, but you certainly can't afford that."

I suck in a breath. "I haven't been drinking," I tell her, my voice a little loud. "I don't drink." More or less true. When do I have time to drink, or care about it?

A small sniff. "Good," she says. "What do you weigh now?"

"What? I don't know!" I say. We're not supposed to weigh ourselves more than once a week. Some girls have scales hidden under their beds. I close my eyes at my annual checkups. Our health and wellness coach praised me for that, but it's not like I'm even tempted to look: Early on I just got tired of crying about numbers that don't have anything to do with how I *feel* about my body.

"Oh, is that what they're teaching you for a hundred thousand dollars a year?" my mother is saying. I don't remind her I'm on scholarship. "That you can just let yourself go and everything will be fine and dandy, and—"

"Mom!" I say. "Mom, why are you saying this?"

"Clive broke up with me!" It's a wail.

"I'm so sorry," I say. A bolt of sadness for her. But I also think, *Well, I guess I can go home this summer if I need to*. Ugh. But also, I'm not going home. I am going to Milan. We have a plan. I jolt up at her next sentence.

"He said he's not attracted to me anymore." There are tears welling up behind her voice.

"What?" My voice is echoing against the white subway tiles.

"It's because I'm too fat," she says sadly. "I've been on a diet for months, but he kept poking my stomach—"

She is *bones* already, god, and my stomach clenches at the idea that she's still trying to lose imaginary weight because of what some asshole thinks, and he's *poking* at her body.

"Look, Mom, you don't need to diet, and you especially don't need to diet for some—" but she interrupts me.

"It doesn't matter anyway, because I'm never going to get as skinny as some little yoga instructor at his gym, so I guess I just—"

Taylor knocks gently at the door, calls my name. I cover the phone, then whisper, "I'll be out in a second."

"Are you there, Addie? Are you listening to me?"

"Of course I am, Mom. What do you mean, yoga instructor?" She's on to the next idea, though, and I close my eyes, lean my forehead against the cool ceramic of the sink.

"I've been telling you your whole life how beautiful you are, no matter what size you are," she says.

"I know, Mom," I say softly.

"But it's just not healthy to be fat."

"I'm a dancer," I protest, sitting up. "I'm *healthy*. I am fat and healthy."

"It's so bad for your knees," she adds.

"My knees are fine," I say, but she's still not listening to anything I say, not really.

"You're so beautiful, baby. But you have to be the size you are for a reason."

Oh my god, Mom.

"What have you been eating?" she continues.

I ignore that. "Maybe this is just my size!"

"Try eating less sugar," she goes on. "And water will flush out the fat," she adds.

"I'm not going on a diet," I say. "And why should I go on a diet if I'm so beautiful?" She's not *hearing* me either.

"You are, honey. I'm just saying. I've been trying to protect you your whole life."

She stormed out of the first ballet studio I was rejected from, raging, *How dare that woman think she's better than us. How dare she call you* fat. *You are beautiful, baby. Don't let anyone tell you different.* (She didn't say I wasn't beautiful, Mom. She just said I was fat.) But we also went to the weight-loss center in the strip mall by our house.

"I know, Mom," I say. Her glass clinks on one of her rings, and her swallow is noisy. I picture her sitting at the kitchen counter, the box of Chablis at her elbow.

"Just think about your movie career," she says. "Or television."

"I want to be a dancer."

"Well, can you be a fat dancer?"

"Yes!" I snap. What have I been doing all this time?

"Professionally, I mean," she says impatiently.

I suck in a breath. "I got Angles. They seem to think I can be."

"And what's that supposed to do for you? You dance in Paris, and then what?"

I stumble. "I don't know," I say, but that's not right. I'm going to Milan. Angles is the start of a huge career.

"I'm just trying to look out for you, Addie," my mom is saying, her voice rising. "I have given everything up for you to be successful—"

"You have done everything for me, and I appreciate you so much," I rush to say. "You have. But—"

"Oh, baby," she says, subsiding, cutting me off at the knees. She sniffles. I guess we're done.

We sit there quietly for a minute. I breathe in the dark. I can hear my friends faintly in the next room, the pulse of music. Finally she sighs. "Well, it's good you'll be off in Paris anyway, because I'm still moving," she says. "I don't need him."

I tell her I'm excited for her, but I don't ask for details. What does it matter where she's going, right? I'll be in Milan.

She talks for a bit more and then tells me she's got to get her beauty rest and that I should be in bed; why am I up so late? When we hang up, I sit there for a second, watching the screen wink out.

I'm back in the parking lot of Madame Pompadour's ballet studio, five or six years old, rushing after my mother, who's storming away. Not understanding why Madame told me I was *trop grosse* for ballet. Remembering how my mother slammed the doors of the car.

"It's just baby fat," she said firmly, gripping the steering wheel. "What does she know? She turned to me, looking fierce. "You're still going to dance, Adeleina."

And I have. I will. I'll dance at every size. I'll have a career at any size. I won't shrink myself to fit the world. I'll make the world shape itself to fit me.

I startle when Taylor knocks on the bathroom door, singsonging, "Yoo-hoo, hot stuff, get your butt out here."

I swing open the door and smile at him. He frowns, and that is not what I intended. He leans in and says, "You okay?"

I shrug, summon up casualness. "My mom. Mom drama. Dra-mama?"

He snorts. "Does she have a new fasting diet to try?"

"She broke up with the new boyfriend," I tell him. I wave it away. I don't want to talk about my mom. "Are we still plotting our choreography?"

"Yes!" he says. "And we have to come up with your act!"

"Right!" I say. I am not going to bring us down with all my worrying about naked skin and spotlights and audiences rejecting me. I'll figure it out. Well, I have to figure it out.

"Dickstorm picking up," Nevaeh is muttering from the couch. She shakes her phone in the air.

"Ugh," Katherine says, peering at the screen.

"Let's not discuss," Nevaeh says, tossing aside her phone. "It's time to figure out an act for Addie!"

I hold up my hands. "Sexy bonsai tree!"

Nevaeh shakes her head at me.

"Well, if you're against that genius idea, I'll have to keep thinking," I say. "In the *meantime*, have you figured out how you're going to transition from the split?"

"Oh yeah, good question!" she says.

They go back to playing around with their own choreography and let me sit on my own plans for the moment, which is great but I'm worried. After all the inspiration at Vaudezilla, and with all the energy and enthusiasm and love right here, I don't understand why my brain is still veering away from imagining myself onstage. Those performers didn't look so different from me. Right?

Eventually I stop even trying and just join them in practicing the little things like hip bumps and bump and grinds and step ball change and shimmying our hips and shaking out our hair and headbanging with our fists in the air, and yelling, "Fuck the haters! Long live Dirty Little Secret!" They're all varying degrees of undressed as we dance, laughing as they try to be graceful while stumbling over their pants leg or getting an arm stuck in their sleeve, but I keep my pajamas on until it's time to call it a night.

"I do not snore," Nevaeh says, heading into the back room, where our sleeping bags are laid out. "For the last time." She whacks Katherine with her hair wrap.

"You sound like a truck," Katherine says, following her.

"Come to bed," Taylor says to me, pulling me by the hand. "Stop worrying about it."

"I can't," I say.

"You won't," he says. "But you should."

Carmen Go said *brag about the thing you like best*. My mom said *you're the size you are for a reason*. Somewhere between there, I'll find an idea.

I flick off the light in the living room and follow them to bed.

9

We have boxes of ball gowns, sheets, and an old sewing machine to load into the car this morning, thanks to Nevaeh's mom. Nevaeh told Virginia they were for a fundraiser—which is true, I remind myself.

"Promise me you'll visit us more often," Virginia says to Nevaeh. Her hair is silky brown and tucked behind her ears, and her lipstick is a dark maroon. She looks so much like Nevaeh, and not much older than her. "Your dad and I miss you."

"I will, Mom," Nevaeh says.

"You too, sweetheart," she says to Katherine. "You are my favorite of all the girls she brings home. Don't tell my daughter."

"Oh my god, Mom!" Nevaeh thumps the trunk closed.

Virginia presses a kiss against Nevaeh's cheek and murmurs, "Love you, baby." Then she hugs us all, tells me how glad she is my bangs have finally grown out, makes Taylor put on his hat, kisses us all goodbye again, and reminds us to be safe and not to forget to get gas and text when we get there.

Back on the road, Katherine flips to another notebook page to write more lists of things we have to think about next and figure out next and do next and find next.

"I'll organize it all into a spreadsheet!" Taylor says.

"What do you know about spreadsheets?" Nevaeh says.

"What *don't* I know about spreadsheets?" He tries to snatch the notebook from Katherine, but she whisks it away from his grabby hands and he sits back, grumbling.

"Text him now," Katherine says to me, putting her face between the seats. She means Jack. Sighing at her very determined expression, I find the poo emoji in my list of messages, and before we've circled around the bottom of the lake, Jack has texted me back, promising that he'll book a safe time for our reconnaissance.

"Reconnaissance!" I say, shaking the phone. Katherine grins.

"He has an excellent vocabulary," she says. "He taught me the word *desiderium*. It means wanting something super desperately."

"That's kind of emo," Taylor says, nudging me with an elbow.

"I also know *mumpsimus*," she says. "It means you are very stubborn and wrong."

Taylor looks offended. "I am *never*."

"That one is useful," Nevaeh says, glancing over at Katherine. "Write that one down."

"I have a whole list," she says cheerfully, turning around to page through her notebook.

"You do?" Nevaeh says.

"But what if he loves *The Lord of the Rings* or something?" I say. "We'll have nothing to talk about."

"I love *The Lord of the Rings*," Nevaeh protests.

"Just the movies," Taylor says.

"The books first!"

"You will like him, Adeleina," Katherine says firmly. I settle back in my seat and sigh.

"I read them when I was in *grade school*," Nevaeh grumbles.

Taylor pats my hand. "And if you don't, you'll still improve your vocabulary."

"*Coddiwomple!*" Katherine says, holding up her journal. "*Efflorescence! Inglenook!* You are *pulchritudinous*," she tells Nevaeh.

"Thank you?" she says.

Jack texts again as we're hustling through the soft snow from the parking lot to the dorms, falling cold and then melting into the neck of my coat. I wind my scarf tighter.

Tomorrow evening.

I scowl at the period. Is he just assuming I'll say yes?

When. I make sure to add a period and am very satisfied with myself.

Seven.

He spells out numbers. I look up to complain to the others, but they've shuffled ahead of me down the path. I know I'm ridiculous, and I sigh. He gets my back up; I don't know. It's stress. I am stressed.

I text back a thumbs-up emoji just to be annoying. He sends back a firework emoji almost immediately. I'm not smiling as I slip my phone back into my pocket, hurry after my friends, and give them the news, but almost.

———

Seven p.m. the next day, as planned, wandering the visual arts building, a maze of bright and busy open studios. Groups of people kneeling on rolls of paper spread across the floor, swiping paint in broad strokes, and others walking down hallways looking serious and artistic. The workshop floor is still busy. I walk by big, open room after room looking for Jack, some smelling like clay and some like paint and then one that smells like chemicals and ink. I peer in. There are long tables with photos spread out, X-Acto knives and mounting boards. Lots of prints taped to the wall, it seems haphazardly. A girl sitting on a stool fussing with a lens looks up and offers me a smile. I think her name is Renee. Jack is sitting at the Mac computer in the corner, his hair falling in his face, but he glances up when I thread through the tables.

"It's time," he says, looking up at the clock over the door. He's wearing a shirt with a happy cartoon giraffe on it under a purple plaid cardigan, and his shoulders are narrow, and his boots are scuffed.

"I'm very prompt," I say awkwardly, my hands in my coat pockets. On the walk over, I told myself I was going to shake off my irritation. I don't care if he doesn't think I'm smart or whatever. I'll just be polite, and we'll do this fast. Nevaeh, Taylor, and I all also secretly agreed in text that I would try to figure out what his deal is. Katherine likes him, so he's cool. But is he cool enough for her?

"Thank you for coming to meet me," he says sincerely, pushing his stool back. I'm distracted by his screen. A photo of the campus at night, swirls of yellow light, orange-and-purple auras fading to black, silhouettes of trees and benches and buildings blooming in the background, light trails from lit-up smartphones.

"Oh!" I say. "That's beautiful!" I don't mean to sound surprised. Maybe I'm surprised that his photos seem to be good. You kind of hope someone you sort of don't like will also be bad at things. But I like it.

"Oh—thanks," he says, glancing back at the screen like he's noticing it for the first time. "I feel like I've been working on them forever." He gives me a half smile. "Sometimes you feel like you don't even know what you're doing, huh?" He leans forward to close his program and clicks through the windows on the computer to shut it down.

"All the time," I say, because I do know. Ask me what choreographing something new is like. Or English.

He shrugs into his peacoat. "You keep going until you figure it out or you hate it. And then you're like, shit, I am going to fail this class."

I laugh at that, and he smiles at me, holding his messenger bag against his chest. After a moment, he gestures at the door behind us.

"Right," I say.

"Sunday night is usually a quieter night on campus if there aren't any performances for the public scheduled," he says as we head out, his voice low. Tonight there aren't any club meetings happening, as far as he was able to determine. And he thought it would make the most sense to start at this quadrant, farthest from the various administration buildings.

I decide that I am going to let him say words like *quadrant* if he wants.

"There are a lot of places to look," he says.

"Let's do this," I say, trying to sound cool and probably missing by a mile.

———

How many out-of-the-way meeting spaces, common rooms, unused classrooms, back-door storage areas, abandoned basement stockrooms, and tucked-away rehearsal rooms that even I didn't know about are there on campus? Approximately ten thousand. I am tired, and my hands and nose and ears are iced over. And, unfortunately, each of these spaces has some kind of issue. The smell of mildew that whacks us when I crack a door open, making Jack have to bolt, or, whoops, the only entrance to this wing is directly across from the teachers' lounge, or I'm pretty sure that mice live here and they will declare war if we try to use the space, not that I'm afraid of mice or anything.

He tells me about each building as we make the circuit, how old it is, and points out things like gargoyles on the roof of the central admin building. The majority of the buildings are from when this place was a nunnery, then a Catholic school, and then the founder and his wife bought it, mostly to start a private dance program but adding other curriculums soon after.

He's not lecturing me—he seems interested in the history and like he wants to tell someone about it. I relax enough to tell him that I'm half convinced most of the old buildings on campus are haunted.

"You believe in ghosts?" he asks me, as we stop in front of the main student lounge. Our breath makes bright plumes in the light streaming from the building, and the tip of my nose feels frozen enough to crack off.

"Of course not," I say. "But I don't not believe in them."

"My night photographs show up a lot of weird stuff," he says. "I don't not believe in them either." He frowns at me. "You're cold. Let's go into the lounge. Get a hot chocolate and regroup."

We haven't found anything too promising, and it's getting close to curfew.

Jack apologizes for that when he sets a steaming paper cup down in front of me.

"I'm sorry this hasn't been very fruitful for you," he says. "I had hoped we'd find something sooner."

"Trying to get rid of me?" I joke.

"I volunteered to do this," he says.

"Oh," I say. "Right."

"I haven't minded it at all," he says seriously, and I have to laugh at that.

"I've only minded it a little," I say. "I mean, it's been okay."

"Thank you," he says, as if I haven't just stumbled over trying to say something nice.

"I am even almost having a good time," I try joking.

"Good," he says. I kind of want him to say he's having a good time, too, but he doesn't.

"Katherine said it would be great," I say.

He looks up from fumbling with his messenger bag. "Katherine's great." His face is a full-blown smile, and his cheeks are windblown too. "She rescued me from failing trig," he says. "And from hating junior year."

"She does that," I say.

"We've had a lot of good conversations," he adds. "She's good to talk to. And open."

Something in me relaxes at that, and I look at him again. I appreciate his serious eyebrows and his crooked nose. His face is okay, I decide. I want to ask him what they talked about, but he pulls out his list of the places we've seen already instead. He is very serious and organized, and his jaw is a little bit stubbly. He also pulls out a well-folded map of campus, neatly marked up with tiny notes and careful *X*s in a variety of colors on most of the buildings.

"This is great," I say. He looks satisfied.

"It's top secret, so you have to burn it when we're done," he says.

I agree solemnly, lean over, and notice that there aren't any Xs on the performing-arts theater, a long, narrow rectangle on the map, a low, two-story rectangle building in real life. I tap on it.

"I assumed you had ruled it out, if you were looking elsewhere for a space," he says. "I should have confirmed that with you."

"I should have thought of it first! It should have been the first place on my mind!" Not the auditorium, obviously. But it's a fair-size building. Maybe the green room, dressing rooms, rehearsal room, shops, or trap room. The storage rooms on the main floor. The storage rooms on the basement floor! Outside, the ground slopes down behind the building, so there's an entrance back there, a short driveway down, and a small loading dock for deliveries. Sometimes musicians sneak out from upstairs to smoke back there, taking the few short steps across the driveway and into the trees.

"Do we have time to go look?" I bounce, excited about the idea.

He checks his watch. I'm faintly amused he wears one, and not surprised. It's old-fashioned, with a brown leather strap and a white-and-gold face.

"We have time," he says. He nods to the right of us. "She's waving at you."

I look up to see Ellory at a table near the tall planters. Wiggling her fingers. Playing cards with Gavin.

"Oh, Ellory," I say. I wiggle my fingers back.

"She's in the modern-dance program, isn't she?"

"She was upset I got Angles and she didn't."

He looks at her for a moment, and then back at me.

"Did you deserve it?"

"Of course," I say, scoffing.

"Well, then," he says.

When Ellory leans forward across the table to draw a card, Gavin catches my eye, smirking at me like he's going to tease me about sitting here with a boy.

I huff. "I used to date him," I say, turning back to Jack. I'm caught between fight and flight. I swear Gavin's staring at the side of my head. I want to win, which means playing it cool. But it's hard not to look back at him, which is annoying.

"Yeah?" Jack says, amused.

"We hung out for a bit over the summer." I lose the fight and glance over, and Gavin looks at me at the same time, so I snap my head away. "I don't like him very much."

Jack stands up, and I look up at him, surprised. "He looks like he's about to come over," he says.

"Oh no," I say.

"Oh yes," he says. "Go. Let's go!"

I push back from the table, and we power walk out of the lounge, break into a run in the lobby, and spill out into the cold again. My hot chocolate has sloshed over my hand, and I'm struggling to get my hat back on my head with the other hand.

"Thank you!" I say delightedly, as we rush down the main sidewalk. "He would have totally ruined everything."

"We were just leaving anyway," Jack says.

"We weren't running away." I nod.

"Exactly," he says. "Now lead on."

"Huzzah!" I say. I am definitely not cool, but he doesn't seem to notice.

10

F oot traffic in the main quad is picking up as freshman curfew starts to count down, but I am glad to see that it thins out more and more the closer we get to the theater. We're quiet, our faces tucked into our scarves, and he's moving fast, long legs and carrot-and-rabbit socks flashing as we slip down the darkened driveway.

Jack has the back performers' entrance open in just a moment, next to the small loading dock and rolling garage door. My heart starts thundering. When the door clicks shut behind us, the dark, musty space is perfectly silent, and the shadows look like they're moving. Jack clears his throat, and I jump nine feet into the air.

"Sorry!" he says. "Where are we?"

I look around as dim security lights slowly bring everything into focus. Here's the receiving area, which seems small. Across the room is the wide door to the storage rooms where the oldest props and sets are archived. We decide against turning on our phones for the flashlights, just in case.

I hesitate, not sure where to start, and he waits for me to decide. After a moment, I lead him up the stairs to the ground floor above us, where the dressing rooms and wardrobe are. One more flight up to the stage and auditorium. I take a breath. There's no sound at all. Not even the air conditioners. It feels absolutely, totally, completely deserted.

The main theater is too big for our purposes—it seats four hundred—but something makes me want to explore it while it's empty and dark, without any other performers. The shadows follow us as we prowl down the narrow passage that runs most of the length of the stage. It opens onto dressing rooms, the rehearsal room, the green room, doors half open into the dark. Jack bumps into me when I peer into the garment room, a little too small, a little too full of stuff, and the prop shop, full of crowded tables.

I open the door at the end into the crossover, where the dim lights on the catwalk and fly system overhead make it a little brighter. We should just go back downstairs, but when I see the call-board by the entrance of the wings, I can't help stepping past it and out onto stage left.

The stage looks enormous, a broad expanse of polished, gleaming wood. The houselights are turned down, but I can make out row after row of empty seats, stretching back, up, and out into the dark, looking like they do when we perform and the footlights are too bright to see any faces.

I want to unlace my boots and shove my coat off and take a running jump into the center of the stage, spin and spin and soar up and spread my arms like wings and dive, skimming across the surface of the stage and twisting to burst into colors like a firework, all the muscles in my body ready for flight, the faceless audience in the darkness out there riveted, their attention a presence I can feel, an energy I pull from.

I glance back at Jack, right at my shoulder. I wonder what he's thinking about, standing here, and maybe he takes my look as an invitation, because he leans over just a little bit, and with his voice pitched low, says, "It feels very daunting to me. All these seats, all filled up, watching you perform."

"I love it," I say. "It feels powerful." He's very quiet, and I keep talking, my words picking up speed. "The nerves, and the—the anticipation, and the excitement. The audience is this anonymous, expectant presence out there, waiting, and all of that together is in your chest. And then you are onstage and everything stops and—" I stop. A breath.

"And?" he says softly.

I look out at the seats, thinking about that.

"And," I say. "And every time there's that perfect moment, where I feel my body and the music almost—click. Click into place. Every time, just for a tiny, tiny second, it's a surprise." I sigh. I can't think of how to describe it. "And whoosh," I say. I cut my hand through the air. I want to say how big and beautiful it is, but I can't find the words.

"Is it ever too nerve-racking?" he asks.

"Never," I say.

But somewhere downstairs, we'll find a place where the four of us can throw a wild show for a different kind of audience. Who will I be when they're right there, so close? When I can see their faces looking at me? Burlesque is supposed to be a give-and-take, an invitation and acceptance of their admiration, and that's the part that still feels so daunting.

"Anyway," I say lightly. "Detour. I just wanted to see what the stage looks like with all the lights out."

"Bigger?" he asks.

"Darker," I say, and hear him laugh a little.

We shuffle back along the corridor to the stairwell and descend two flights to the loading area, through the heavy doors and into the storage-room corridor, lit by security lights. The long-term storage area runs the length of the building. It's the place where they store scenery once it's been retired for a season. The rooms and nooks are well-insulated to protect the bulky stuff in storage—which means quiet enough to muffle music and maybe applause, enough room for a small audience. I've been here before with other dancers—hunting for backdrops to use in our showcases, looking for props, grabbing a tiara to prance around in between takes until the prop master plucks it off your head to pack away again. Broken-down set pieces are stored here, construction materials, huge bolts of fabric for the costume department, and in the last room, through the wide doors all the way at the end, the backdrops that don't fit anywhere else. No one ever comes here. Mostly it's where old props come to peacefully retire.

I turn the knob of the left door carefully, and it clicks open, sweeps outward. Very dim motion-sensor lights click on, and Jack stops inside the door.

"Oh, wow," he says, and the surge of triumph is real.

The room is large, and the ceiling is unfinished, rough beams. Stacked along each wall are painted backdrops—the ones that get repainted over and over, every season or even between shows, by theater kids and dance kids and even the music kids when they're feeling fancy. Some of them dingy, some of them bright strokes of color—fluffy white clouds in a blue sky, a sketchy forest, a graffitied subway station—padded around the edges and stacked several deep. There's also a painted arch, with columns on either side, and I rush underneath it, spin to beam at Jack, and throw my arms wide.

"We've found it!"

"Do we have to whisper?" Jack asks in a normal voice.

"Fuck no," I say, and turn to examine my find. String up a curtain between the columns, build a little space behind it, spread out cushions for the audience. Drape fairy lights and fabric garlands across the jungle of backdrops. Hang pretty paper lanterns overhead for light.

"So this is the place," he says.

"This is definitely the place," I say, and those words are my favorite words all day.

I snap photos of everything to show the rest of the group, and see that there's no cell service down here, which I like, which makes us feel more separate and safe from the world, and also there will be no live tweeting.

When my phone alarm goes off, my curfew warning, I sigh, and we head through the dark to the back exit.

"It's easy to get here from the dorms," I tell him, lowering my voice automatically. The exit sign is flickering, making the shadows stutter strangely. We're whispering about how people can reach the stage door by taking a path through the woods, when—

Boom!

The noise echoes from somewhere else in the building.

Jack and I freeze. Solid ice. Rigid, staring huge-eyed at each other, clutching our jackets to our chests. A heartbeat.

My tiny voice is frantic. "No one is supposed to be here. No one is supposed to be here!"

"The wind," he suggests. His forehead is knotted up, and his eyes are wide and black in the light.

Another boom. And then a rattle. We both jump.

"Shit, shit, I think that's the elevator," I say.

We both look over to the closed elevator doors and up at the ceiling, like we're going to see it moving down. I'm shaking. We're going to get caught.

"Run," he whispers. He hasn't blinked. He doesn't move. I push him. He fumbles at the exit door, but he can't get the keys out.

I glance over my shoulder and see a door—maybe a closet? Better than standing here in the open.

"Hide," I whisper. I lunge across the room, dragging him behind me, fling open the door, shove him in ahead of me, crash into him from behind, yank the door closed behind me, and stumble right into his chest.

We're in the dark, in a tiny supply closet, and there's no room to move, and I realize I am pressing my face into the side of his neck, my palms against his shoulders, my boobs jammed right into his chest. Both of us breathing hard, neither of us moving.

In a moment he takes in a deep breath and shifts, and his arms come around me. His hands settle on my hips. He whispers, "Sorry, sorry," but there's nowhere else for them to go. We're pressed flat against each other. He swallows and catches his breath when my cheek brushes his jaw, and his hands tighten on my hips. It's too intimate. He's too warm.

Oh. He smells so, so good. I can feel how hot my neck and cheeks are, his stubble against my jaw, the soft sigh that flutters a curl of hair against my ear. I'm so aware of his body against mine and the skin of his neck just millimeters away from my lips. Can he feel how hard my heart is pumping? I can feel his. Do I have hot-cocoa breath? This is horribly, terribly, agonizingly awkward. But *oh god*—I realize I could lose myself in how warm and solid and good-smelling he is, and being pressed against him feels so *snuggly*, ugh, and oh my god. In a flash, I wish Katherine didn't like him.

Oh. Oh no.

The coast has to be clear by now, doesn't it?

I freeze, trying not to breathe and trying not to think about our bodies. Eyes closed, ears strained listening to the outside, definitely not softening against his body.

Centuries of quivering in the dark later, he starts shifting, burrowing his shoulders back away from me the tiniest bit so there's just a little more room between us, but not much, so he can turn his head to look at me. His face is an inch from mine, and our noses are brushing. His eyes are dark in the dim light that filters through the crack around the door.

I want to kiss him. He leans forward.

"I think we're safe," he says almost silently, and his lips just barely skate against the corner of my lips, a feather touch that makes me gasp the tiniest bit, sends an electric-shock flinch shuddering through him. He jerks back.

For a spark of an instant we are frozen again. Then frantically I scrabble behind me, looking for the doorknob, wrench it, lean hard against the door, and spill out backward, stumbling a few steps and then catching myself, freezing.

We're both completely silent, waiting for an angry security guard to grab us by the hair and haul us off to prison, but there's nothing. Then another boom, the familiar sound of the ventilation system roaring on. I gasp, pressing a hand against my chest like I'm in a melodrama. My heart's never had a workout like this.

I swallow and choke out in a whisper, "The ventilation system. It was the ventilation system. Not the elevator." Relief.

Jack closes his eyes, then straightens and tugs his jacket down. "Right," he says. "Ventilation. Of course." He's a little breathless too.

He digs in his pocket for his hat and jams that back on his head too. He shoves the door closed with a thump. We stare at each other for another long moment, and when I nod at the exit, we sprint to it, run up the driveway, and dive for the trees, ducking behind one like it's going to offer any protection. Snow shakes off a branch and lands with a plop on my head, and I yelp.

"Shit!" I choke, because I can't stuff it all down anymore.

In our escape we keep to the wooded area for a little bit, and I feel ridiculous creeping from tree to tree, and then we bounce back onto the paved walking path and meander like it's any old night, swing left between the math and arts building and back onto the main thoroughfare. I stop and suck in a big, big breath.

"Holy crap!" I say, bouncing on my toes. "That was terrifying. I thought we were going to die. I thought we were going to jail." I'm grinning at him, but he looks serious.

I stop, reach out to touch his shoulder, but pull back. "We're okay, right?" I say in a low tone. "It was just the—system?"

"HVAC," he says. I'm not surprised he knows. He nods. "I think it'll work," he says, businesslike. Does he mean the space? He turns and we're walking, back to the dorms, I guess. My shoulder bumps against his, and he pulls away.

"You're okay?" I ask him. "That was a big scare at the end."

"Oh, yeah," he says.

I want to push, poke at him until he tells me why he is acting like a weirdo. I want to look at him in the light, because my mouth still feels like it is tingling. There is so much in my head.

I say hi to some people who pass from behind us. I turn to Jack to say something casual, but he's stopped. We're at the door of the girls' dorm.

"Okay," he says.

"Okay!" I say.

He's just looking at me. He's standing there, and kids are passing around us, and his face is very serious. He opens his mouth, closes it.

"The closet," he finally says.

Aw, hell. "I know!" I rush to say. "I'm so sorry! That was ridiculous, right?"

He hesitates. "Okay," he says, nodding.

"It was kind of hilarious," I go on. "I promise I'll never drag you into a closet again."

"Okay, then," he says, still nodding. "Right." He pulls out the tightly folded map he made, presses it into my hand, and lifts his hand in an awkward half wave. "Good night," he says.

Then he yanks down his hat firmly and walks away. Gone.

11

I'm sitting cross-legged in bed, still cold but with a blanket around my shoulders. I message everyone the pictures of our little bootleg theater and rip Twizzlers apart with my teeth. There's a flurry of excited emojis, and Katherine has already redecorated the place in her mind, and Nevaeh is arranging our trip to the thrift store tomorrow to debrief and scout for costume pieces to add to the beautiful stuff we got from her mom and because she really, really wants to look for her suit, and to start loading up on any scenery and sparkly things we can get our hands on, because who knows what we'll need.

Everyone is excited again, so I hesitate before I type, *things got super awkward at the end though.*

I sketch out the basics like I find it hilarious—*we jammed ourselves in the closet can you believe it, I'll tell you the whole story tomorrow.*

I have come to realize, the more I think about it, that he hated it. He hated every second of it. He was so embarrassed to be smashed in with me so tight, he didn't even know what to say. And then I'm so embarrassed I liked being so close to him. Katherine likes him! He likes her! And there I am jammed like a wad of gum between them.

And I bet he was horrified to touch me, my body all mashed against his. *Maybe he just thinks I'm fat*, I think angrily—but I smash that train of thought.

We can talk about it at the thrift store tomorrow, where we can jump up and down about our brand-new, ready-to-be-decorated, about-to-be-legendary burlesque club, and that's what I'm going to think about.

———

The next afternoon when we push open the door to New Again, the thrift store, the balding clerk behind the counter is flipping through a magazine without looking up, and humming to the Christmas songs playing, for some reason, over the speakers. Maybe that's why we have the place to ourselves.

Taylor asks, "Why do all thrift stores smell exactly the same?"

"My suit is here," Nevaeh says. Her eyes are gleaming. "I can feel it." She pulls off her hat and shakes out her Afro, fluffing it with her fingers, then takes off toward the men's section. Katherine heads to the racks of lingerie. We need to assemble the under-pieces to strip down to, between stuff we buy and stuff we own. Taylor grabs a shopping basket to pile it with things from the home section.

I follow him, because I'm still no closer to figuring out my act, and until I do there's no point in trying to figure out a costume.

I glide my fingers along the length of hanging textiles, more than enough tapestry-like curtains to layer on the walls to make our performance space feel warm and intimate. Then the giant crates filled with pillows for seating. A velvet love seat cushion, a tasseled, embroidered throw pillow, a silk quilted pouf. Taylor is in the next aisle wearing a glittery reindeer-horn headband, sweeping votive candleholders and clear glass vases to fill up with fairy lights into his basket, and anything else shiny that catches his magpie eye. We're lining up full baskets at the counter, slightly alarming the clerk.

Nevaeh whoops.

"Fourteen-dollar three-piece suit!" She thrusts a loaded hanger into the air. "It has *pinstripes*, y'all. And a vest!" She's already found her hat, a fedora-looking thing she's wearing cocked over one eye.

"Try it on right now," Taylor commands, and hustles her into the dressing room, a closet with fabric stapled in front of it, almost knocking off the headband.

Katherine's cheerfully singing along to the Christmas carols somewhere on the other side of the room, hangers clacking together as she browses, and I leave my stack of pillows to go find her.

There are a couple of prom gowns on top of her basket, bustier-style, ready for crafting into fabulous bustiers for burlesque performers. Now she's browsing the floor-to-ceiling shoe shelves, examining a pair of cowboy boots.

"These would be so good for a cowboy act! Or a rodeo thing. Ooh, with a lasso," she says, and you can see her brain start to scheme. In thirty seconds she'll have the choreography planned out for me. We've been trying to brainstorm an act since Friday night, and they're not impatient yet, every time I shake my head, but I worry they will be soon.

Katherine offers the boot to me. I take it but shake my head. "I don't think I'm very country."

"Ooh, maybe you're rock 'n' roll," she says. She snatches a busted lace-up black boot and waggles it at me.

I open my mouth to say *Probably not that, either*, but instead what comes out is, "I'm sorry about Jack."

She looks at me, head tilted. "Why? What's going on?"

"That closet thing I texted you all about last night. I shoved him into it and then squished my boobs right up against him," I say. "I'm worried he thinks I did it on purpose. He seemed a little upset about it last night." *Thinks I'm fat*, drifts into my head. I shake it off.

"Aw, no, I don't think so," Katherine says. "All he told me was that it was a good night and we'll like the space."

"That's it?" I say. She pats my arm, nodding. "But we were jammed in tight. My boobs—" I gesture at them.

She shakes her head at me, smiling. "Your boobs are great."

"I want you to know that I will never do that again," I say, and then she looks confused. I try to clarify. "Rub up against him. You know. If you. And he. I don't know if you—but maybe if you did. And if he did. If you two—"

It takes a second, and then her face goes bright.

"I don't have a crush on him!" she says, laughing. "I mean I do—"

"You do!"

She didn't mean to say that, I can tell, and I am filled with a rush of excitement.

"No! Not him," she says, her voice even lower. We're both crouching down behind the racks, whispering in excited hisses. Or at least I am. We're ridiculous.

Oh. Oh!

"Who?" I say. She has *never* said this or anything like it. "Do the others know? Should I not say anything? Have you told anyone? Katherine!"

She's shaking her head, and her cheeks are so red, and she waves her hand at me.

"No," she hisses. "Don't say anything! I shouldn't have said anything! I'm so embarrassed. Aw, shit," she says, very sincerely.

"Katherine!"

Across the room Taylor hoots again, and we both jump a little. Katherine leaps up and heads over that way, and I follow after putting the cowboy boot back with its mate, my head whistling. I won't say anything. To anyone. I will just die of all the not saying until she says something. As for Jack, he still probably really likes her, and I'm going to have to let that be his problem. And my liking him—I have so much self-preservation, I can sell it for profit at this point. And it's all a mess, but luckily there's stuff to distract me because *whoa*—the suit looks like it was made for Nevaeh. Slim pinstripe trousers in slate gray, a single-breasted jacket, a vest.

"Amazing," I say.

Nevaeh does a slow, sexy spin so we can appreciate her from all angles.

"Are you going to try anything on?" she asks me. Argh.

"Twilight burlesque," I joke. "When I take off all my clothes, I sparkle!"

"Really?" Katherine says, her brow wrinkled.

"No, not really," I say, sighing.

"No pressure," Taylor says, "but we have only weeks to figure out how to look good when we rip off our clothes." He pauses. "Okay, a lot of pressure."

The Angles deposit deadline is near the end of the month, which I know, which is why we are rocketing full-speed ahead.

"Tomorrow," I tell them. "I'll have an idea by—"

"Breakfast!" Taylor says.

"Taylor!" Katherine says.

"Dinner," I say, glaring at him.

"Dinner," he agrees.

"Hey, we watched all those YouTube videos. Maybe do something inspired by one of them?" Katherine says to me as we haul up the rest of the stuff to pay, and I am carefully not saying anything! At! All! about her exciting revelation.

"Steal an act?" I say to her.

"Borrow!"

"But I want to do something brilliant, genius, groundbreaking, amazing," I tell her, a little joking but I realize absolutely kind of not.

"All art is theft," Taylor says, and Nevaeh starts arguing with him.

Because the whole burlesque club idea was mine in the first place, I haven't told them that part of my problem is my hesitation about this whole naked-skin, audience-looking-right-at-me thing. It's my problem to get over, this fear that when I invite the audience to enjoy me, they'll say *check, please*, because they're mad I'm fat.

Die mad, I think, straightening up.

"No matter what you do, it will be brilliant," Nevaeh says then, hoisting an enormous plastic bag over her shoulder. "We're not here because we're average and ordinary, right?" She waves back in the direction of campus. "Honestly, I can't wait to see what you decide on. No pressure."

"Remember, Carmen Go basically totally said your boobs were made for burlesque," Katherine reminds me. "You can't let her down."

"No pressure," Taylor says.

"Okay, none of you are allowed to talk any more," I say. "Get out; get out." The door chimes and chimes again as we tumble back into the cold, staggering under our bags.

Fluttery indecision is not my brand. I go for what I want. I admit to myself that I want to be captivating, and sexy. And nothing is off-limits for me.

I slam the trunk of Nevaeh's car shut. I'm fat and gorgeous. I'm going to be filled with inspiration any second now.

Sexy postal service worker, I text the group the next afternoon, as I wait for history class to begin. I am not filled with inspiration. Since breakfast this morning, all three of them have been bugging me about what I've decided on for my act. I haven't come up with anything yet, but I believe in last-minute flashes of genius.

A dairy cow, I type. *An accountant*.

Taylor is kind of into the giant-robot idea, but generally their horrified reactions keep making me laugh.

Even though I'm distracted by my phone, I still see the flash of bright socks at the front of the room and look up, see Jack making his way to his usual seat. He plops down without looking back at me. He might not have noticed I'm here. This isn't my normal spot, this seat in the back corner—I took it because I don't think I absorbed any of the reading last night.

Then again, he might have noticed.

A sad T. rex, I type.

Neither Jack or I speak up in class, and I'm surprised to find him waiting outside the door when it's over, leaning against the wall.

"Did you know Shirley Chisholm was the first Black woman

elected to Congress?" he says, straightening up. "And the first woman to run for the Democratic nomination for president. Mr. Hoffman forgot to mention that," he adds.

"Great," I say. Lecturing mode hasn't vanished entirely, even if it's stiffer than usual. Socks: Orange. Unicorns and narwhals.

I'm so sorry that was terrible and awkward fills up my mouth, but saying that will make it more awkward. And I'm sad we've lost all our easiness together. And that I want to lean forward and sniff his neck. If he's not a fatphobe. "Where do you get all your socks?" I say instead.

"Online," he says. "I wanted to talk to you about the invitations."

"The—oh!" Students are streaming by us. He offered to design the invitations the night we went scouting. And I had totally forgotten about that, all the really important details like that blown out of my head by the embarrassing awkwardness at the end.

He follows my gaze, swings back to me, and leans in so I see his eyes are just plain ordinary brown, even though they've got gold starbursts radiating from the center. "Sorry," he says in a low voice. "The project I'm handling for you."

Our invitations, the small cards we'll slip into the mailboxes and backpacks and notebooks of our invitees, people we think will be excited, who will keep it under wraps. Private Insta page, cash app, details on show night.

"I had an idea," he continues. "Pictures of you as the backdrop."

"Me?" It's more of a yelp.

"The four of you, I mean," he says quickly, as we move away from the door of the classroom for some kind of privacy. I'll be late to ecology, but I usually am. "I want to take a series of close-ups in order to capture the spirit and glamour of the performance. Nothing that will be identifiable, of course."

Oh no. Pictures.

"What about our accessories?" I say. "Sexy shoes. A feather boa?"

"I think we need something more intense," he explains.

Great. Intense, naked close-up photos.

"Not naked," he says, like he heard my thought or read it on my face. "Skin is important, of course—that's part of the rebellion of the art." He's struggling to be very professional and not awkward, but we're both quivering with the uncomfortableness of this discussion.

"Oh, sure," I say. "The naked art." I don't even know what I'm saying, but he nods like it makes sense. "I'll ask everyone," I tell him. "I'll text you. Or Katherine will."

"Right," he says. We stand there for a moment, waiting for the other person to talk. Then he lifts his hand and turns toward the stairwell, letting me watch him go.

I sigh and lean back against the wall to pull out my phone. I type *sexy dump truck* to the group, for the usual flurry of groans, and then fill them in on the invitation plans, if they're up for it, my heart bumping along as I type. Within seconds, they're all in. *But photos!* I want to say. Still pictures. Every divot and pimple and fold and dimple. An accidental double chin, a roll of fat on my belly, all captured forever for someone to judge. I'm judging, and I hate that.

dirty photos for my portfolio, Taylor types.

need to hem my dress this afternoon, Katherine types.

Nevaeh says, *glue gun and glitter party before the real fun.*

We're headed over to the theater tonight, after dark, so they can see the place themselves. Then we can start bringing over supplies and materials, crafting our plan to transform the space into something glamorous and gleaming, a darkened, secret burlesque club, the one I see pretty much every time I close my eyes now.

Photos, though. And Jack the one who's taking them.

Settling my bag on my back, I tromp down the stairs.

12

Dry tech is more nerve-racking than opening night sometimes, and my heart is rattling. Curfew is an hour away but we're going to sneak our way from the dorm to the theater, a practice round just to make sure there are no surprises, and that we'll be able to smuggle in the supplies we need before the show. Jack texted to offer a distraction—he could set a small fire somewhere! But I assured him we'd be okay and were very brave, my thumbs flying over the keyboard, grinning despite myself.

Nevaeh, Katherine, and I all haul our laundry bags down to the dorm basement, because they're a great cover. Taylor leads the way, holding open doors. But we have to loiter by the machines for a few minutes, Nevaeh pretending to mess with her laundry card, waiting for Amy to leave. I'm bouncing up and down the whole time, filled with ants and grasshoppers and butterflies.

When Amy clears out, we're down the corridor, sidling through the double doors to the furnace room. Then out the cellar door, racing up the concrete steps and rushing the few feet up and over the solid, snowplowed drifts and down into the trees behind the building. No one has been caught sneaking out this way yet, that we know of. (Please, please don't let anyone get caught.)

We're silent as we weave our way through the leaning pine trees, taking the long, long way. Laughter and shouted conversations from campus spill into the spaces between buildings, echoing. Ordinary life is right there, close and loud and bright. But this moment feels louder and brighter. Nevaeh and Katherine holding hands, their plumes of breath caught in the light that reaches us. Taylor with his arm through mine, keeping me steady, the crunch of the snow and glimpses of the dark, glittering lake to our left. I grin up at Taylor, big and bright, and squeeze his arm. His smile in return is huge. He feels it too. We all do.

It takes forever and also only seconds to make our way to the theater. We all crowd together in the trees across from the performers' door. The small gravel parking area feels like an endless abyss. It's a little dark back here, the streetlight in the driveway not quite reaching.

I squeeze Taylor's hand and he says, "On your mark—"

And then I launch, trying not to laugh wildly, skitter to a halt on the driveway, flattening against the rough basement wall, the rest of them following. Muffled giggles and gravel scattering.

"This is ridiculous," Nevaeh whispers, and she is grinning, still holding on to Katherine's hand.

"Just wait," I whisper back, and crack open the door to usher them inside.

We make our way to the warren of storage rooms. I push open the door to our little hidden theater and flip the switches, and dim can lights flicker on overhead. I step aside so they can emerge into the broad room, cozy-snug, so apart from the world and with so much potential.

"Holy shit," Nevaeh says, her arms crossed, her smile coming slowly, and then it's a beam.

Taylor heads straight for the arch, the painted columns. "Holy wow," he says, running his hands over a column and nodding like he's coming up with a plan.

Katherine slips her hand into mine, a sheen of glitter across her cheeks. "You found it."

I squeeze her hand, and my heart is full and warm. They like it! I knew they would, but it's such a relief that they do.

After the brief moments of quiet awe, we're a whirlwind of planning. Taylor sits in the middle of the room, writing frantically in his notebook. Nevaeh has a measuring tape, because of course she does, and is shouting out numbers and ideas. Katherine is single-handedly shifting backdrops around to envision different possibilities for the stage setup. I'm filling them in on all the thoughts I've had since finding this place.

When I'm suggesting we add a curtain to the entrance that we can sweep aside for added drama, I get distracted by a clothes rack in the corner. I reach down to touch a bit of slightly faded pale pink tulle poking out of the bottom of a garment bag. It sparkles. I peer under the bag and then gently pull it up over the stiff fabric. The tutu is old, but still glowing. Heavy beads and crystals that trail down into sparkles glittering across a tulle skirt. I lift it off the rod with a little bit of a grunt and hold it up in the light of the room.

It's spectacular. A practically vintage performance tutu, the romantic kind that falls to your calves, lush and full and over-the-top. The kind of tutu you dance as Giselle in so you can die beautifully of betrayal and heartbreak, sinking down into a heap of fluff and sparkles. It's so full it is spilling out of my arms, beaded heavily and shining with diamond-like rhinestones. The velvety pale pink silk underlay glimmers beneath layers and layers of shining silvery tulle, softer and fuller than any tutu I've ever worn. It's the most gorgeous skirt I've ever seen up close, expensive and lush and extravagant. I couldn't borrow it—measured across my waist, it's about half my size. But the gleam and glitter fill me with such an idea.

I can imagine myself in something like this, confident and brave and beautiful and breathtaking. Aloof, the audience leaning forward, wanting to catch my eye, get my attention, holding their breath. And then . . . *boom.*

I gather the tutu into my arms and hug it close to my chest. Taylor looks up from his notebook, his serious expression melting into a questioning one.

"From ballerina to badass," I tell him. I shake out the beautiful tutu in front of me, hold it up so it glints in the light. "I'm going to strip out of a fabulous tutu and rock the audience's world."

Taylor's face blooms into a grin. "Oh, shit!" he says, jumping to his feet to run his hands admiringly over the beading. "It's such a perfect idea. It is so perfect for you, Addiebear; how did we not think of this before?"

"I don't know!" I say. "But now I have some planning to do." It feels like I can stop worrying—ballet is my home. I can imagine myself dancing confidently onstage, familiar steps baked into my bones, building up my confidence, a store of confidence before the big reveal. This feels right.

I call over Nevaeh and Katherine, so relieved I've found an idea, a costume I can imagine myself in. They're bursting with ideas for bedazzling a tutu, for making it easy to whip off.

I can't stand still anymore, and I bounce and spin into chaîné turns across the room, and there is the story in my head: I'll emerge as the traditional ballerina, dance with precision and control in every move—then tear off the skirt and whip into burlesque extravagance. Strip down to—sequined booty shorts and a bralette. It's not any more naked than the shorts and lacy sports bras we wore for the Fosse piece in junior year, right? Maybe a little more sparkly. I'm doing this!

"Okay! Last vote," I say, smiling. "Ballerina burlesque or robot come to destroy the earth?"

Taylor lifts his hand. "Come on. The robot. Lasers! A smoke machine." He sighs, shaking his head mournfully. "Such a missed opportunity."

I whack him with my notebook. He's outvoted, and Katherine hugs me.

"I love it. You are so beautiful. You will be so beautiful!"

"I will!" I say. I fumble, trying to work the clasps on the hanger and wrestle the tutu back into its place.

I smooth the skirts down as the others gather up their stuff. The costume we put together—it'll be gorgeous. We even have some pieces already, I think. A wedding dress from the thrift shop with a bustier top that we can hack, maybe. I already own a dress tutu that I can wiggle out of. We can figure out underthings. That part will be fine. Can I take it all off gracefully? There's a good question for me. And then, of course, there's the other one that's been following me around—can I take it all off gracefully in front of an audience?

"You ready, Addiebear?" Taylor says, holding up my coat.

He settles the coat around my shoulders as I slip my arms through the sleeves. When I turn, his face is serious.

"That's your 'I'm worried but I am not going to tell anyone about it because I am so brave and stoic,' face, which is your most annoying of faces," he says.

"Ugh, I'm fine," I say, flapping my hand at him.

"Your idea really is great," he says, his hands shoved in his pockets. "And you know, we're all going to be there. We're in this together. Like we always are. We're annoying like that." He regards me for a second. "Yeah?"

"Yeah," I say. "Jerk."

"Stuff it," he says. "You love me." He slaps my butt as he passes by, and I whirl to whack him with my hat. The girls follow after him, hugging me, telling me they're excited and that I did so good.

I really did.

I flip off the light and swing the door closed with a click, leaving the room dark and quiet and waiting for us, the music, the audience, for showtime.

13

There's so much to worry about. The adrenaline from our escapade makes it hard to sleep, and hard to sleep means hard to dance the next morning. Crack of dawn, because I woke in a panic, realizing how little work I've done on my showcase piece lately, how far behind I suddenly feel. Nothing but burlesque on my mind, but what about the rest of my life?

My steps are illuminated; shadows follow behind me on the pale sprung wood floor of the studio as I extend and bend and stretch through my piece. Flying up, landing solidly, relieved that the choreography's still branded into my muscles, pushing through the low sweep and the broad leap. Still, even though my body is performing, I keep having to ignore thoughts that slide into my brain about things other than the showcase. Also have to ignore my phone, which I should have left screen-side down, because every so often I see it light up, and at a pause in my choreography, I give in to temptation.

Magic, the preview of Taylor's message reads, and then *no, Taylor* from Nevaeh below that.

And then *photo shoot tonight*, from Katherine.

My stomach does the thing where it springs up and spins in a circle, bumping against my heart and making it wobble. Katherine has booked a basement rehearsal room for after dinner, and Jack will come around eight. Hard to say which part of all this is making my heart wobble the most: being photographed, being photographed by Jack, or the deadline for choreographing this act that not only requires removing my clothes, but removing them in an exciting and creative and clever enough way that people are happy to have spent their money on watching me do it.

But then I think of that video, the one of me at the party. And how confident and amazing I look in it. I set my phone back down on the floor, shut my eyes, and picture myself prowling around Taylor like a lioness. Visualizing the scene, I let myself open up into that new space where I am delightfully free, undeniably hot, and full of joy or something like it. Not bulletproof, because that's having a protective shell. Just not needing one at all.

"New showcase moves?" Carly's amused voice rings out over the music.

Startled, I turn to see her in the open door, smiling, and realize that I've lifted up my hair and have one hip cocked out, and I didn't even hear her come in. Obviously.

"Oh, hi!" I say, dropping my arms. "No, just thinking."

"It's nice to see you practicing. I feel like I never see you around," she says.

"I've been here!" I wave my hand around to indicate the building. But it's true—I haven't been here enough.

"Everything okay?"

"Yeah, of course," I say. "So much going on."

She nods. "I know you're always on top of things," she says. "Don't forget I'm still here to talk if you need to."

Warmth in my chest.

"I know you are," I say. I hug her impulsively, making her *oof* and laugh, but she hugs me back. "Sorry!" I say.

"You're okay," she says. "You can come see me just to chat," she says.

The thought of that—it sounds like such a relief. She always makes tea and lets me put my face down on her couch, or pace around the room, or cover my face and moan about life. I always leave feeling better. But I can't go until we're done with the show. I can't lie to her about it.

"I'll visit," I say. "I'll catch you up on everything."

And I really do wish I could confide in her, tell her I've found a way to get to Angles, that it's a cooler, sparklier, more nerve-racking, and potentially wonderful idea than I could have imagined, and all the angst, so many costumes, this new style of dance that is so exciting. But then she catches me off balance.

"We also still have to talk about your funding," she adds, and my thoughts screech to a halt.

"Right," I say, bobbing my head. Hoping I don't look as guilty and panicked as I feel.

"I have some calls in," she says. "It's going to be okay."

"I know it will," I tell her, my stomach twisting in half. I just can't tell her why.

The rehearsal room that Katherine booked isn't the biggest or the nicest, but it's in the basement and at the end of a corridor, so we think it's probably safe to work on acts that clearly aren't related to our showcases or ensemble pieces or anything else that seniors like us should be spending time on. Katherine is in her leotard, whipping her Hula-Hoop around her waist. She can work the hoop all the way up to her armpits and down her thighs, and then step out on one side and hula-hoop with her leg extended in front of her and her toe pointed. She grins at us. She's showing off.

"We could have just sold tickets to this," Taylor says. "No, please, keep going," he tells her when she starts to slow down.

She kicks the hoop into the air and catches it with one hand.

"I can hula-hoop," she says. "But can I hula-hoop and take my clothes off?"

"Yes," I assure her. She is very dexterous.

"I guess we're going to find out," Nevaeh says.

They're almost done with their costumes, since they've been working on them longer, but they're still tweaking. We'll probably keep messing with them until opening night. We've all been sifting through the dresses we have from Nevvie's mom, the stuff we've dug out of our own wardrobes, the thrift-store things, the things they've already ordered online, like wigs and gloves and rolls of Velcro tape. Watching YouTube videos about how to make costumes that are easy to take off—that's where the Velcro comes in. I whacked the skirt off the wedding dress with a big pair of scissors, feeling almost a little sad about it, but I have a bustier now. And a whole lot of satin skirt. I just have to add some of that fabric as a panel behind the laces, so it fits me a little better. But from the front, it already looks ravishing. I didn't bring it tonight—it's not as ready as everyone else's costume pieces, so I have something else to be worried about, for picture taking.

The door isn't quite closed, and when Jack appears, my heart stutters, as if I had a crush on him, which I don't.

"Jack!" Katherine cries. She pulls him into the room.

Katherine might not like him that way, but the way he looks

at her—if I wasn't sure he was smitten with her before, I'd be wondering now. Why wouldn't he be? She's beautiful and kind and smart, and didn't he say they have a lot in common? And they had a lot to talk about. And she's skinny, and—no. Not going there.

Anyway, I am too smart to have a thing for someone who will never like me back.

When he leans down to kiss Katherine on the cheek, she grabs his hand, animatedly telling him about all the costume stuff we have, how excited we are, how much we appreciate him, and he's gazing down at her with the sweetest smile, hair mussed, and I sigh.

Or at least try *not to have a thing.*

Performance smile, activate.

"I expected you all to be naked," Jack says, setting his bags down, propping a white plastic tube against the wall and observing us.

"Disappointed?" Taylor says. He crosses his arms over his chest. He has such nice shoulders. You can see that even in his warm-ups.

Jack blushes.

"Well, there's still time," he tells Taylor.

"You bet there is," Taylor says, and Jack's blush gets darker.

While Jack sets up his lights and the white screen that was in the tube, flicks off the overheads, and shuffles things around, the rest of us start getting into the costume pieces we have. We decide that Katherine will be photographed first.

He starts shooting as Nevaeh brushes Katherine's curls and pulls them into a tall, fountaining ponytail on her head that she can whip around. She's so unexpectedly punk rock in her thrift-store stuff. She's got a poofy black-and-purple petticoat, a tight off-the-shoulder tee, and a kid-size motorcycle jacket that's just cropped on her. Black pleather fingerless gloves from the internet, plus sparkly purple hot pants and a spangled black bikini top for the grand finale. Wicked black eyeliner, pink mouth. Nevaeh dabs the bow of her lips with a little bit of gloss, and Katherine spins to us.

"What do you think?" She smooths down the petticoat, pulls at the end of her ponytail. She looks just like herself, but even more so.

"Oh, wow," Jack says, breaking the silence.

"I love it," Nevaeh tells Katherine, smiling.

"You look great," Jack says, seeming a little shy for just a second, because his crush looks super pretty, I assume, or maybe just because he's a little awkward. It's kind of cute, honestly. And I try not to sigh at myself.

"Want to see me hula-hoop in it?" she asks him.

"Heck yes!" he says, giving her two thumbs up. Yeah, he's a little dorkward.

I grab the hoop to hand to Katherine, and she spins it into motion around her waist, up her torso, down to her hips, and he's shooting, adjusting his settings, shooting again, looking at the screen of the camera and adjusting his settings and moving again. Jack gives her directions, and they take shots without the hoop, moving around her, close up, moving back to capture a pose from behind, from the side with her head turned away. She's confident, melting through poses, elegant arms and wrists, her throat a long line, her leg stretched long and lean. I try not to compare her almost-done costume to the sad bustier and old performance tutu I'll have to work with.

Nevaeh, Taylor, and I watch shoulder to shoulder against the wall in the shadows thrown by the spotlight. My nerves are building up.

Nevaeh seems perfectly confident and cool. Of course, she takes videos and selfies of herself all the time, is so at ease with how she looks in them. All the parts of her collected, resting easily together. I hope if I stand here, leaning quietly, maybe I'll soak that up.

"Katherine has such a crush on him," Nevaeh says in a very low voice, bumping her shoulder against mine. It's not my secret to tell, but I really want to.

"She's sweet to everyone," I say.

"True," she says, tilting her head. "But I think he's got to be into her."

My stomach goes *oof*, but I scold myself. Doesn't matter, remember?

"Do you blame him?" I say.

"Obviously not," she says. "Wouldn't anyone be?"

"What are we whispering about?" Taylor leans over to whisper very loudly.

"Addie thinks that—"

I elbow her, and she stops, laughing. She takes a quick selfie of the three of us.

"Nevaeh next!" Katherine calls.

Nevaeh scoops up her hat, shakes out the sleeves of her suit jacket, and holds out her hand to Katherine, who accepts it gracefully. She spins and dips Katherine while Jack shoots. Then he gets close to shoot the brim of her hat, her bow tie, the bedazzled cuff links that are just for show, her slim ankles, and the tap shoes.

"What were you whispering about?" Taylor whispers, distracting me from my nerves.

"Nothing really," I say. He lifts an eyebrow. It's a skeptical eyebrow.

I don't say anything more, and soon I'm off the hook because it's Taylor's turn. Nevaeh helps him into the wild black-and-white curls of his wig, which he assembled out of two wigs. He's wearing a flowing Greek-style dress of green satin with a very daring thigh slit. He's got that biteable neck and that kissable jaw and the flawless skin of his throat and shoulder.

"I kind of want to make out with you," I tell him.

"Only kind of?" he says, tapping my chin. "I'm disappointed in myself." He swoops me into his arms and gazes dramatically into my eyes. I let my head fall back, flinging my arm behind me, and he makes *om-nom* noises at the base of my throat that tickle so much I start laughing.

Jack clears his throat and interrupts us, and Taylor sets me back on my feet, rubbing off the lipstick on my collarbone with a thumb and pinching my cheek. He is wonderfully elegant, dramatic, and powerful, and they're chatting while Jack takes pictures.

Katherine takes my hand and whispers in my ear. "You're going to be okay!"

"Do I look that scared?"

She smiles sympathetically. "I know you hate pictures."

"It'll be fine," I say.

Then Jack points at me.

"Don't we have enough photos?" I say.

His forehead crinkles. He looks down at the screen of his camera, back up at me. "Well . . ."

"We do not," Nevaeh says firmly, tugging me away from the wall. "We need photos of all of us."

"But *why* do we need—"

"I need them," Jack says. Then clears his throat. "I'd like to have as many as possible to choose from," he explains.

"The more the better," Nevaeh says. The two professionals nod at each other.

"I don't really have much of a costume yet," I hedge.

"We have those dangly earrings!" Katherine says, swinging around and grabbing the bag of costume stuff.

"And you can use the black satin gloves," Nevaeh adds, peering into the bag. Katherine bought them before she decided to go with the short gloves.

"I think there's a necklace in there too," Taylor says. "Here, let me look—"

Katherine pulls the bag away. "I can look!"

"You don't have to take pictures if you don't want to," Jack says softly to me.

"I'm nervous," I find myself admitting to him. "About not having a costume," I add quickly.

"We don't need a whole costume," he says. "You'll be beautiful. I mean, it'll be fine. Great."

I laugh. His voice is rumbly and reassuring and kind, and it helps.

I slip into the long crystal earring drops and the large crystal neckpiece, keep my leo on but climb into my tutu. Nevaeh poofs me with glittery powder, adds eyelashes, eyeliner swoops, and red lips. She's biting her lip and working fast. It's the fastest behind-the-stage costume change I've ever been a part of.

"Hm," Jack says.

"Thanks," I say, with my hands on my hips.

"Oh! Oh, no, no, I was thinking about how to capture—you look great, I mean." He's a little flustered.

I take a deep breath and move in front of the light, which is bright enough to make me blink. Then I turn and look at him lifting the camera and realize I don't know what to do with my hands. I try to remember what the others were doing, besides looking graceful and totally comfortable in front of a camera.

I move into fifth position, pose with my hands above my head, and he clicks. I drop my arms and turn and look over my shoulder, and he clicks. I spin, so my tutu flares out, and he clicks. I stop. I'm out of ideas. And I know I'm stiff. I'm flushed with embarrassment, hating not being good at this, everyone watching me be not good at it, feeling underdressed and awkward.

"I'm sorry," I say. "Can you—can you maybe tell me what you want me to do?" He's the photographer. He ought to have a vision or something, right?

He looks at the screen of the camera, looks back at me.

"Can you dance for me?"

I hesitate. But, oh, *dancing*. Oh yes, I can do that. I nod.

"Music!" Nevaeh says, and grabs Taylor's phone. She's still using her phone for selfies. They put their heads together over his music app.

Jack comes close, lifts his hand, hesitates. "Can I?"

I nod.

He adjusts a curl at my ear, his fingers gentle, and nods to himself, then steps back.

The music, when it starts, is familiar enough to make my eyes prick with tears. It's my audition piece for Angles. My choreography was heavily ballet-inspired, to capture all my dance interests, to show them my breadth of experience and ability. And now it fills me with a quiet kind of joy.

"Thank you," I say to them, and Nevaeh blows me a kiss.

Jack smiles wide at me. I think he can tell that I'm so much less nervous. I nod, lift my chin, and lift up on my toes, a graceful swoop of my arms, a turn, a bend, my back arched, closing my eyes to listen to the music as I move. I won't dance my audition piece, but I'll let it move me. It's easier to pretend that Jack pointing his lens at me is the same as Nevaeh snapping photos at the coffee shop, but the shutter noise is flickering fast. When he slips behind me, I get goose bumps, then shake them off, pull all of myself around me like a cloak, and I dance, in the spotlight, throwing off shadows behind me.

Jack and I are kind of dancing as he slips around me, moving in close as I sway to the side, rising to his feet as I go into a spin, catching his eye for long, long moments, and then I leap, gliding through the air, landing softly, turning my head and lifting my chin.

With a graceful twist of my wrists, I sweep my hands down my bodice to my waist, slowly sink to the floor, skirt puddling around me, and bow, arms extended to each side.

I jump when the shutter goes off loud at my ear. "Holy crap!" I say, twisting around.

"Sorry!" Jack says. He rises to his feet and lifts his camera again, gets a picture of my upturned face. He looks at the screen and then back at me. "Good," he says. He's really close to me, and he's not moving.

"Can I see?" I ask, holding out my hand, but he shakes his head.

"Not yet," he says.

"Would you show them to me first, before you show anyone?"

"Of course," he says.

"But don't photoshop them."

"I'd never," he says. "I promise you'll like them."

I nod but don't respond.

"Just a few more," he says. "Then we'll be good."

He suggests one final pose. I sit on a stool and shrug out of my cami, hold it clasped to my chest. Nevaeh arranges my hair against my naked back and sweeps powder, maybe glitter, over my shoulders. When I look down, I see my love handles, and the need to clap my hands over my midriff is overpowering. I take a breath, keep perfectly soft and still.

Nevaeh steps back and tells me how beautiful I am. Jack's shutter clicks as I look over my shoulder, down at the floor mysteriously. A breath in and out, my belly expanding and contracting. A wave of goose bumps sweeps over me at being more naked than I've ever felt before. I close my eyes. The room is quiet, the murmuring music, the others talking, Jack's shutter. It feels good.

Bunches of kids are all headed back to the dorms, buffeting our own little group as we make our way together. Jack and Taylor are in front, in deep conversation about, I think, Taylor's new socks, or soccer. Katherine and Nevaeh are behind them, arms linked. Katherine is glowing, Nevaeh laughing at her.

Snow is falling, giant fat flakes that land with a plop on your hood, not graceful at all, but the smell is so fresh, a sharp coldness in the air. Something about the snow makes all the students rowdy, everyone running screaming down the paths, skidding across the slippery parts, digging into the old snowbanks piled up along the sides of the walkways and throwing snowballs that are half ice. I slow down, fall behind because I get nervous when things get slippery.

I catch up with everyone where the sidewalk branches off toward the girls' dorm. I sidle over to Jack and tug his sleeve.

"Hey," I say, my voice pitched low, and I realize I'm not sure what I'm going to say. It's loud out here, a group of kids hurtling by us, shouting, a chorus of singing.

Jack leans toward me, bringing his mouth close to my ear. "You were great."

I shiver. I don't think that's what I was going to ask. But I'm not going to deny that it is nice to hear.

"Just FYI," he says quickly. He glances up as the clock tower starts to strike ten. Taylor offers to race him back to the boys' dorm, and they're off, and that's okay.

Katherine, Nevaeh, and I sprint down the path to ours before the clock finishes its countdown.

14

The following evening, I'm curled up next to the window in the common room, trying to finish *The Bell Jar* and unexpectedly having feelings about it, when I can keep my eyes on the page. The snow is still piling up outside, on and off since last night. It's hard to do anything but scrunch down in the chair and drift with the snowflakes and daydream about my dance, my clothes, our club.

When my phone buzzes in my lap, I jump, flip it over. My mother.

"Finally you pick up. Do you need money?" Her face is pinched, her lips all pruney.

"Nice to talk to you, too, Mom." My voice is wry, and I keep it low because there are other students in here.

"Don't take that tone with me," she says. "You know I'm only *joking*."

"I know," I say, even though I'm not quite sure she was joking.

"I'm glad to hear your voice," she says.

"I miss you," I say. And it is true.

She sniffs, and then she says, "I miss you, too, little ladybug. I suppose I should just get used to you being gone forever." A text message notification pops up on my screen as she talks. It's from the poo emoji. Jack. The preview says, *As per our agree—*

"Addie?" my mother is saying. "Are you listening to me?"

"Sorry, Mom," I say, struggling to sit up straight, catching my book and then catching the phone when I drop it. "Just a second, I have a—"

"—trying to tell you—"

"Just a second, Mom," I say.

"—don't understand why you have to—"

As per our agreement, I'd like to show you the photo I've picked as the backdrop of the invitation card first. I stare at the screen and type back, *of course.*

My mother is still talking. I tap back to our call.

"I'm so, so sorry, Mom; it was just a text message. About, uh, a test."

"A message from who?" she says. "From *whom*," she corrects herself.

"Oh, just—" I start to say, and another notification pops up, with an attachment.

"Hold on," I say to my mom.

"Addie!" she says.

Tap on the attachment. Full-screen photo.

Against a glittery, golden light, slightly shadowed: the outline of a back, bent to the side in a graceful curve, shadow of a spine and shoulder blades, soft folds of skin at the bend of the waist. Shadows and light but real skin, touchable and the feeling of movement and a strong, fat body. And it's my back. It's my back, looking like art. It is gorgeous, and it's my back, unretouched and unphotoshopped, and look at that.

"Addie," my mother says.

"Hi, Mom," I say. "I'm here."

"What's wrong?" she says. "You sound strange! What's going on, Addie?"

"I'm sorry," I say. "There's just so much going on. Can I call you later?" I hang up before she answers, and I look at the photo again, try to remember I'm in a public space. I take a deep breath, and then another, looking at this photo.

What do you think?

The message pops up, and I switch over to my texts to see that he's still typing.

A long moment, then he stops typing, and then he types, and then he stops typing, and I want to shake the phone and make the words come out.

Do you like it?

Approve of it, I mean

More typing, but then it stops again.

Yes, I type back. Should I have added an exclamation point? I send an exclamation point.

!

I will finish the invitation tonight, then.

I hesitate, then send him a smiley face. Then a firework emoji.

I am filled up with helium looking at this photo, which doesn't seem real. Which is funny because it's so real in that kinetic curve and that fold of fat at the waist and the trace of scars and the texture of skin and how alive it is, the bright shine of sparkles reflecting in the spotlight. Bright shine of me, reflected in the camera lens. It's me.

I forward the photo to Nevaeh, Katherine, Taylor without comment and put my phone facedown on the arm of my chair. I'll read for a while longer, before I see what they think, my hands shaking. I knock the phone off the arm and scramble down to pick it up. Sitting cross-legged on the carpet, I see our group chat exploding with exclamation points.

that is your back, Taylor types.

More caps lock and exclamation points.

what are you doing? Nevaeh asks.

i don't know, I type, and then I do.

get your coats get your hats let's go outside I want to go make snow angels go go go

Minutes later, I burst into the dark, snow-filled air, twirl and let the flakes fall on my lashes, on my tongue. Nevaeh tackles me from behind, not wearing a hat, and there's Katherine with two hats, her arms around my neck.

"That is your back!" she yells.

"I know!" I yell. "These invitations!" A running start, and I jump into the snow, whooshing up and landing with a poof that knocks the wind out of me, makes me laugh breathlessly. I turn over and lie on my back.

Katherine lands next to me, and Nevaeh swan dives on top of both of us, burying us deeper. She smacks a kiss on Katherine's cheek, leaving a glittery purple print, and then mine.

"Snow angel!" she cries, plowing through the snow to another untouched spot, Katherine stumbling after her.

I'm smiling up at the sky, low dark clouds and snow still drifting, until someone charges past and I get a faceful. I sit up, spitting and brushing the icy crystals off my cheeks and nose and eyes, and then someone is reaching for me, hauling me up. It's Christopher, and once I wobble up to stand he puts his arm around my shoulders. My face is stinging.

"So bad at this snow thing," he says. "You look ridiculous. Like a big old drowned rat." He's leading me to the walkway.

"I'm okay," I say. "You can let me go." I twist away, move a step apart from him, keep lurching ahead through the piled-up snow.

"I'm not sure I should," he says.

"I'm fine," I tell him.

"Why are you getting so worked up?" he says, maddeningly. He's right next to me again, matching my steps.

"I'm *not*," I say.

"Okay, well, have your temper tantrum."

"I'm not having a temper tantrum!" I try to keep my voice even.

"Oh yeah?" he says. "You look like Ursula the sea witch, flopping around onshore." He mimics me flailing again.

"Oh, fuck off," I snap. Nevaeh and Katherine are marching over.

He snorts at me. "Seriously? Get a sense of humor, Addie."

"I don't want you to talk to me, and you keep talking to me."

"I can talk to you if I want."

"But I don't want you to!" I'm angry, which makes me near tears, which makes it even worse.

"Aw, just calm down," he says, slipping his heavy arm around my shoulders. "I'm a nice guy."

"She said go away," Katherine says, pushing him off me. Nevaeh grabs his hand as I duck away. She's clamped on to his wrist.

"You," she says. "Holy shit, it's you. *Look at this.*" She yanks his arm again, thrusting it toward us. We're near one of the tall light posts that illuminate the path, and I see it immediately—a big blood blister under his thumbnail, black and blue and yellow and gross, and familiar. He yanks his hand back, saying something, but I can't hear it over this revelation.

"You've been sending dick pics," I say, and I laugh. "What is wrong with you?"

"Prove it," he says.

Nevaeh's already got her camera out, and she's got a picture of him, his hand, his face, which changes when he realizes what she's doing. He grabs at the phone and Nevaeh dances back, stumbling a little in the snow. He grabs her wrist with one hand, shaking her arm, and Nevaeh is yanking back, snarling something. I'm trying to grab his coat, I'm yelling something, I don't know what.

And then Katherine tackles him into the snow, howling.

With a mighty heave, he pushes her off, and Nevaeh catches her around the waist, pulls her up and away. Katherine is angry-crying, red-cheeked, and Nevaeh is whispering urgently into her ear, trying to guide her away. Christopher is back on his feet, and he's laughing, his jeans wet from the snow.

"That's right, run, you fucking—"

And then Taylor tackles him.

Christopher thrashes, and Taylor's got his shoulders pushed down in the snow. I dive in, trying to pull Taylor's arm, get a grip on his coat, and I slide sideways and land hard on my elbow and kick away out from under their struggling bodies, scrambling back. Nevaeh catches my hand and helps me upright, Katherine close at my back. She says something, but I can't make it out. Other students have gathered around, and it's a general roar of voices where everyone is shouting something and no one can hear one another until there's Mr. Banerjee, his deep voice cracking through the air and breaking Taylor and Christopher apart, panting, covered in snow, groping their way to their feet.

"What is going on?" Mr. Banerjee asks, his eyebrows scrunching down low under his beanie.

"We were wrestling," Christopher says. He's panting. He slaps Taylor on the back.

"Yeah," Taylor says flatly, yanking down the hem of his coat. "Friendly wrestling."

Christopher spreads his hands wide. "And you'll be glad to know he started it."

Taylor jolts at that but doesn't say anything.

Mr. Banerjee shakes his head, a sharp jerk, a sweep of his hand like he's done with them. "Jhang. Davenport. You'll be hearing from the dean. Back to your dorm. Now."

Christopher is smirking, and Taylor's eyes are narrow, furious. His shoulder is stiff when I touch him, try to guide him back over to us.

"Yes, sir," Christopher says, brushing snow off his coat. He wiggles his eyebrows at me as he leaves, because of course he does.

"Jhang?" Mr. Banerjee says.

"We'll walk him back," I say. "It was my fault."

Katherine takes Taylor's hand, and I slip my hand around his elbow and squeeze, and he is rigid and furious. Nevaeh stalks next to us, sputtering. "The nerve. That creep. That absolute asshole."

"So that's cleared up," Taylor says. "He's sending dick pics. And now I've gotten a second strike."

I stop on the wet sidewalk. His second strike—that means one more and he's out. One more demerit—a mark on your record—and he is literally out. As in expelled. So if we get caught sneaking out after curfew . . .

"You can't do the show," I say to him.

"No," Nevaeh says. "Oh no."

"Of course I can," he says to me, irritated, then mutters, "I'm freezing."

"There is no way in hell you're risking getting kicked out," I say urgently.

He frowns at me and gestures toward the dorm. "Can we go?"

"Your NYU acceptance," I say, furious, my voice louder. "If you get expelled—"

He closes his eyes. Shakes his head.

"I'm so sorry," I say.

"I can't do the show." He sighs. His face is grim, and I feel like I can hear the sound of all our hearts, broken into pieces and rattling in our chests, and it's bullshit.

Katherine takes Taylor's other hand, so she's holding both now, and he looks at her. "I'm going to hot glue Christopher's dick to his thigh," she says, and we all gasp, shocked into laughter.

"Katherine!" Nevaeh says, snickering. "Language!"

"Don't come for my friends," she says darkly.

And the snow just keeps falling and falling, covering everything.

On Friday morning after arts block, Taylor texts us: They're grounded to their dorm for a week, aside from classes and meals. And he's on warning status for the rest of the year, can't breathe wrong or he's out.

we should just cancel, I type. *i don't want to do it without you. i don't want anyone to get caught. i can't take this*

it's fine, Taylor types back. *don't you dare.* And I'm distracted from the rest of the message when my dorm elevator door opens on a crowd in the lobby. I step out into a ton of kids gathered around the bulletin board, taking photos, laughing, the RA trying to shoo folks out of the way, pulling down papers and folding them over, asking students to back off. I crane my neck to see what they're looking at, then push through the crowd.

The bulletin board is plastered with black-and-white dick-pic prints. Ones that seem familiar. The thumbnail with the blood blister. In marker, in handwriting, in caps, the words at the bottom of every single picture read *CHRISTOPHER DAVENPORT LIKES TO SEND DICK PICS.*

I clap my hand over my mouth, glance to either side of me. Everyone's taking pictures as fast as the RA can shuffle them out of the way, and I quickly snap my own, then back off and out of the crowd.

And in the quad there are more: dick pics on lampposts and on the entrance doors of the science building next door, and the giggles are exploding in my chest. I message my photo of the bulletin board to our group.

Almost immediately, Katherine types back. *SURPRISE!*

Nevaeh texts, *my beautiful Katherine is BRILLIANT AND MY HERO*

we win! Taylor texts.

A blushing face emoji from Katherine.

Then the eggplant emoji and the knife emoji.

can't explain how much I love you, Katherine, I type.

Jack helped, she texts.

Taylor types, *his penis is viral!*

probably literally, Nevaeh types.

Oooooo from Taylor.

I look up to see a couple of guys tearing down flyers from lampposts. And a couple more, farther up the path, doing the same. Christopher's friends? There's a knot in my stomach. A sudden thought: If Christopher finds out about the show, would he be pissed enough now to screw us over? I hesitate, watching the messages slide by from my friends, all full of glee, and me too, but.

we should be careful

we should back off and just avoid him

don't just let him bully you, Katherine writes.

no. i'll avoid

will he avoid you

I don't know how to answer that.

will he stop sending the photos?

i guess we'll find out

I'm not really smiling anymore as I head to class through a sea of dick pics.

15

The next two weeks feel like ten minutes.

On Saturday we're stuffing envelopes with invites. They're stunning. A small card with a soft black background, an aura of gold around the sweep of my back, the words *Dirty Little Secret* curling down in red. Instructions brief: Tell no one. Join us. An Instagram handle. We've already made an invitation list: all genders, only arts-program people we think we can trust—only seniors, no exes, no one with grudges against any of us. When it's nearing senior curfew, Katherine and Nevaeh distract our resident assistant so I can slip the cards into chosen students' mailboxes without being noticed. Then I run over to distract Jack's RA as he slips behind the desk and distributes the boys' batch, and then it's done.

In the middle of the night, I wake up restless and open Instagram.

Fourteen friend requests already.

I sit up, beat my heels against the mattress, push my face into the pillow because I've got to make noise.

Sunday morning we wait downstairs in the boys' dorm lobby with breakfast from the campus coffee shop while Taylor drags himself out of bed. Nevaeh goes down the list to accept the requests, one by one.

"Okay, then," she says. "I guess now we see if they actually send the money. Could I have coffee, please?"

I hand her the to-go cup.

When Taylor finally bounces out of the elevator, his hair wet and standing straight up, he's waving his phone at us.

"Look at that!" he says, pointing at the screen, beaming.

"Your phone is off," Nevaeh observes.

"That is a black screen," Katherine affirms.

"Look at what?" I ask.

He grunts, pokes at the screen, and turns it back to us triumphantly. "There!"

"That's your boyfriend on FaceTime," Nevaeh says. "Hi, Damien!"

"Hi, gorgeouses!" Damien says, his voice tinny through the speaker. We all wave.

"No!" Taylor says, punching at the screen again. "I'll call you back!"

"That was mean," I say, pulling my hat on.

"Okay," he says, frowning at the screen. "Here!"

The three of us lean forward. It's the cash app account-balance. It says $400. Nevaeh accepted the friend requests only fifteen minutes ago.

"That's—" I stop, and then look around. The common room is crowded, and the other chairs are close. *That's our first four ticket sales, so fast*, the sudden tension in my shoulders says.

"Yes," Taylor says triumphantly.

"That means—" Nevaeh says, very intently. Her eyes say, *that means the invites worked*, and Katherine grabs her hand, pulls her close.

"So people are—" Katherine says. She waves her other arm around in a signal that we all know means *people are buying tickets already, holy crap!*

"And this is—" I say. My flapping hands say, *and this is going to work!*

"Yes, yes, yes!" Taylor says, punctuating each shout with a pound of his fists on the coffee table. The next group of chairs, full of soccer players, all turn around. "I love yogurt *so much*!" Taylor says. "Yes!" He grabs the cherry yogurt container off the coffee table and cuddles it passionately.

They give us dirty looks, shake their heads as they turn back around to whisper about how weird we are.

Katherine throws her arms around Nevaeh's neck and smacks a kiss on the corner of her mouth, and they are smiling delightedly at each other.

"Does Jack know?" I ask Taylor when it occurs to me, and he shrugs. I text him, and he sends a string of firework emojis, which is exactly right.

All day Sunday the ticket count keeps racking up, one ticket and then a flurry. I smile to see the names: three dancers from my improv class, the treasurer and two others from Nevaeh's BIPOC-Speaks club, a senior from my English class—all names I recognize. Another flurry of people we like, and then another flurry, and then we call it. We're sold out. That's $2,000. Rehearsals start this week, because we've got a show coming up fast.

It's hard to keep the smile off my face, so I don't try, bouncing out of classes all week, slinging my bag over my shoulder, practicing my burlesque routine in my head. My fingertips are sore because I keep pricking myself with needles, making hemming my bustier slow going, and I still can't pull the slipknot and fling off my skirt in any kind of graceful way—sometimes it lands at my feet and I get tangled in it, and sometimes it lands on my head, and none of my friends can help laughing at that. Katherine keeps dropping her hoop, and Nevaeh had to tear apart her suit pants yet again and remake them because they won't slide off properly, and she doesn't want to talk about how she keeps stumbling on her hat.

The gestures and attitude of burlesque are easy for us to pick up. The body language, the smiles—we got over being embarrassed about smiling at each other sexily real fast, and we find ourselves reveling in those versions of ourselves who aren't afraid to gleefully accept your admiration and adoration: *Yes, we know we're amazing and talented and beautiful too.*

The hard part is literally the pulling off the clothes. We may have mastered the sexy smile, but we still sometimes clench our teeth instead because it is so, so hard to strip and dance. And also remember to study for midterms and finish the readings and practice things that aren't burlesque, but oh my god, stripping off a corset.

There's a new, weird rhythm to our lives, in this countdown to the first show: rehearsal, class, study, fall over trying to take a corset off, rinse, repeat, and all of it seems normal and like it'll be this way forever, so we forget we shouldn't be complaining out loud in the coffee line about the painful red marks the boning has left along our rib cages and torsos, but honestly that could be from any of our rehearsal costumes over the years, and we're all getting a little hysterical from the buildup and excitement.

Wednesday, our final costume craft night in Katherine and Nevaeh's room, we're being rowdy, and all of a sudden a sharp knock comes on the door. Katherine throws her entire body off the bunk bed to snatch our wigs and a corset off the desktop and plop down on top of them.

"Come in," she says, barely suppressing her laughter. Nevaeh and I can't suppress ours at all, seeing her flailing around like that.

"Studying?" the RA says.

"Explosions," I gasp.

"Formulas," Katherine chokes out.

"*Science*," cries Nevaeh, and we're cackling again.

"Right," the RA says, but we can't answer her, and she gives up on us. "Keep it down a bit, will you?"

On Thursday, I'm so distracted in technique that Madame George has to correct the angle of my neck and shoulders, as if I'm a first-year. I'm still flushed a bit with embarrassment when I collide with Gavin outside the locker room.

"I was thinking," he says.

"Aw, good for you!" I say pretend-cheerfully, patting his shoulder and not paying a lot of attention.

"And I thought, *why does she look so familiar?*"

I scrunch up my face at him. "I don't know what you mean."

He falls into step with me as I head down the hall, pulling out my bobby pins. I always mean to just leave my hair up all day, since I'll be practicing again after dinner, but it starts to bother me thirteen seconds after I leave rehearsal in the morning.

"On the invitation," he says. "That's you."

We stop in the stairwell.

"What invitation?" I say. Shit, shit, shit. He is literally, actually literally, the last person I would want knowing about this. Okay, besides Christopher. But still, I'm frozen, eyes wide, staring at him with no idea what to say and my heart whapping faster than it should be.

"When did you start doing burlesque?"

"I don't know what you're talking about." I'm so bad at playing clueless, and he doesn't even pretend to take me seriously.

"I wish I had gotten an invite," he says.

"There's no invite," I say, pulling out my phone.

"But I would very much prefer a very private, just-Addie show anyway. What do you say?"

"I say it's a real pity you dumped me, I guess," I say, and leave him in the stairwell.

In the quad I call Nevaeh to ask if we should panic, and she tells me she's panicking at that question.

"I'm sorry! I should have killed him immediately and left his body for the janitor!" I only one-eighteenth joke. We know this is a small school and that we are not collectively James Bond and that our invitation plan isn't flawlessly cryptic and secretive, and we've been keeping an ear out for rumors. But we hadn't looked right in the face of what it would mean to be so directly confronted, even in such a ham-handed way by someone who isn't a threat.

"No, no," she says. "Murder would just add to our worries."

"So what should we do?" I ask. "Should we cancel it?" I know we're not going to, but feel like I need to hear her say it.

"Of course not," she scoffs.

"Okay," I say. "Okay." And I try to breathe past it, but can't help feeling like I'm not going to relax again until this whole thing is successfully behind us.

When Jack pulls out a chair at our dinner table, the evening of our second-to-last dress rehearsal, he seems very pleased with himself. His socks are purple and have kittens playing with yarn balls, and his haircut is too short.

"No, why did you do that?" I say, reaching out. He's startled, touches his head. I shake mine. "No, I'm sorry, I like it. I liked your curls, is all."

"Did you?" he says, and he's really smiling at that. "I didn't know that."

"Uh, yeah," I say, awkwardly. Usual reminder to myself that I don't like someone who likes my friend.

"Anyway, I wanted to tell you all I was really excited about tonight," he says earnestly, and my heart is squeezing so hard. "Where should I meet you? When should I be there?"

Without Taylor's act, we worried that the show would be a bit short, so we're each going to come back onstage to do a mini demonstration—Katherine will pull someone out of the audience to teach them a Hula-Hoop move, Nevaeh will demonstrate some tap dancing steps, and I was going to grab a nondancer from the audience to teach them the basic ballet positions. But Jack volunteered to let me teach him. And then he agreed to be the emcee, much to our surprise—it had started as a joke. I can't imagine him doing it, honestly—he doesn't seem like the performing type. But everyone is enthusiastic about the idea, and I'm sure it'll be fine. I hope.

"Are you still sure?" Nevaeh says. Maybe she's not sure either.

"He'll show us tonight, right?" Katherine says. "Have my banana," she says to him.

He clutches it awkwardly. "Right," he says, pointing it at us. "It's going to be great."

———

I am sitting in the audience watching Nevaeh and Katherine work on raising the curtain when Jack arrives. We don't have any decorations up, going all supersecret in between rehearsals. We've tested our ideas out, the fairy lights and swaths of fabric, richly embroidered cotton and silk and satins and velvets all sewn together, thrown over the scenery pieces leaning along the walls, paper lanterns and some battery candles scattered around the room. Fabric on the floor like picnic blankets, throw pillows thrown down—voilà, a performance space.

Jack pauses at the entrance and glances around at the very undecorated space.

"This isn't what it's going to look like," Katherine calls over.

"It has a dystopian charm," he tells her. Does he look nervous?

"Are you nervous?" I ask him.

"No," he says. And then a slow smile.

He's really not nervous at all.

"Are you drunk?"

That surprises him a bit, and I grin at him cheekily.

"*No*," he says, mock scandalized.

Katherine shows him the musical setup, the remote control, the little Bluetooth microphone we have turned way down, because we just need a little boost to sound authoritative, but not much. She points out the ON and OFF switches very dramatically, because even low screeching when you put the mic down is terrible, and so is drowning out someone's music.

"Are you ready?" Nevaeh says to him.

"Of course," he says.

He's wearing a dark gray suit, fitted perfectly slim. Green socks, though I can't see the pattern, a very dark green shirt. Button opened at the throat. He sees me staring at him, and he gives me an upward nod with his chin.

"Go time," Katherine says, throwing her arms in the air. She and Nevaeh plop down next to me. My stomach is made of surly bees, inexplicably nervous for him.

But he doesn't even pull out index cards, like I expect.

He launches into thanking the audience for coming, and it's funny. His voice is smooth and warm, and I notice he's got an accent I can't quite place, a little roundness of the vowels, almost midwestern, that is delightful. He's smooth, too, slipping into an introduction to Dirty Little Secret, Lakeshore's one and only underground burlesque show, as far as we know.

We laugh at that, caught up in his act, and he smiles back.

"Our performers tonight are extraordinary," he says. He asks us if we're ready for an incredible amount of talent, extraordinary charm and wit, breathtaking beauty and grace, or something like that. I lose track of all the adjectives, but I keep elbowing Nevaeh in the side until she puts her arm around me to make me stop.

We jump to our feet to applaud.

"There's more," he says, carefully turning off the mic. "I have introductions for all of you, but you can approve them, if you like, and I thought we could go over your interstitial acts to make sure I've got the timing down and so on." He pauses. "If I've still got the job."

Katherine runs up to hug him. "You have got the job!"

"Taylor helped me practice," he says. My heart squeezes again and again.

We run through the whole thing in one go for the first time after he leaves, and then again. We've got it down flawlessly.

Friday we are a mess, and I slip off my chair when I try to roll down my stocking, and I want to cry, and we keep going until we give up.

"You know how it works," Katherine says, lifting off her wig. "Bad dress rehearsal, great performance."

"That's a cliché," I say.

"Well, yes," she says.

"Is it too late to quit?"

"Oh my god, Addie, no," Nevaeh says.

"We're going to do it," Katherine says. "It'll be great."

"Oh my god, Addie, yes," I say, and let the curtain fall behind us.

16

When my alarm buzzes in the dark of my dorm room, I bolt straight up and only just manage to not scream. It's not that late so I haven't been sleeping, just staring up at the dark ceiling, rehearsing my act in my head, trying to breathe deep and stay loose.

I love you, Taylor messages us. *Be careful! Break a leg! THIS ISN'T FAIR*

We meet in the dimly lit hall, Nevaeh, Katherine, and I, and they're as breathless as I am, wide-eyed, full of barely suppressed glee. We catch one another's hands, squeeze, creep down the emergency stairs. I crack the cellar door open, and a boom of wind grabs it out of my hand, swings it wide into the dark, and we all gasp at the door being snatched wide, the way the wind feels bladed with ice, and then it's hard to stop giggling. Katherine and Nevaeh hustle into the shadows beneath the trees, their hands clapped over their mouths, and I ease the door shut and rush after them, hunched into my coat, shaking a little from the chill, from the nerves, how quiet it is, how loud our boots sound, how heavy I feel like I'm breathing, how long it seems to take to make our way, stumbling over roots and rocks because it's so much darker without the buildings we pass being all lit up.

Such a relief to make it to the theater, scramble down the driveway and down the hall, into a room that we're surprised to find is already lit and blazing with electric candles and lanterns, pillows scattered across the floor, curtain up. And Jack, standing there smiling.

"I was too excited to wait," Jack says.

And then we're off.

It's the fastest hour of my life: hair, makeup, costumes, props, setting up our little spotlights, slow, steady breathing. Jack is off to greet the audience members at the outer door. The music is low and sexy. I pop out to take a look at what we've done, this little jewel box of a guerrilla punk rock theater spreading out in front of us, this huge private room that feels intimate and warm and textured and glowing yellow.

Katherine in full punk rock makeup, skirt floofed, chain necklaces glinting in the light, and Nevaeh tilting her hat over one eye, hair pulled back tight, slick and gorgeous in her suit. I smooth down my tutu. We're all in half masks, delicate things just covering our eyes, tied in bows behind our heads, giving us plausible deniability. The two of them look lusciously mysterious, beautiful almost-strangers. We huddle together as the hour ticks closer to midnight. We miss Taylor so much. Katherine checks the time on her phone, and we jump behind the curtain. Soon the sound of voices. Gasps. Excited murmurs and talking and laughing and shuffling as everyone finds a place to sit, scoots around, and points out things to one another.

Jack slides behind the curtain.

"Are you ready?" he says. That sweet, excited smile.

"Are you?" I ask, touching his hand.

"Of course," he says. He turns his hand over, squeezes mine, surprising me. "You're going to be amazing." He means all of us, I know.

And then his voice is rolling out over the audience, and there is actual hooting and hollering. Katherine takes a deep breath and steps out onto the stage to even more whooping. Nevaeh and I peer through the gap in the curtain to watch, whooping along with the crowd when she spins the hoop into motion around her waist. They cheer every move, but when she whips her right arm out gracefully and the hoop spirals to her gloved wrist and spins there in frantic circles as she bites, one by one, the fingertips of her other glove to strip it off in one smooth motion, there are actual howls.

It goes too fast. Katherine bows to wild applause at the end of her performance and springs backstage into Nevaeh's arms, absolutely incandescent and giddy. She jumps back out in her tap shorts and pretty bra to demonstrate hula-hooping to the whoops and applause and surprise of the crowd, takes a bow, comes back for another bow and another. Then Nevaeh, sent off with a kiss on the cheek from Katherine. She struts into the light, tipping her hat to an audience that wolf whistles with approval, calling her name when she whips off her coat, but when she starts flicking open the buttons on her shirt, they start to lose it completely. Someone shouts "Fuck yeah!" when she tosses it into the crowd. They're totally in love with her onstage, heartbroken when she leaves them, comes back to us to bury her face in Katherine's neck and squeeze my hand tight, laughing wildly, overcome by the noise and the glee, and it's absolute magic. She jumps back out to kick-ball-step across the stage, bantering with

Jack. Katherine is peering around the curtain. So much laughter, and then a roar, and she's breathless, laughing too.

And now the audience is waiting for me. I hear Jack's voice, and I catch Katherine's and Nevaeh's eyes, glittering bright, buoyed up by that spirit that takes you over when you know you have just had the performance of your life.

I am frozen. I am iced over. I am a solid brick of fear.

The audience is white noise.

Nevaeh takes my hands. She waits until I look at her. She bends close to say in my ear, "You got Angles, Addiebear. You got this."

I squeeze her hands tight. I kiss Katherine's cheek. "Knock them dead," she says, seizing me in a fierce hug. I straighten up, yelp when Nevaeh slaps my butt, and laugh.

"Friends . . ." Finally, Jack's familiar voice booms over the microphone, warm and rich, settling my nerves and silencing any murmuring, throat clearing, laughing. "Let's put our hands together for the ravishing, delightful, delicious, diverting dance sensation, Arabesque L'Amour!"

Like the silence was flammable and Jack struck a match, the room explodes with cheers, and my heart explodes in a shower of sparks, because no turning back now.

Showtime.

I suck in a breath and step out from behind the curtain, into the light.

17

I pose, my arms a delicate arch over my head in their pale, pale blue satin elbow-length gloves. My tutu glitters. My lips glisten pink. I am a ballerina doll.

I think about that first ballet master who told my mother, "She is too fat. She will never be a dancer."

But I danced. I took lesson after lesson and found the music wanted my body and my body wanted the music, and it changed me, shaped me, dug into me and curled around my bones and knit into my muscles and made me stronger and brighter and more alive. This is the promise I've tried to keep to myself: that my body is perfect—larger than most dancers', "*fat*" in the eyes of too many people, people who don't understand bodies, who don't know how beautiful they are. I'll take the word *fat*, and I'll keep it next to my heart, and I'll own it. And I'll take up the space in the world that I take up and not apologize for it.

I have never stopped dancing. And I will never stop dancing. And I will never stop reveling in the feel of the music, those first few bars that shower over you, lift you up to your toes, sing down your spine, keep you suspended in time, and then explode out of your skin, out of your stillness, help you inscribe the movement of your limbs and the tilt of your head and the length of your neck and the shape of your feet and the joy and concentration in your face into the hearts of the audience.

Now the tinkly opening notes of the *Nutcracker* music I'm using spill onto the stage, but this isn't going to be any Christmas pageant.

One last deep breath.

Up onto my toes, I rise.

There's no hesitation; my body follows the music, chasing the bell-like notes, nimble, delicate little steps, flitting across the stage, neck long, arms graceful, skirt shimmering. (Flash of memory: *How many sequins do I really need?* I ask; *All of them!* Katherine cries.) I breathe into the ripple of the music, moving around the chair and across the stage again, the classic choreography thrown away.

Dainty pas de bourrée *couru* in sixth position. *Tendu devant* in plié. *Relevé*.

At every moment, I'm aware of the audience, buzzing and alive, in a way I never am while performing. I can tell they're captivated. Surprised. This isn't what they expected, a fat ballerina. And where the hell is the burlesque? I feel my mouth quirk the tiniest bit.

I'm giving you a taste of delicate and demure, my friends, steps I'm told aren't meant for a body like mine, showing you I can be your perfect music box ballerina. Lift the lid, and I will spin and spin and spin for you.

But that doesn't mean I'm going to stay there.

Grande jeté. Arabesque, slowly, slowly, counting down because in three, two, one—

The beat drops.

And I drop to my knees.

And there is such a roar.

So long, ballet.

The deep thrumming bass of a heavy, bone-shaking dubstep "Sugarplum Fairy" remix, familiar classical music gone bonkers, crashes over all of us.

It sweeps away my sweet performer's smile, and in its place is me, Addie, slightly wicked, grinning out at the audience and telling them, *You ain't seen nothing yet.*

Sweeping my hand up along my side, the length of my neck, asking with my hand, with my smile, *You ready to see ballerina doll go burlesque?* All in one move and right on the beat, I release the sparkling rhinestone clip pinning my hair into a prim updo, and I fling it into the air. My hair tumbles down around my shoulders in waves, and I whip it around, arching my back, whip it around again, my mass of dark curls glittering silver and gold, wild and untamed, and I'm really grinning now. Because this is what I want, to show you how beautiful I feel.

Gathering all my hair up, I lift it off my neck as I roll my shoulders, moving to the thunder that's filled up the whole room. A pirouette like the world has never seen, sinuous, letting my hips swing around with the force of the turn, leaning it into the force of what my body can do, a tornado, the ballerina unleashed. Then stomp to a halt at my musical cue.

Hips moving to the beat, I trace my fingers down my arm to my shimmering glove, now teasing the first reveal, and suddenly, with the thought of it—*the first reveal*—I almost rock to a halt, almost stop, almost *freeze*, almost go up in flames. The beat goes on without me, and I am out of sync. Can anyone tell?

I spin again, roll my hips, buying time.

It's just an arm. Just a hand.

Still, my mind flashes on names: *Shima, Juan, Alice* . . . I know they're out there, saw them coming in. *Sarah, Elise, Eleanor* . . . I have to be with them Monday in math, in technique, in English . . .

My stomach is in free fall now, but no one could ever tell. I won't fail, I'll never fail, even if this feels like the bravest thing I've ever done. I catch the beat and haul myself back into it, prowling across the stage, stroking the length of my glove, easing the fingers off one by one, slide it off slowly with my teeth—why does satin have to taste so terrible?—and swing it into the air.

"YES!" someone shouts, and it fills the room. I don't even know who, but it's a voice full of triumph, and my glove is now a flag of victory.

And there it is, my naked arm, skin glowing in the spotlight. Yes, just an arm, but right here, right now, I decide it's the most delicious thing I've ever seen. I let the roar of the crowd, the roar of my breath in my ears, the roar of my heart in my chest, fill me up, as I strip off the second glove too.

"YES, GIRL, GET IT!"

I throw both naked arms in the air and spin, do that thing where I just take up all my space.

Oh yes.

The rest of it, it goes so fast, but every second is burned in.

A sequence of pirouettes to the dubstep beat land me at the chair. I shimmy down into it and stretch one impossibly long leg up to the ceiling. The audience knows what's coming as I give them a wink and begin to untie and unwind the ribbon of my dance shoe. I playfully kick it off, and next is the thigh-high stocking. I roll it down and there it is, the ballerina's strong, naked leg and wickedly arched foot. And it shouldn't be sexy, that bare foot, with its calluses and blisters and misshapen toes. It shouldn't be sexy, my normal, naked skin, not airbrush smooth, not model-thin, too many muscles, so many white-and-pink scars, beauty marks, and ordinary dents and bruises, cellulite and pores and realness. But here we are. Under a spotlight, and goddamn perfect.

"WOOOOOOO, YEAH!"

I repeat the reveal with the second leg, then jump lightly to the seat of the chair.

Grinning at the audience, I move my hands down my sides, along the waistband of my tutu, unfasten it in a flash, and whip it off with a flourish. I'm in my corset now and a short tulle petticoat, but I don't let the audience catch a breath. Leaping off the chair and bounding across the stage, wrap skirt a banner in my hands, I'm spinning and whipping the skirt around my body like it's a bullfighter's cape.

I'm laughing. They're cheering. This is joy, leaning into this roar from the audience. Here, right now, for always, my body is *mine*—it isn't bare skin; it's not nudity. It's ownership. It's feeling absolutely, deliciously, wildly sexy, totally in control. Letting the audience come along for the ride because I'm nice like that.

I thought I would feel naked. Frozen, embarrassed. *Naked*. But I don't. And it's with that total, utter joy that I let them watch me put my foot up on that little chair and glide that garter off, flip it into the air with a toe, wiggle out of my corset and down to a glittery bralette, dance my way out of the petticoat, revealing my satin tap pants and even more sequins, all flashing in the light, almost as bright as my smile.

And finally, standing there—having shared all the secrets this audience is lucky enough to see, filled with happiness and pride and disbelief at my own luck to be me, here at this moment—finally, I bow.

18

I'm glowing. Glowing, full of bursting, shining, shimmering sparkles that snap and pop, revved up in a way I've never been after a performance. The light inside me should be lighting up the whole room, spilling out into the hallway, but I'm still just me. Except somehow *more*. Electrified, powered up. *We did it.* We threw our arms around one another, breathless, and jumped up and down and we screamed, *Holy shit, we did it, we did it.* And I said, *Thank you, thank you, thank you so much* and they said, *This was amazing.* We did it, and every moment—the roar as Nevaeh whipped her tie off, the laughter when Katherine spun her Hula-Hoop all the way along the length of her body, the way Jack kept the audience directly in the palm of his hand with just his voice, his terrible puns that had us snickering behind the curtain, where we stood hand in hand, amped up with adrenaline. The hot light sparking off my skin, and the pure love and admiration from the audience. Like nothing I've ever felt before. Almost addictive.

I'm smiling as I dance with the broom through the performance space, which feels too empty now, thinking about teaching Jack to get into first position and plié. Stumbling a little bit, the audience laughing, holding his hand as we dipped down and he came back up smoothly to a cheering crowd. He took an enormous bow, grinning, eyes bright, and I was socked with the need to cup the angle of his jaw and kiss the annoying, lush curve of his bottom lip when he smiled at me, amused and delighted by his own performance, warm calloused fingers squeezing mine tight.

Shake it off, because it was just heatstroke under the hot lights, I tell myself.

Jack is in the storage room next to ours, putting away the pillows, and Katherine and Nevaeh are at the loading dock, packing up everything that needs to be taken back to the dorm. They've been awhile, and there's not *that* much to pack. When I make my way down the corridor and push open the EXIT door, I think I manage to smother my gasp and let it close quickly and quietly.

Entwined, under the dim gold light. Nevaeh's hands tangling in Katherine's curls.

I spin and bang straight into Jack's chest, catch myself. "We can't go out there!" I whisper. "Go! Go!" I push him backward, my hands on his chest, down the hallway.

When he stops, I crash into him. He covers my hands with his. "What's going on?" he whispers.

I bounce on my toes, and I can't stop smiling. "Nevaeh and Katherine are totally making out!"

"Oh, no way!" he says, grinning. "This is the wildest night."

"It's so great, and I am so happy—and you're happy too!?" I say, completely surprised when it occurs to me.

"Of course I'm happy! I'm not a monster." He frowns.

"But you—don't you like Katherine?" I swore he was half

in love with Katherine, I did. Or at least—that he could never choose me, when we were standing side by side. But something in me shifts.

"Katherine?" he says. "Of course I like Katherine." And now he's looking at me like I am totally demented.

"I mean a crush!" I wave my hands around, trying to explain. Trying to make sure. "Like-her, like her! Want to kiss her!"

He's shaking his head. "Like-like her?" He smiles at that. "Want to kiss her? No. Not Katherine," he says. He's waiting for me. Hopeful. A little nervous?

I thought, of course he'd prefer someone smaller than me. Not fat. The perfect classical ballerina I could never be. An assumption as easy and automatic as breathing.

But the way he's looking at me now, eyes lovely, dark, and intense, and that smile and that hope.

And me. Tonight. Dazzling, gorgeous—delightful, delicious, all those things he introduced me as and more. I can't believe I ever thought he'd never be into me. I can believe that look in his eyes.

When I take a step closer to him, he seems to catch his breath. The whole world seems to catch its breath.

"So," I say softly. "Just to be clear. Not Katherine."

"No," he says. I watch his face carefully, the tiny smile that's crooking his lip. "Not her."

I hadn't wanted to have feelings for him. Too serious. Too tightly wound. Arrogant, I thought. Closed off.

Kind. Thoughtful. Earnest. Unexpectedly funny. Intense.

That arch of his eyebrow. That biteable curve of his lip.

A step, an inch away. His eyes are wide and bright, and he is breathing the tiniest bit fast.

My heart is hammering. I sway just the slightest bit closer, close enough to smell the warmth of his skin, the comforting clean smell of his shirt. Our eyes lock.

"So," I say, "I wonder who."

And then I get to feel that catch in his breath when I slide my hands up his chest, slip my fingers around the back of his neck and let them rest there gently. Him in shoes, me in socks, so he is a little bit taller than me. I rise up on my toes and bring my mouth close to his, knowing exactly what I want. Knowing exactly how desirable I am. What a feeling that is.

"Because I like you," I breathe, balancing there, my lips just barely brushing his. "Like that."

He swallows. He trembles the tiniest bit.

"I like you too," he says, his lips moving against mine. He closes his eyes. "So, so much."

"Good," I whisper. I kiss him.

And he kisses me back, lips and sighs and his hands roaming the length of my spine, pulling me tight against him, me pressing against him, climbing closer, into his arms, kissing for I don't know how long.

When we break, foreheads pressed together, he whispers, "This was unexpected." He's catching his breath, and I feel his smile.

I laugh softly and kiss him again. "Wasn't it?" My voice isn't entirely steady, and my heart isn't either. "We can't stay here," I say after a moment. I kiss him one more time, and he wraps his arms around my waist, nestling his nose against my neck.

"Really?" He sounds so wistful. I feel wistful too.

"Really," I say. I step back with a sigh, smile at him. I am lit up and so is his face. His hair is all over, and I want to kiss him again.

"Tomorrow?" he says. I nod, and his smile is huge.

I follow him down to the EXIT door and peer around it.

Katherine and Nevaeh are zipping up backpacks and not kissing at all, so I clear my throat and push the door open, Jack following behind me.

"I am just going to head out," he says cheerfully, kissing them each on the cheek and letting the heavy door close behind him quietly, and it's just the three of us, and I don't even know where to start, but I can't stop grinning.

"So!" I say. "Hi! Guess who I just saw totally making out?"

They glance at each other and back at me, stage makeup still sparkling bright in the dim light. Nevaeh bursts into laughter, and Katherine hides her face against Nevaeh's arm.

"We were totally making out," Nevaeh says, her cheeks berry dark, a slowly blooming smile.

I throw myself at them, hugging hard, and then they can't talk fast enough. About how Katherine couldn't stand anymore not telling Nevaeh how she felt. How she had never felt that way before about anyone, ever, didn't even recognize it. Or know what to do with it, for the longest time. But she was so overwhelmed by it tonight, by this incredible person on the stage with the brilliant, beautiful smile. She was so afraid she was ruining their friendship. And then Nevaeh kissed her, and they lost track of time.

They make fun of me for crying, but they're crying too.

"It was Nevaeh," I say to Katherine. Her crush, I mean.

"It was always Nevaeh," Katherine says to me with a sweet smile.

When I confess what happened with Jack, they laugh at me because I'm still a little dazed, and my heart is still kind of fluttering. But we can't talk about it more; we have to go, we know we do. It is getting so late and being here is dangerous, but it feels like we're in a glittering, twinkling bubble, so we take just one selfie, heads close together, our eyes shining, and then we slip back to the dorm through the dark with our hearts as bright and full as the moon behind the trees.

19

et up, get up, get up!" Nevaeh is singing. She's peering over my bunk, shaking me awake, and I groan, cling to Rachel the tiger, try to burrow into my pillow. She crawls up into bed and bounces. I squint up at her. Her face is above me, framed by a lightning-and-thundercloud of hair, smile as bright as my heart.

"How could you still be sleeping?" she demands.

I sit up, drag my fingers through my hair. "Did that really happen?"

"I told you we'd do it."

We did, didn't we? We threw an *amazing* performance, and we were gorgeous and people bought tickets and they cheered and laughed, and right, we were gorgeous, and it worked. And Nevaeh and Katherine! And—yes, I kissed Jack. I am pretty sure that isn't something I dreamed.

"We did it!" I grab her and hug her. "We did it. I never doubted that we'd do it."

She snorts at that. "And," she says, "guess who's going to Milan this summer?"

She hands me her phone. I blink at the number in our cash app. We are almost halfway to our goal. Halfway to Angles. Burst of joy in my heart, and I hug Nevaeh again.

"Taylor got the next batch of invites out while you slept the morning away, because that boy just won't listen and stay safe," Nevaeh says, brushing my hair behind my ear. She grins. "I guess the rumors are spreading."

"This is unbelievable," I say.

"I believe it!" she says, bouncing down off the bed.

With a flurry of blown kisses, she's off to her club. I'm still a little dazed as I grope for my phone. Congrats from Jack and an invite to lunch, and forty-nine million message notifications between Taylor and Nevaeh.

we missed you, I message him.

i'm your behind the scenes operative, he says. *(((((but my act would have killed))))*

I'm not convinced Angles is a go, not yet, but I am bubbling up with a little bit of hope. And what feels like absolute, undiluted pride in myself for killing it, in my friends, who never stopped working, in how beautifully we pulled this all off.

In the shower, midscrub, I have a sudden urge to tell Carly about it. About everything—that feeling of letting loose, how playing this ballerina character who breaks free makes me feel more real and raw, more honestly *me*, beautiful and radiant onstage. Completely seen, inside and out. How strange it is. Overwhelming. Scary. Good. Overwhelming. Good. I want to spill these jumbled thoughts out, share all those feelings with her, like I always have after performances, after my Angles auditions. I want her to be proud of me. Proud of the ways I've grown.

But . . . what do I really expect her to say? I stop, washcloth in hand and water pouring hot over my shoulders. What would she really think about us up onstage? Would she see that we were shining, beautiful, proud of our bodies and skin, funny and clever and expressing ourselves in ways we were never taught in class? Not caring about who's looking at us, only about how we see ourselves. Would she understand? It just feels like this wild epiphany, and I want so badly for her to understand. I think she would. I really do.

Before I can change my mind, I dress fast and find her in her office, prepping for the week. She looks up with a big smile, scolds me for going outside without drying my hair when she sees that it's all icy, then jumps up to push a cup of tea into my hands. She looks a little tired, her face pale. Her shoulders look narrow in the old beigy-pink cardigan she keeps on her chair, and she's in the black tunic, black leggings uniform she wears even on the weekend. I think I'd die of shock to see her in anything else.

"Is this a bad time?" I ask her, cupping the tea mug in my hands.

"Lots of coordination with donors. Lots of arguing with parents. The usual." She smiles at me. "But you look happy this morning."

"I'm happy," I say.

She settles next to me on the couch. "Well, then tell me about it."

Her face is open, expectant. She's waiting. Where do I start?

"Addie?" she says, tilting her head.

"Well," I say cheekily. "What do you think about burlesque?"

"Burlesque?" she repeats. She looks confused. "What do I think about it?" She waves an elegant hand, lost for words. "I don't know, I guess I just think it's creative stripping? Why are you asking me about burlesque?"

"It's an art form," I start to argue.

"Art? It's entertainment," she says. "Sexy entertainment."

"It's more than that!" I say, heatedly. "It's about finding total confidence in your body, and—" I stop, because she looks skeptical and a little confused.

"And?" she prompts.

I shake my head. "Sorry," I say. "It's just—something I was thinking about."

"Anyway, you've already got confidence on lockdown," she says, toasting me with her mug.

That startles me. Do I? Is that what it looks like to her? Because compared with the feeling I had last night, it feels like I've just been pretending. Being onstage felt like a miracle. I want to always feel like I did onstage last night, totally seen and totally accepted and beautiful. I want to always feel that beautiful all the time—beautiful in who I am, I mean. But I'm realizing Carly isn't going to hear me if I say that.

She gestures with the teapot, and I hold my cup out. "So, seriously, why did you bring up burlesque? That smile you walked in with was something."

Last night and velvet curtains and twinkle lights and applause and hugging Katherine and Nevaeh, and Katherine and Nevaeh kissing and . . .

"Oh, nothing really," I say. "We went to a show in Chicago. And it was great. But also . . . there's a boy." I'm disappointed in her reaction about burlesque, but my smile is real.

Her eyes light up. "Tell me everything," she says.

"Well," I say. "I spent a lot of time being annoyed by him, but it turns out"—and I am kind of amazed by this, now that I've realized it—"he might have been trying to impress me."

"Good on him," she says. "I'm surprised you didn't realize sooner."

How could I have?

She urges me to tell her more, and there's a lot to skirt around, but she seems delighted with everything I tell her and teases me about how pink my cheeks are.

"Bring him to meet me! In a very casual way," she's quick to add. "But stay focused, okay?"

I nod. "Of course. Obviously. I am laser focused."

"You just have so much going on." She's shaking her head.

I point to myself. "Laser focused."

"Now go! Shoo!" she says. "I have to dig out from under my email, and you have entirely too much to do to be sitting here with me."

I'm halfway out the door when she calls out.

"I almost forgot!" she says. "Angles funding!"

I turn, holding the doorframe. "Right! What about it?"

She looks worried. "I've meant to check on you. I should have checked sooner—we're coming up on the deadline, and—"

"Oh! Right! It's fine!"

"It is?" She doesn't look any less worried. But now she's added "skeptical" to the mix.

"Oh yeah," I say. "I should've said something. My friends are helping me."

"That's wonderful!" she says. "How generous of them!"

"You have no idea," I say.

"You're so lucky to have such great friends."

Sudden, totally unexpected feeling like I'm going to tear up. "I know it," I say, my voice breaking a little. "I really do."

———

When I leave her office, it's past noon, and the quad is busy with students making their way toward the caf or headed to the off-campus buses that take us to the next-biggest town (with at least two more restaurants than our local main street). I'm meeting Jack for lunch soon, even though I would kind of rather go hide in my bed now, still a little dejected by Carly's dismissal of burlesque. The others will tell me to forget about it, it doesn't matter what she thinks, and right now I wish that felt true.

I can't find Jack in the clumps of boys coming down the stairs and ramp outside their dorm, but I do see Gavin. I duck my head, slipping to the other side of the lamppost like it's actually going to hide me, which it doesn't. He makes his way over to me.

"Hey, Addie-Addie," he says, and then lowers his voice dramatically, leaning in like he's going to tell me a secret. My stomach flips. "I heard that you are *amazing*."

"Of course I'm amazing," I say immediately, lifting my chin, pretending that I'm not totally startled he's heard about it already, even on a campus this size. "How sad are you that you couldn't come?"

"Just waiting for my private show," he says.

"That is never going to happen," I say.

"Are you really sure?" he says.

"Addie!" someone calls, before I can tell Gavin exactly how sure I am. I lift my hand to wave at Jack. He beams at me, and there's the real flutter in my stomach. Happy to see him—he likes me! I like him! We actually talked about it! But those nerves are still there, too, the waiting-for-the-other-shoe-to-drop feeling. I've never understood that metaphor so well as right now—I don't like how the feeling, the fear, can stick so hard to you.

"Hi," I say, when he stops in front of us, and I can feel how big I'm smiling.

"Hi!" Gavin says.

"Gavin was just leaving," I explain to Jack.

"No, I was just arranging my private show," Gavin says.

"Have I said never in a million years yet?"

"I hope you change your mind," he says.

"I know," I tell him, surprised I actually believe it. "Ready?" I say to Jack, and take him by the elbow to drag him away.

When did that happen, the confidence that Gavin really wants me? There's a little bit of glee in it, a lot of smugness.

"So should I ask what that was about?" Jack asks after a moment, breaking into my thoughts.

I release his arm when I realize I am rudely power walking us down the path toward the caf and tuck my cold hands in my pockets. I've forgotten my mittens again.

I shake my head. "No," I say firmly. "He's not important."

"Okay," he says, and then smiles. "Hi."

I like his face. How could I have pretended not to like him?

He holds his gloved hand out, and I take it with my bare one.

"So you appear to be glowing today," he says. "Is there any particular reason why?"

I laugh. "I feel like I'm glowing," I say. "I feel like we did something extraordinary, and how are we ever going to top this?"

"I feel that you will all find a way," he says.

"You also have a career on the stage, Mr. Suave and Charismatic."

He appears low-key mortified by that, ducking his head. "I'm fairly surprised I pulled it off, to be honest."

"It never showed for a second," I say, squeezing his hand.

"Tell me about what's next. Milan."

"Milan," I say, and my heart skips. "But first, two more shows. Midterms. Rehearsal. Showcases. Graduate. And *then* go to Milan for the summer to work with the best dancers in the world and launch a brilliant career, whatever that looks like." I pause.

"My mom thinks that means I'll become the world's most famous dancer and buy her an island. No pressure. Her *other* plan is that we'll go on gluten-free diets, I'll lose eighty pounds, and then we're off to LA."

He slants a glance at me. "That's a lot," he says, pulling open the door to the caf. "And it's fairly absolutely ridiculous."

I shrug. "You can tell her that. She wants everything for me. She doesn't stop to think which part of everything I want. I'm starting to believe she never will." I want to change the subject. Not think about it all right now. "That got very serious!" I say.

"Parent talk is very serious!" he says. "Let's talk about something much better."

"Baby animals," I say.

"No, no, far too frivolous and not at all manly. English literature!"

"I have feelings about Shakespeare, and none of them are positive."

"No!" he says. "The bard weeps."

"The bard can die mad." I consider that. "Maybe he did."

We talk about what to talk about until we're just talking, all through getting food and finding empty seats and eating sandwiches that we barely notice, too focused on each other to care about something as trivial as lunch meats.

He walks me back to my dorm, where modern American literature waits for me. ("I love *The Bell Jar*," he says. "Of course you do," I say.)

"Can I talk about seeing you again soon?" he says, taking both my hands.

I don't want to stop talking to him. I do want to kiss him, and he blushes when I do.

"Oh yes," I say.

This—our hands together, the brief kiss he brushes over my lips, the smile, that little part of my heart that's cheerleading, somersaulting, doing splits, and throwing confetti instead of worrying. This is coming dangerously close to dreamy. It's a new thing on top of the pile of two more shows, and sneaking through the dark, of midterms, of our senior recitals, of the future racing toward us, however that's going to look. Of deciding what I want—me. Not my mother and not Carly. Angles. My bad Italian.

I want it all. I want to wrap my arms around it and jump up and down. I want to see what's next.

20

The following week is nonstop: study for midterms, rehearsal, go to class, inhale food, rehearse showcase, brush glitter out of everything, ignore Gavin's increasingly flirty messages, even when I can't make myself delete them. They make me smile, and they shouldn't. I should block him, and I don't know why I haven't yet. Why every time my finger hovers over the button, I stop.

Text all day with Jack, though (his contact name is still a poo emoji, but Taylor has added a heart), rehearse more, study more, fall into bed and sleep for way less time than I want to, wake up, repeat. Gavin is still teasing me about wanting a private show, proposing more and more ridiculous places for us to be alone, making me laugh. But Jack and I text about all the things that are real. He's still worried about his math midterm and hates that he's bad at it; he wants to be a photojournalist and wonders whether he's good enough. We talk about imposter syndrome and that feeling when you're onstage and killing it, and Angles. He tells me how he only started talking at four, and in complete sentences. I tell him about losing my first dance competition and more about my mom. When he hears a rumor I love puns, he is relentless.

Saturday night, our second show—this time it's all anticipation before the performance, no fear, scurrying around to set out the electric candles and Velcro up the swaths of fabric and the lanterns overhead, exchanging a quick kiss with Jack when we pass each other (to the eye-rolling hilarity of Katherine and Nevaeh, who are sneaking their own kisses behind curtains).

The show is pure happiness, the audience electric and buzzing, the three of us blowing up the stage. I revel in the gleeful shouting, the gasps, the applause as wild as my hair curling around my shoulders, my bare skin catching the spotlight, glittering and glowing winter white-person pale. My final pose, arms in the air, is so defiant I could stop an army. I get a roller-coaster-drop feeling in my belly listening to Jack banter with the crowd in his smooth, deep voice between our main acts. My cheeks ache from smiling when I flip the curtain aside to join him onstage for our plié lesson, and my hand tingles, so ridiculous, when I take his to steady him, a little skip-beat when he smiles at me.

The amount in our cash app gives me a thrill but also makes me feel almost guilty. So much money just for me. I'll find a way to pay it forward somehow. Cautious happiness now, though. In bed, too wired to sleep, I let myself download the language app again.

I drift off listening to a comforting, soft voice whisper *buon giorno*, *buon pomeriggio*, *buona sera* in my ears. *Conosci il sindaco?* Do you know the mayor? *Quell'anatra é in piedi sulla mia pizza.* That duck is standing on my pizza. *Buona notte.*

———

"You are smiling at your phone again," Katherine says on Sunday night, waving her stack of calculus flash cards at me. She's sitting on my bunk bed with Rachel in her lap, running Nevaeh through equations as Nevaeh works on my "looks like no makeup" makeup.

I'm still leaving Gavin on read and smiling as I text Jack back, even though I'm going to see him in about an hour. He wants to show me his favorite nerd movie, *Baraka*, which he says I will love and guarantees will change my life. I made him promise he'd watch *Center Stage* with me, which is terrible and has so many problems, but I love it, and I've watched it ten thousand times since I was a kid.

When my mother's Skype ID pops up, I groan.

"Don't pick up," Nevaeh says. "You'll regret it."

"It could ruin your date!" Katherine says.

I grimace at them. "I have to."

Nevaeh sighs and leans back, tapping her makeup brush against the open lid of her palette and poking it behind her ear. "Your funeral."

"And it's not a date," I insist as I answer.

"What's not a date?" my mother asks. She's wearing a sheet mask and looks like a terrifying lagoon zombie.

"Is it Sunday Night Beauty Hour?" I ask.

"Always," she says, and takes a sip of the drink at her elbow. "Beauty is hard work, Addie."

"And the harder you work, the more beautiful you are," I say in a singsong voice. Her ritual is comforting. I can imagine the smell of grapefruit coming from her mask.

"Exactly," she says, mask crinkling around her mouth. "Now, where are you going? I see you're wearing a little lip gloss, at least."

At least? Nevaeh mouths.

Mom squints at the screen. "Make sure you powder that nose. Shine is never your friend."

Nevaeh looks hilariously outraged at that. She has made me perfectly fresh and dewy, not shiny.

"Thanks," I tell my mom. "I just wanted to pick up and say hi—"

"Is it a date?" she interrupts.

"I didn't say it was a date," I tell her.

"Hm," she says. Her serious look is a little undermined by the mask hiding her expression, but there's a lot of disapproval in that short sound. "You certainly do not have time for dating, Adeleina. What about rehearsal?"

"I *am* rehearsing—" I say.

"And taking care of yourself. Look at your face. I think your cheeks have gotten a little—"

My stomach plummets because I know what she's going to say. Nevaeh snatches the phone from my hand before my mother can finish. "Hi, Mrs. Grant! I like the beauty mask!"

"Oh, hi!" my mother says, her voice lifting. "Nevvie! Look at how pretty you are!" Nevaeh's still made-up from her Insta tutorial this evening, in shades of gold and purple. "How are you girls? Is Katy there?"

Nevaeh lifts the phone, and Katherine waves from the bunk bed.

"We're just studying for a big test tomorrow," Nevaeh says truthfully. She, Taylor, and Katherine have a calculus exam. "So we'll just let you go. Enjoy your beauty night!"

"You two smart cookies have a good night!" she says. "Addie," she calls, "don't forget to—"

But Nevaeh has hit the END button and tosses the phone on the desk behind her.

"You were right; I regret it," I say cheerfully, pretending I don't feel a little shoulder-slumped.

"Regret what? We've just been here sassing you up for your date," Nevaeh says, pulling her brush from behind her ear. "Close your eyes for me."

I am glowing when she's done. Katherine fluffs my hair out, making it huge, pulling long curls over my shoulders, a mass of waves falling down my back. Nevaeh tugs the neckline of my cropped sweater down a bit to add a dusting of shimmer to my collarbones, and they declare me perfect over the rising buzz of butterfly wings in my stomach.

They walk me downstairs and wave me off like they're sending me on a cruise, instead of just over to Jack's room to watch a weird movie. It doesn't matter that this is the first time we're hanging out together alone, I insist, and they nod at me, knowing I'm full of crap.

They text me encouragement throughout my short walk in the sharp cold.

bone town! Taylor says.

TAYLOR, Katherine says.

I grin. Probably not boning. But I did like kissing him, a lot. My stomach does a little dip, nervous and excited and nervous around and round. It's not entirely unpleasant.

I am a little bit shifty as I wait by the front desk for Jack to come sign me in, pretending to examine the bulletin board and hoping I don't see Gavin or Christopher. Nodding back at the students passing by who nod and smile and give me a thumbs-up, students who weren't there but who must have heard about the club. And it's thrilling. I should be worried that so many people seem to know, but honestly—it's *cool*.

Rumors spreading, I tell the group, smiling as I type.

we're underground legends, Taylor says.

oh i like that, Katherine says. *i have never been a legend.*

The elevator dings, and I look up to see Jack's face light up when he notices me. After he signs me in, we do an awkward shuffle but finally manage a hug. "You smell very good," he says, stepping back, guiding me into the elevator.

"You do too!" I say. "Do you know what you smell like?"

"I have never considered it seriously," he says.

"Vanilla and laundry. Clean laundry," I rush to say when his eyebrows go up a little. "Laundry detergent. Good! You smell good."

Oh, I am so awkward, but he does not seem to mind.

"Good," he says. "I am glad you like it."

When we reach his room, he opens the door and lets me go in first. The overhead light is off, so the room is dim, the desk lamp throwing a circle of warm yellow light, and he leans down to press a kiss against my lips, the corner of my lips, and smile at me. Another kiss on my cheek, and then he is all business, taking my coat and explaining that his roommate is out with his girlfriend, so I can just use his chair, which is pulled up to the desk. He jumps into his own chair to peer at his laptop.

I don't move from the open door yet. I try really hard not to think *bone town!* He's wearing his glasses and an actual sweater-vest and dark denim jeans. And he is just cute. I like him, I think, as he talks enthusiastically about how the movie was shot in twenty-four countries on six continents, gesturing at the screen and squinting to read small text. I like to talk to him. I like to make him laugh. And I want to kiss him again.

I'm feeling myself with my hair down, my lips glossy. I like the curves of my body and the length of my legs. And I want him to notice. He's leaning forward and frowning at his laptop, telling me he thought he had the movie queued up but it'll just be a moment, he thinks, he's almost got it here. He looks up to smile at me, still standing at the door.

I smile back at him, a long slow smile.

He sputters to a stop, his fingers stilling over the keyboard. Eyes locked on mine.

"So. Okay if I close the door?" I say. Very slowly, very deliberately, I step back against it, swinging it shut gently.

He is still staring at me, his lips a little bit parted.

"I—what?" he says. "Oh."

I shrug out of my cardigan, let it slip slowly off my shoulders, puddle on the floor. This is better than Saturday night, when Jack looks at the sweater and then at me, leaning against the door, feeling lush in my clingy tunic and leggings. He seems arrested, a little dazed, and that sends a rush of fire through me. But then a crackle-pinch of doubt, like a shock of static electricity, blazingly unexpected. But maybe I don't—maybe he doesn't—I cut that thought off, swallow. Where did that come from? I reject it. I toss my hair, and he just blinks at me.

"Jack?"

He blinks again and shakes his head just the tiniest bit, a smile crooking the corner of his lip. Looking at me. He sees me.

"Hi," he says softly.

"Hi," I say, just as softly.

He's out of his chair so fast it's still spinning when he gathers me up against the door, his nose in the curl of hair behind my ear, the relief of it. He sighs my name, a humming, satisfied noise, when I slip my arms around his neck and press back against him close as I can and when I say, my voice breathless, "Kiss me, please," his mouth is on mine and it's even better this time, hot and sweet and full of urgency and roaming hands and breath coming hard, and I want more. Yes. I nudge him backward, and he shuffles us to the bed, kissing all the while, and we sink onto the bottom mattress.

I pull back after just a second and whisper, "This is your bed, right?"

"Sure," he says, his eyes kind of unfocused, and then glances down. "I mean, yes, right, my bed."

He's going to say something else, but I take his face in my hands and kiss him again.

We stretch out, kissing slowly, quickly, soft bites and pecks and long, slow soft presses of our lips, and it feels too good and still I want more. More skin, and more touching. I feel greedy, and I feel a little wild, and I feel like that doubt could never possibly come back.

Arching against him, I slide my hands under the hem of his shirt and feel him tremble. I skim my fingertips along his stomach and the muscles twitch, and I kiss the side of his neck. He cuts off a groan, takes my face to kiss me again and again until it feels like I'm being baked by the sun, warm summer and hot sand.

When I sit up, he reaches for me, then stops and leans back on his elbows to watch. To look at me as I lift the hem of my tunic and pull it off in one smooth move, shaking my hair out. The dark curls fall over my shoulders.

I'm wearing my prettiest bra, which is still some serious hardware, but lavender lace, "balconette-style," Katherine informed me, which translates to *check out my really amazing rack*. My pale skin looks kind of *luminous*, maybe, maybe that's the word, and

I feel sexy and gorgeous and delicious and all those good things you're supposed to think about your own body.

"Oh," Jack says, still leaning back against the pillows. His glasses have disappeared somewhere. His eyes skim over my curves and my skin—no stage makeup and no glitter, I'm suddenly aware. This is me totally exposed, in the dim yellow desk-lamp light.

He hasn't touched me yet. He stares, his breath is coming hard, and I'm trying to catch my breath too. And then, out of nowhere, he rolls over, falls out of bed, murmurs something— "Sorry," maybe, or "I have to go" and then scrambles out of the room, door thumping shut behind him, leaving me kneeling alone, half naked, on his bed.

For a moment, I am frozen.

He just ran away from me.

I took off my shirt, and he looked at me, my fat body, the real-ness of my body, and he ran away.

He actually ran out of his own room to get away from me.

The stairwell door bangs shut behind me, and then bangs again, other students pushing through, voices echoing up and down the stairs. I'm still wrestling with my sweater, yanking it down, finally just dragging my coat on and tugging it across my chest. I refuse to cry. This is ridiculous. I don't care what he thinks of my body, if he had second thoughts when he saw me up close, looking exactly like who I am, not wanting to touch me. When I swipe notifications up on my phone, trying to distract myself, I see Gavin's name on top.

i don't think i've ever really seen you dance, he's written, this boy who keeps flirting with me, and before I think about what

I'm doing, I'm typing *where are you* and hitting SEND, and before a half second has gone by, the reply pops up—he's in his room. He's got a test tomorrow. Do I want to come give him a study break, winky emojis.

I'm stopped on a landing in the stairwell, my back pressed against the cinder block wall, and I stare at the screen and that history of texts from him, the flirting that has made me smile despite myself. His slow-motion pursuit. Why I never told him to stop. Or thought about why I don't just delete the texts. Or really blocked him.

I can't deny that these texts, these ridiculous texts I should have deleted, were good for my ego. I remind myself he flirts with everyone. He likes everyone. He claims to like me. He says he wants me, right up front, no bullshit. And he's really hot.

be there in five, I type, before I can stop myself.

avin is leaning against his doorjamb when I arrive at his room. He smiles when he sees me and says in a low, teasing voice, "So have you finally come to give me my private show?" as I move past him, into his room, a double with a shared bathroom that I covet.

I shove down the immediate thought of Jack as the emcee, watching our show. Watching me dance. I don't want to think about Jack right now.

"Yes, I'm here to dance! There's just so much room," I say.

I gesture to the small space. It's so familiar. His cologne—his soap? Wherever it comes from, slightly woodsy but not overwhelming. Theater posters cover all four walls, classic musicals and Shakespeare dramas and Broadway hits. His bed is made, the comforter the same navies and grays he wears. The pile of pillows. *Why do you need so many pillows?* I asked him once, and he pulled me back into the nest of them so we were lying on our sides, face-to-face, sinking down. *This is why!* he said, and kissed me.

He slips my coat off my shoulders. "Okay, that was a ridiculous idea." He pushes the door closed, hangs my coat on the hook behind it. When he turns, he holds his arms out to me like we're going to waltz. "Though we could slow dance."

He's smiling at me, that sweet Gavin smile, the intense attention that always makes me feel like there's no one he'd rather be talking to.

He's surprised when I take his outstretched hand, move his other hand to my waist, but he smiles big and steps closer, sets us swaying.

When he slides his arm around my waist, I slip my hands over his broad shoulders and wrap my arms around his neck, letting him pull me closer, and I have to work to stop myself from comparing them, how their arms feel around me, how I feel in their arms.

"So why did you really come?" he asks, turning me slowly so I get a 360-degree tour of his room.

Why did I come here? To let him look at me like he wants to kiss me, run his hand down my back, and pull me closer instead of running away. I could let him.

I shrug. "To say hi?"

"Ah," he says, and pulls back to scan my outfit, my face. "Well, you look beautiful," he tells me.

"Yeah?" I say.

"Obviously," he says. "Ellory and I broke up last week," he adds.

"Oh, Gavin." I push at his chest, and he laughs at me.

"You'll be happy to hear she dumped me," he continues.

"Of course I'm not!" I say.

"Maybe a little," he says.

"A little," I admit, which makes him grin.

"So why did you just—decide to end things with me?" I ask. The question falls out of my mouth, out of nowhere.

He stops, so we're standing instead of dancing. He's as surprised by the question as I am that I asked it.

"I always thought it was because you were afraid of people making fun of you for dating a fat chick," I say, finally voicing my worst fear. Bringing it right out into the open.

His face changes. Shock, and then anger. "That's ridiculous," he says indignantly. "Why the hell would you think something ridiculous like that?"

"What was I supposed to think?" He doesn't understand; of course he doesn't. It's a fear that will always stalk you, just a little bit, when you're fat. The ugliness from other people who think fat people aren't worthy of love because they're fat. Their awfulness is not my problem. I know that, and I won't let it stop me. But sometimes it snipes at me, follows me. Tells me it's outrageous to think I'm beautiful. It's outrageous to not care what other people think. It still gets me when I'm not looking, and sometimes I don't even notice it's gotten me: How long did it take me to believe Jack actually liked me? (*No, god, I'm not thinking about him.*)

I'm sure Gavin has his own insecurities. But I don't know how to make someone understand, if they've never been told by strangers, by people who are supposed to be on their side, that they don't deserve what they have because of their size.

Gavin sighs and nudges us back into our slow dance. "I was afraid you liked me too much," he admits.

"That's even more ridiculous," I say.

"I was afraid I liked you too much too."

"Ridiculous," I say again.

"And Ellory was going to be in my French class."

"You ass."

He laughs at that.

"I didn't like you that much anyway," I say, lifting my chin, and his smile is smug.

"Well, I always thought you were gorgeous," he says. Part of my heart lifts at that. And when his palm finds the naked skin at the small of my back, I shiver.

Why did I come here? For this. Sometimes I feel so solid, and sometimes like a delicate shell, so easy to crack. Sometimes I let it get to me.

I don't need someone to tell me I'm beautiful, I decide, right as he leans forward to kiss me, slow and sweet.

It's nice. Nothing like kissing Jack—no urgency, no wanting to get closer, to touch him, pull him close, keep kissing him.

It feels good, being kissed. But I don't want to find validation in a boy. Or look for validation because I've been rejected and it hurts. It really hurts. But I can still find a better way to remember that I am hot, that I am a catch. Or I'll try, the way I always do. I stumble, and it hurts, but I always find my way back to who I really am. But I don't need to be caught to do it.

I let myself enjoy his kiss, just for another moment, and then pull back, put a finger on his lips.

And tell him, "I have to go."

———

It's still ridiculously early, and I head straight to Katherine and Nevaeh's room. Nevaeh is sitting up in her bunk, a textbook open across her knees, but as soon as she sees me, she tosses it aside.

"What is it, baby?" she says, holding out her arms. "Come here."

Relief floods me, after so much anxiety, and second-guessing myself, and hurt. It hurt, so much, when he left. The sadness is there, behind everything else.

I kick off my boots and drop my coat and clamber up, huddle in. She strokes my hair and I hold her hand, and it's hard to describe that feeling of solid safety. How it has become so much a part of me.

"So I'm feeling like there's a reason you're back so soon," she says.

"I almost made a terrible mistake," I tell her, starting with the easy part. She laughs at that.

"Oh no, Addie."

"Oh yes. You know how Gavin is always waltzing around saying the most ridiculous things to me about how beautiful I am?"

"He's not wrong, but he's still a jerk."

"Well," I say.

"But why was Gavin the Jerk on your date?"

I start to tell her everything. When we get to the part where I'm kneeling on Jack's bed, my shirt off, his wide eyes, that look on his face and the way he rolled off the mattress and out of the room, we start to giggle at the image until we are collapsed on the bed, shoulder to shoulder. It feels good to laugh at how absurd it was. It helps to tell Nevaeh how much it hurt. She doesn't try to excuse him or tell me he might have a good reason. She agrees that he's an ass. And she doesn't push it when I say no, I don't want to talk to him. Not yet.

And then there's Gavin. And that need for validation that's so hard to resist.

"Why is it so tied up like that, the sex and the self-doubt and our bodies?" Nevaeh says.

We agree that we're still waiting for the epiphany. That permanent transformation, where confidence isn't just a bulletproof shell. Where you've transformed into someone who has cut loose everyone else's opinion and can never be hurt again.

A place where the microaggressions that build up turn to ash instead of turning inside, Nevaeh tells me.

"It's like a million tiny cuts that never scar, because the cuts keep coming," she says. "They're reminders that I'm living in a world that doesn't love me, that is actively built to reject me, remind me that I'm not white and that is the ugliest thing about me. Next ugliest is being a Black woman who knows she's beautiful."

She trusts me enough to tell me this, and I know that's an honor.

We slide down under the covers, our heads tilted together, and I hold her hand, and there aren't any words left. It has been such a long night.

Katherine arrives after finishing a late rehearsal. Once she climbs up on the bunk, she hesitates, looking at me, and then doesn't ask how the date went. I'm okay with not thinking about it for a while. We make a blanket fort, which can be the place where we're safe for a little while. Tonight.

Nevaeh applies a different expensive, sponsored soothing sheet mask on each of us, and we take selfies and watch endless videos of soothingly peaceful, calm capybaras that have other animals standing calmly on their backs, and everyone involved is very happy about the whole situation. It is *capibara* in Italian. I know because they're my favorite animal, and I looked it up.

When it's clear that we're all exhausted and ready for bed, I make my way down the hall and let myself look at my phone, both hoping I've heard from Jack and hoping I haven't. My thumb hovers over the notification—a text from him.

I don't know how to have this conversation. I'm not ready to hear about why he ran away from me, or sure I want to know. But maybe it's not me; maybe it's his own thing. Maybe it's something we can talk about when I feel less like I'm sunburned when I remember how he froze, how he fled. All the validation in the world, and the recognition that I don't need it, can't blow that picture away. Not yet, anyway. I go to bed without opening the text. When I wake up, I'm still not sure I can read it or want to hear what he says. Somehow I go all day, through fine-tuning all the bends and twists and arcs of our showcase. Defying gravity over and over again. Lunch and classes, dinner and rehearsal and bedtime, avoiding his text until it feels ridiculous.

I want to apologize, he says in the first one. *Can we talk?* The second is another apology, an offer to meet up for coffee. In the third one, he tells me it's complicated. In the fourth, he says he has to explain in person. In the fifth, he apologizes again and says he'll wait until I'm ready to talk.

I'm not ready. But I'll see him in history tomorrow.

I chicken out and skip class.

"He's asking me if I know why you won't talk to him," Katherine says gently at dinner. Nevaeh has filled her in, with my blessing.

Why won't I talk to him? I'm afraid that I do care what he thinks. I don't want to hear what he thought when he looked at me. What a terrible feeling.

I come to class late on Thursday on purpose, but I let him stop me after. His socks have flowers on them. And he looks worried, sad, anxious. My heart squeezes. I like him. I am a monster for putting it off. But I can't let myself be vulnerable, or get hurt, or get my confidence shaken. Not right now. Too much going on and too much riding on it. But it's hard to stay angry at him when he looks like he wants to reach for me.

"After the last show," I tell him, stepping back. "Let's talk when everything is over."

He nods at that, looking sad. I feel like a coward.

It's the third and final show, though, and I tell myself I want to be able to focus on it. The excitement of performing again, the sadness that it's our last. A tiny part of me has maybe been looking forward to the show being over, because being onstage, performing in such a brand-new way, having to develop a brand-new kind of faith in myself has been so overwhelming, so hard to process. But it has also felt so shockingly good and been such a surprising rush. I don't want all those feelings to disappear when we take our final bow.

On Saturday morning, the last show just hours away, I wake up to a chill, snow building up on my windowsill. Thick flakes, falling fast, muffling everything. The other three are already at breakfast, so I wiggle into my heaviest turtleneck and wrap myself in scarves and remember to put on my mittens halfway to the cafeteria, snow dimming the sun and biting my nose and spilling into the ankles of my boots as I clomp along a path that hasn't been shoveled yet.

I'm wet and freezing when I blow into the caf, which is quiet and almost empty. I am not surprised. Tree branches are whipping in the wind out there, tiny bits of ice and snow blowing in my face, my eyes, as I pushed my way across the quad. Taylor, Nevaeh, and Katherine are gathered at the big picture window, watching the grounds crew try to dig the sidewalks out faster than the snow falls.

Taylor pulls up the weather app.

"Well, we're about to be buried alive," he says. "Sounds like a party."

"Forty-mile-an-hour winds tonight," Katherine reads from her phone. "Whiteouts. That is not a real number of inches of snow that can fall in three hours!" She shows the phone to Nevaeh.

"That's a blizzard," Nevaeh says.

We all turn to look out through the window again. Bundled-up people trudge down the salted paths that keep getting snowed over, and there's a snowball fight over on the quad, other students plowing furrows through the knee-high snow as they chase one another down.

Oh no.

"We can't do it tonight," I blurt, startling Katherine and Taylor out of their argument about what *windchill* actually means. I gesture to the scene outside, remembering to lower my voice. "We can't have people digging trails." Their footprints would make an arrow that points right to the back door of the performing-arts building and the suspicion that something shady is going on. Amping up the likelihood of being caught.

"Aw, shit," Nevaeh says, grimacing at that. She sighs and turns to snap a photo of the snow through the window, blustering under the glow of the lampposts outside. "We'll postpone. I'll post in the group."

"I'll text Jack, okay?" Katherine says. I nod.

It pushes off our conversation for one more week. The idea makes me antsy, I'm surprised to realize. But I don't like feeling like a jerk, like a chicken. My excuses seem thinner and thinner.

Later, at dinner, looking out that same picture window, we know we made the right decision. It's still snowing. Absolutely no way our midnight trails wouldn't be noticed. After eating, we drift over into the rec room, manage to claim the couches by the window. Katherine settles down on one end, pulls me down next to her to curl up on my side with my head in her lap. Her hand is cool on my forehead. Taylor lifts up my feet and snugs in next to us, his hand around my ankle. Nevaeh is leaning against Katherine's legs, her cheek on her knee and her arm wrapped around her calf.

Soft, terrible music is playing over the speakers in the corner, and there are a bunch of dudes yelling at the foosball table and a girl kicking the antique *Ms. Pac-Man* machine. Voices are echoing in the lobby, and there are so many stomping boots and shouts and bangs from the lobby doors. But I feel like we're in a bubble here, looking out at the storm. We're quiet, watching the snow fall hard, the wind letting up for a bit so that big fat flakes are now taking up the whole world.

"God, I hope no one missed the post and thinks it's a good idea to go out tonight," Nevaeh says quietly, leaning against Katherine's knees. She's chewing the inside of her lip, staring out the window.

"What if someone does?" I say, twisting my fingers in the hem of my sweater.

"I'll get up early and stomp out footprints," Taylor says. "And then I'll figure out who had the bright idea to go out in a storm and kick their ass."

"I am not sure that would be less suspicious," Katherine says.

There's no reason to think footsteps from curfew breakers would point to us. There's no reason, necessarily, to think if someone was caught they'd give us away.

"We just have to wait," Nevaeh says.

No reason to think that, but not easy to stop.

Anxiety shakes me awake early on Sunday to find a photo from Jack to our group. He took it from the top floor of the arts building, and it shows that the snow is unbroken all the way around the sides of the theater, and along the side of the art building too. Just a gleaming expanse of bright white.

Oh, thank god.

We are a little giddy for the rest of the day. There's always been an element of getting away with something about this whole whackadoo plan, from being able to pull off burlesque acts in just a few weeks to getting people to show up to never getting caught.

It feels like we're almost in the homestretch, that we might even make it, that our luck might hold out, until the dick pics arrive in all three of our DMs on Monday night. No hand in the frame to give away who it is, and none of us want to look closely enough to see if we recognize it.

The caption is *sorry not sorry*.

"I'm really sorry I had to look at that picture," Nevaeh says at dinner, pushing her phone away to pick up her fork. "Why don't they ever give up?"

"I don't like the 'sorry not sorry' thing," Taylor says.

"I'm trying to not panic," I say.

"Maybe it's just 'sorry not sorry I sent all of you a photo of my penis'?" Katherine suggests.

Nevaeh shakes her head. "Maybe." She sounds doubtful.

I think all of us are worried about the same thing. No tracks in the snow, no evidence. No reason to believe it's a real threat. But no way to respond.

We try to shrug it off. But the idea that it could be Christopher—Mr. "I like to send dick pics"—the idea that he might know about the burlesque show, sticks with me the rest of the evening and through the day on Tuesday, making me a little bit of a wreck. I don't want to share my panic with the rest of them. I don't want them to worry.

I'm off my game when we rehearse our performances on Tuesday night; in technique on Wednesday morning, I fumble a triple turn, teeter to a messy halt, only barely missing the dancers to either side of me. My heart is pounding and the shock keeps me frozen—how could I have lost my focus like that?—and the look on Madame George's face is thunderous.

"Adeleina," she says in a rock-hard voice, and I brace myself for the lecture but look up with everyone else when the studio door opens and another student appears, hands an envelope to Madame George, and waits, staring at all of us like she's never seen a roomful of dancers.

"Adeleina," Madame George says again, looking up from the yellow sheet of paper. Her voice isn't any less terrible. "Gather up your things and go to the dean's office."

I stare at her, my brain trying to catch up to the pounding of my heart. The rest of me already knows—my body is in fight-or-flight already. We've been caught.

Angles.

My thoughts are slow. Disconnected. Far away. We were so close. It was just one more show. How can time be up already, inches from the finish line?

The class is murmuring, and I feel them staring, and the gossip machine is ticking into gear, gearing up to be a roar, if anyone connects this summons to the whispers about the burlesque club.

"Addie," Madame George says. "Right now."

"Yes, sorry," I stammer, shaking my head, pushing myself to move, to clear out the ringing in my head. I'm clumsy as I pull on my warm-ups. My hands are shaking. We knew it could happen. We knew we could be caught, but it didn't truly seem possible. Katherine and Nevaeh, a few doors down—have they gotten theirs? I can still hope that it'll just be me, my idea, my punishment.

Maybe this is nothing. Maybe it won't be so bad. Maybe my heart will stop clawing at my breastbone and give me space to take a full breath.

Worth it, it was worth it, I remind myself. Whatever happens, it was worth it.

22

When I push through the door of the locker room to get my stuff, Nevaeh and Katherine are there, packing up their things. Nevaeh looks perfectly calm, and if you didn't know her, you'd think she was bored. Katherine looks furious, her lips tucked in and bright spots of color on her cheeks.

"I'm so sorry," I say.

Katherine flings her arms around me. "I am not sorry at all," she says fiercely. "And I am going to tell them that."

"It'll be okay," Nevaeh says. "They could've waited just one more week, but it'll be okay."

She squeezes my hand.

"I texted Taylor. He's pissed," Katherine says as we stuff our feet into our boots. We don't bother changing, because we don't know what's going to happen yet. Maybe we'll come back here for the rest of our morning classes. "He says to plead the Fifth."

"I don't think we can do that," I say, pausing midlacing. "Can we?"

"I would like to know who turned us in," Katherine says.

Then adds, "Although, I think I do know," and I look at her, surprised. I had hoped I'd be the only one to think the dick pic was a threat.

"'Sorry not sorry,'" I say.

"There is still time to superglue his—"

"Katherine!" I say.

"We will just keep that in mind as plan B, then," she says darkly.

"It's possible the school, whoever, doesn't know anything," Nevaeh murmurs. "That it's hearsay."

"We were never stopped with a box full of feather boas," I say.

"What if they found our stash of costumes?" Katherine says. "Our props. Our decorations."

"They don't have our names on them," Nevaeh says.

I sit on the bench, stare at my scuffed-up, salt-stained boots. I can't make myself stand up yet.

Nevaeh slams her locker shut. "Are we ready?"

"No," I say. "Am I being too obvious if I say this sucks?"

"A little obvious," Katherine admits.

"At least I'm staying on brand."

We burst into the cold, bright day, which seems way too cheerful for our grim mood. There's no sense rushing across campus to get yelled at, so we dawdle, try to enjoy the thin sunshine, and hesitate at the bottom of the admin building's stone steps.

"Still time to flee," I tell them.

"Let's just get detention over with," Nevaeh says, poking me ahead of her, up to the heavy double doors of the admin building. We shuffle in single file, our boots squeaking on the marble floors of the foyer. My heart is humming, and the guilt, that these two are here with me, is a drumbeat under everything.

We crack open the door to the dean's office. The waiting area has hulking furniture and heavy curtains and thick carpet we leave salt stains on. From the high corners of the room, plaster cherubs are frowning down at us. There's that dark, electric feeling before the worst storms, when you stand on the beach and watch the black waves whip up into a froth, crash at your feet, lashing rain and thunder not far behind.

We are alone in here, no one at the administrative assistant's desk. Katherine and Nevaeh slide into the hard-backed wooden visitors' chairs, hand in hand. They both look a little dazed. I can't sit, can't stop moving, pacing up and down the length of heavy patterned carpet, clunky boot steps muffled, hair raised at the back of my neck.

"Jack," I say. He should be here with us. "Have you heard from Jack?" I ask Katherine. She shakes her head.

"I texted him," she says.

"Maybe he's already inside," Nevaeh says, nodding at the closed door that I assume leads to the dean's actual office.

I'm glad Taylor's not here, not caught, not in trouble for helping us. But I also wish he were here to say something ridiculous and distracting. Something unexpectedly rallying.

I sit, fighting the urge to hunch down. Trying to think straight. Right, we should have talked before we came inside. Some kind of plan, maybe. I don't know how much time we have now.

"If they don't know, really—if they don't have any evidence, we have to bluff."

Nevaeh takes a breath. "Burlesque club? What burlesque club?"

"If they know, if they really know—it was all my idea. You don't know why you're here. Pretend you don't know what they're talking about."

Katherine snorts at that. "I am proud of what we did. Why would I pretend I'm not?"

"You have my sword," Nevaeh says. She nudges Katherine. "Now say, 'and my bow.'"

"Oh, my favorite nerd." I put my head on her shoulder. "Will you still love me when we are sentenced to a dungeon of potatoes to peel?" I whisper.

Her laugh jostles me.

"Only if you peel my half," she whispers back.

The door to the dean's office opens after a century and a half, and Ms. Flores, the office admin, smiles at us like we're here for a nice visit and ushers us inside. The office is as airless as the waiting area, with a big wooden desk and dark bookcases lining the walls.

The dean is a small man, older, with narrow shoulders. His fine gray hair is always parted deeply to the side. He's got thick gray-and-black eyebrows, and usually has a pleasant face, but right now he looks like he's been chewing on gravel. He gestures at the three heavy chairs in front of his desk that are waiting for us. Ms. Flores sits by the window with a clipboard on her knees, and the dean settles on the corner of his desk with his hands clasped in front of him.

Katherine reaches over for my hand, and I smile gratefully at her.

"Hello, girls," the dean says. His voice has the slightest smooth southern ring to it, and it's very gentle. He looks at each of us in turn. "I'm very sorry to see you here." He's smiling a little, and something about it turns the background hum of fear into a buzz in my ears.

I don't know if we're supposed to respond to that. I shift in my chair, glance over at Ms. Flores, who smiles at me kindly.

"Do you three know why I needed to call you in?"

"Dean Pembrooke, whatever it is, I'm sure it's just me you should be talking to," I say steadily, my voice serious.

"Is that right, Ms. Grant?" He lifts a salt-and-pepper eyebrow. "Because I am certainly looking forward to understanding this situation."

I suck in a breath, a flicker of dread in my chest. "Dean, I can explain whatever it is you think—"

"Seniors are capricious," he says to us, voice still gentle in a way that makes me want to duck. "They let off steam. They do teenager things. Maybe a little sneaking out past curfew." He pauses, gazing out the window for a moment. "I remember doing that when I was your age."

A thousand years ago, I imagine Taylor saying, and I struggle to keep my face motionless, push down the wild urge to laugh. Katherine squeezes my hand, and I shake my head the tiniest bit, looking at the neat creases on the dean's navy slacks instead of at her.

"Could I understand that?" the dean says.

No, I think, still swallowing the panic-laughing.

"Perhaps," he goes on, and then sighs. "What I don't understand is three girls sneaking out after hours to turn private school property into a *strip club*." His voice hasn't changed—steady, musical. Kind. But he throws the last two words down with a thud.

I am on my feet before I know what I'm doing, my head roaring.

"No!" I shout, then lower my voice, willing it not to tremble. "No, that's not—"

"Ms. Grant!" he snaps. "Sit down!"

"Dean Pembrooke," I say, swallowing. "I don't know what you think—"

"I think, if I'm not mistaken, that the three of you were taking off your clothes in front of an audience and charging money?"

I open my mouth but nothing comes out, and in my head Taylor's voice says *well, technically*, and then Nevaeh and Katherine are standing, Katherine's shoulder against mine and her voice steely.

"Who claimed we were doing a strip show?" she demands.

Now the dean is up on his feet, jabbing a finger at us, his mouth tight.

"Sit down. Right now. All three of you."

We look at one another, stand there for a moment longer, until he snaps, "Now." And then we sink back onto our chairs. He stalks around to the other side of the desk and snatches up a sheet of paper to gesture with.

"It has come to my attention that you three girls violated curfew, broke your dorm bylaws, broke into and entered school property, in order to illegally charge fellow students for a sex show—"

"That is a lie," Nevaeh says, leaning forward.

"Watch your tone," the dean snaps at her.

"Where did you get this information?" I say desperately, but he ignores me.

"I have never, in all my years here, encountered such an egregious violation of school rules and school conduct, standards, and principles."

"No," I say, razor-throated.

"I am shocked. And I am sorry to hear that any of my students would do such a thing. Violate the code of ethics in such a reckless manner," he says. "And not just violate it. *Flaunt* your violation."

"Who claims we were—we were running a sex show?" Katherine says, swallowing.

He looks at her for a long moment. "You're going to claim otherwise, I see," he says.

"It was not a sex show—" I say, my voice raised, before I can stop myself. Stupid, stupid, stupid.

He smiles at me.

"Well, then. In my judgment, the accusation brought to me against you is credible, Ms. Grant. All of you."

I swallow.

"Just me—" I say, but he doesn't let me finish.

"You are all being formally charged with immoral conduct—"

The rest of his sentence was blotted out by the thunder in my ears. I feel Katherine jerk, and Nevaeh is raising her voice, but all I can think is *immoral conduct.*

His voice breaks in. "The three of you girls will be appearing before the honor board on Monday," he says.

I can't let this happen. If I do, they'll lose everything. *Everything.*

Immoral conduct is a serious violation. That's not detention on Saturdays.

I ball my hands into fists, willing him to listen to me.

"Dean Pembrooke!" Raising my voice to drown his out. His eyebrows climb all the way up into his hairline, and his lips disappear. "They didn't do anything," I say desperately. "Whoever said so was wrong. It was just me. All of it."

He narrows his eyes at me. "I believe I was clear."

"But I'm the one who—"

"You will have to tell it to the honor board," he says.

"But you can't do this," I say.

He smiles at that one.

"I'm sorry to say I can, Ms. Grant," he says, shaking his head at me. "I truly am. I don't want to do this. I want to believe in all my students. I want to think you have good judgment. That you're trustworthy. That you will make me proud—honor Lakeshore Academy."

None of us reply to that. Katherine's hand is still tight around mine.

"Well, then," the dean says. "I don't think I have to tell you that there will be serious consequences for your future because of your poor judgment."

"What's going to happen to us?" I ask. I can't even look at Katherine and Nevaeh. They did this for me. I know it's bad, but I don't know how bad.

"You should have worried about that, and your college acceptances, a little sooner. For now, you're all on campus restriction until next Monday," he says, taking a seat and pulling a notebook in front of him. "After that, it will be up to the honor board. Maybe if you had read your student handbook, you'd understand the consequences of your actions a little more clearly."

I flush, and Katherine tugs my hand before I can blurt out something rude. The dean looks up, nods at us. "Ms. Flores, if you could escort them out."

———

"Real power move, having us escorted from the room," Nevaeh says, dragging her scarf around her neck, our boots squeaking again on the marble hallway.

"Your college acceptances," I say to them. My chest feels hollow. "It can't be true. I'm so sorry."

Nevaeh whacks me in the arm.

"We know," she says. "First, we're not going to panic until

we look at the handbook. Second, you don't get to take all the blame." She sighs. "I'm pissed, but I'm not pissed at you."

I nod, but the loop in my head is clanging. *My fault. Their futures. My fault. Their* college acceptances, *and it's all my fault.* Angles is gone, and it's all my own fault. If I hadn't pissed off Christopher. Maybe I should have been nice to him. Maybe I could have pretended. The thought makes me sick. Everything about this is making me feel sick. I can't stand this.

We push outside into the glaringly white quad. Katherine takes my mittens out of my pocket and hands them to me as we crunch back down the sidewalk to our dorm. My hands are shaking, but I manage to shove my mittens on.

"I only know of one kid who got an immoral-conduct charge," Katherine says, startling me out of my doom spiral. "The cameras in the girls' room in the north gymnasium. That sophomore boy."

"That's actual immoral conduct," Nevaeh says. "They're charging us as if we'd done something that repulsive and beyond the pale."

"Do you remember those seniors last year, with the bonfire by the lake—they were down there drinking and half of them ended up in the water naked," Katherine says. "I'm pretty sure they just got demerits."

We were supposed to be bored out of our minds in detention for the rest of the year, not terrified about being expelled, and about everything else we're likely to lose. I shouldn't be berating myself for not being nice to a dude who didn't deserve a second of my time. I shouldn't feel so hopeless right now.

"Jack wasn't in there," I say, remembering.

"I'll text him," Katherine says, glancing at me. "Find out whether he's been there yet."

"Maybe he'll enjoy being called immoral," Nevaeh says. "He's such a nice boy."

I snort at that, and she laughs.

We should talk, me and Jack. God, we should talk about all of this, from what happened in his room to what happened in the dean's office, but the idea feels like too much right now. Everything feels like too much. From here, the rumors and the gossip about us that have already been trickling out are going to flood campus, and we'll have to wade through it all like everything is normal. I'm not ready to think about that yet, but I don't think that's going to matter.

"Christopher must have found out," Katherine is saying as we swing left to go around the dance building. "It's the only thing that makes sense."

Another knee-jerk twitch in my head—*if only I hadn't brushed him off and made him angry.*

Nevaeh waves her phone at us, blowing a soft drift of hair from her forehead.

"Or it could be one of these people," she says. She shows us the notifications coming through, texts and messages from friends and some from names I barely recognize, everyone wanting to know what's going on, because they heard something might be going on. Everyone wanting the whole story. "Everyone in this school likes to talk. Someone who heard about the show and didn't mind their own business? I don't know! How are we supposed to know?"

"Christopher," I say.

"Maybe! Who knows! It's bullshit, no matter who gave us away." She stuffs her phone back in her pocket with an impatient sound and grabs Katherine's hand. "Can I tell you how much I don't want to look at my Instagram comments?"

"Or go to class right now," Katherine says.

"No, it's lunch now," Nevaeh says, pointing at the clock tower on the library building. "I am going to eat a cheeseburger. No, today it will be two cheeseburgers. Cheese fries. And we are going to finish studying for our chem tests."

They walk me back to the dorm—I want to change out of my leo and warm-ups into a giant, bulky, armor-like sweater. And I won't just crawl into my bed and put a pillow on my head and try to not die of guilt, which I didn't realize was possible, or hadn't thought about it before, but there you go.

"It will be okay," Katherine tells me with a squeeze, though I'm the one who's supposed to be telling them that. Nevaeh tucks my hair back into my hood and presses her cheek against mine.

When I bring myself to look at my phone screen, there's a text from Jack—*can we talk?* he asks. I hesitate, before I respond.

yes, I type back. The relief is unexpected.

would you believe i've never gotten a single demerit before?

of course not

and now i have enough to keep me going through the end of the year

But—just demerits? That's all he's gotten? No. We'll talk about it tomorrow. He'll explain.

Now it's the next message—from Carly already. She wants to see me. She already knows. I don't want to see her face. Sexy entertainment, she said, dismissing it. Creative stripping. She won't have changed her mind. Can I pretend I didn't see her text?

Sitting on the floor of my room with my coat still on, my bottom dresser drawer pulled out, listening to the sounds of the dorm—someone laughing, someone yelling that they can't find their boots, someone flipping fast through their music playlist, doors closing—I can't find anything I want to wear, nothing clean, anyway. I haven't had time to do laundry in a month, have I? We've been racing from thing to thing to thing, trying to keep up with class and rehearsal and still pull off this whole production behind the scenes and sometimes crawl into bed for a few hours. We did it together, the four of us.

"We should all move to New York and open a burlesque club together," Katherine said one evening, leaning back on her elbows on the floor of the rehearsal room with her feet out straight in front of her and her Hula-Hoop around her hips.

"Are burlesque clubs particularly lucrative?" Taylor said. "Will we be rich and famous?"

"We would be paid in friendship," Nevaeh said, deftly applying a coat of red to her lips in front of the mirror and stepping back to assess it critically. "And we would all live in a one-room apartment and steal bread crusts from the birds, but it would be okay because of the magic of dance."

"I can move to New York after Milan," I said. "We can do it as a hobby. We can teach burlesque. We can make the world a better place!"

"We already make the world a better place," Taylor said. "Because we are so ridiculously good-looking."

I get up now and kick my door closed, dig into the back of my closet for the garment bag with my costume, and hang it on the back of the door and unzip it, and it's like turning on the light when the white tulle spills out, the pastel sequins, the rhinestones.

I stare at it, remembering how amazing I felt in it. How beautiful and powerful I felt throwing it off. Inviting the audience to admire my naked skin—my thick thighs, the curve of my belly, the width of my hips and the jiggle of my butt. None of it perfect, but it doesn't have to be. Learning, as we planned and schemed and rehearsed and then danced, that my body, and whatever you want to call a flaw, is nothing I am ashamed of or want to hide.

And there we were, sitting there in front of the dean, listening to him tell us, out of nowhere, that we have been caught. That our behavior was lewd. That our naked skin is immoral. Not knowing how to tell him how wrong he is.

My satin gloves have fallen onto the carpet, still inside out from the last performance. I scoop them up to turn them right side out, but—no. My stomach clenches because of course it doesn't matter if I fix them. I ball the gloves up in my fist and throw them across the room. I yank the hanger off the back of the door because I want to throw that, too, ball up the whole thing and stuff it in the garbage compactor downstairs, but then that thought is terrible also. Never wearing it again. No one ever seeing me wear it again. How could the dean ever understand what it meant, to wear it?

Showing our skin is immoral. The thought a steady thump.

Detention for bare shoulders. Detention if our skirts are too short. Sent away to change, because hiding all that skin is more important than our education. Because our arms distract boys. Maybe they should be taught that we're literally not sexual objects who spend our lives trying to give them boners. Maybe they should get told to focus and leave us alone. Maybe all this is bullshit, and I'm tired of it. *My skin is not immoral.*

———

Carly's not in her office, but the door is open. I hesitate for a second, and then set my bag on the couch, sit next to it. Pull the pillow into my lap like I've done a thousand times. She doesn't seem surprised when she finds me waiting for her. She makes me tea, sits across from me with a glance at the garment bag.

A cup of tea doesn't mean she understands, though. She was supposed to understand.

"What were you thinking, Addie?" she says. "You risked your entire future for this!" Her voice is tired. Frustrated. Angry.

"I was trying to save my future!"

"This wasn't the way to do it," she snaps.

"The immoral-conduct charge is crap."

"The dean doesn't think so." She throws her glasses on her desk and leans back against it, rubbing her eyes.

"He's wrong," I say. "Look at this!" I stand and unzip the bag, lift out my glittering tutu skirt, the breakaway bustier, and lay them over the couch.

"What is this?" she says.

"My sex-show costume." I feel like I can't catch my breath.

She crosses her arms, frowns at the garments on the couch.

"Burlesque," I say. "I tried to tell you about burlesque. It's beautiful." I wave my hand at my costume. "I danced in this." I pull out the tap pants and the sparkling strapless bra, throw them down on top. "I took them off. And this is what I was wearing underneath."

"Addie," Carly says.

"I have never felt better onstage. Or more in control. Or more beautiful, or powerful," I say. "I loved feeling sexy on my own terms."

"Addie—"

"A sex show. They're calling it a sex show. I don't understand why they're trying to make this ugly!"

I crumple down next to the pile of tulle, completely overwhelmed, rock forward and clasp my arms around my stomach.

I begin to sob, my shoulders shaking, and Carly is quickly beside me, handing me a tissue. She puts both arms around me and lets me cry until I am hiccuping, hands me another tissue to blow my nose. When I am just dripping, trying to catch my breath, she stands up to plug the kettle in, rips open a new box of tea from her bottom drawer, watches the sidewalk below her window while the water bubbles.

I suck in a deep breath, and she turns.

"I don't know what to do," I say. I don't think I've ever felt this lost. I silently plead for Carly to have an answer, any answer for me. She's always known what to do.

She's quiet for a moment, pours water in a mug for herself and adds more water and a fresh bag to mine. She replaces the kettle and sits next to me.

After a moment she says, "I don't know what you should do either."

I laugh. "I hate that answer," I say.

She laughs. "I do too." She shakes her head. "Drink your tea." She sighs and puts her hand on mine. "I'm on your side," she says softly.

I didn't know how very badly I needed to hear that. I want to cry again, but I pull in a shaky breath.

"My mother thought the tuition for Angles was a scam and I should just walk away," I say. "Did I tell you that? She said you were trying to scam me and that I shouldn't let you get away with it."

She chokes at that, and I grin at her a little.

"We did this—our burlesque club—so I could go. Because the idea of losing this opportunity was the worst thing I could think of. Because my friends didn't want me to lose my chance." I shake my head. "It didn't feel like I had any choice, Carly." I stop. "But can I tell you how much we loved the idea?"

She laughs again. "A burlesque show."

"An underground burlesque club."

"The sheer nerve," she says, shaking her head. Smiling at me. "Unbelievable. You have always been so go big or go home."

"It was that or sell a kidney," I say.

"Why didn't you wait for me, Addie?" Frowning now. "I was working on it."

I shrug, looking into the bottom of my cup. Look back at her. Her face is scrunched up with worry and sad, her bun in disarray.

"I couldn't," I say. I breathe in deep. "And I'm glad I didn't. I loved it. I wish I could make you understand what it was like. And how good we felt." I am sick and scared about what's going to happen to us—but I wouldn't change anything. I would still have done it. I still would've loved every moment of it.

Carly's quiet for a moment. "I know, Addie," she says. "That doesn't mean you didn't break the rules. You know you deserve demerits."

"I know," I say. "We were ready for them!"

"Demerits," she says. "Suspension. Then detention for the rest of the year. An official warning on your—"

"Okay!" I say. "I know! All those things."

"All those things," she agrees. "But, from what you've told me, the immoral-conduct charge sounds like bullshit."

I love her so much in that moment. I squeeze her hand.

"I don't know what to do about it," I tell her.

"You can speak at the hearing," she says. "You have to speak at the hearing. It's possible you might be able to get them to back away from the more serious charge."

I sit up at that, heart somewhere around my throat and beating all wrong.

"Maybe," she says, seeing the look on my face. "I don't want to get you excited about something that might not happen."

"But maybe," I say.

"Maybe," she agrees. "You'd have to be thoughtful when you speak about it. Clear. Convincing."

"We can do that," I say. "I can do that." I can do that. I have to do it, anyway. Pretend that I'm someone who speaks up in class, who can give moving speeches, who can ask a room full of people to really listen to her and be powerful and convincing when they do.

I could do that. I could make sure my friends are safe.

"And Addie," she says. She hesitates and I brace myself. "I haven't gotten the official word yet. But I know they're going to tell me to pull you out of the mentor program."

Pull me out of the mentor program? Oh god, Zoe. My freshmen girls. I've been so proud to work with them, and so proud of them. And now, unexpectedly, a blow to the heart, I've lost them.

"I'm sorry," she says.

I bite my bottom lip to stop it from trembling again. "Well, that makes sense, right?"

"God, Addie. I can't stand this. I admire your bravery, I do. But, god, it was reckless," she says, sighing.

I start stuffing my things back into the garment bag and shrug. "Go big or go home," I say. "Right? Shape the world to fit me." I zip it up.

Carly smiles at that. "Well, I guess I know you were listening."

"To every word," I say.

And with that, I stand and head out the door, determined to make the world hear me.

Taylor, who spends the dinner hour circling the table, hugging each of us in turn until we beg him to stop, tells us that Carly's right—they should have told us we get time to talk at the hearing and "present our own side of the situation." He's been doing the research. He's been reading the handbook.

"Our side is, 'you are wrong and this is misogynistic garbage,'" Katherine says, scowling.

"I'll present our case," I say. "If you'll let me. I want to do it. I know I can do it."

"Are you sure?" Katherine says. "This is going to be way worse than speaking in class."

I am 100 percent not sure, absolutely terrified, maybe going to die. But this was my idea from the start, so I have to be the one to end it.

"Yes," I say. "I'm sure I'm sure."

There are so many things to say, and I'm going to stand up and make sure everyone hears every single word of it, because all of it is important. Everything we've said to one another. Everything we've yelled about and everything we've thought and felt, all of it bubbling up in me. Ready to be set loose.

My mother calls after dinner, keeps ringing until I pick up. She wants me to know that I should have stayed in Miami if I wanted to be a stripper.

"You demanded that I send you to this school for what, Adeleina?"

Her words scoop my heart out. I'm hunched at my desk, my arms wrapped tight around my stomach.

It's dark behind her. With her makeup off, her skin looks too pale, the freckles, the pale crescents under her eyes, glowing in the light of her screen. Her flip-flops squeak on the tile floor as she crosses the living room to pull out a stool at the kitchen bar. She reaches over to flick on the overhead light, and her face floods with color again. "So you could pull something like this?"

"Mom——" I say, but she's not done.

"I was shocked when the school called, Adeleina, and embarrassed, and I told them it could not possibly be my daughter, because you'd never do something revolting like that to me, that they were mistaken, that they had the wrong number. I insisted that they had the wrong number."

She's fumbling around on the counter, and I recognize the sound. Sure enough, she drags an ashtray closer.

"Are you smoking again?"

"What if I am?" she snaps. She shoves her hair behind her ear, pops a Virginia Slim in her mouth and flicks a lighter in the same single smooth move, blows out a cloud. Her voice is hoarse. "How do you think I felt, when they told me what you had been doing? I've been bragging to my friends about Paris——"

"*Milan*," I say, something breaking in me. *Milan*.

"——and instead you're out there wasting all that time and all that money? What about Paris, Adeleina——"

But she's not listening, because she never listens, and something's broken free, and I'm leaning forward into my screen, gritting my teeth.

"Listen, Mom. Mom!" I say, to catch her attention, make her look at me. She sniffs. "Mom. I have worked so hard, every day. You know that. You know I worked hard to get a scholarship to this school. I worked my ass off to get into Angles. In *Milan*. It's a dance troupe in Milan. I have been grateful every single day, for how lucky I've been. But I screwed up; I know I did. I thought I could find a way to spend the summer in Milan. And I lost it.

It felt like my only chance to become a dancer, Mom. A professional. I needed to meet Mohadesa Rabei. I told you about her. The fat dancer who—"

I stop when my mother visibly winces, trying to rein in my anger.

"Well, this is the first I'm hearing about some woman," she says.

"It's not, Mom! It's not. You don't listen. I'm scared about my future, and I'm scared for my friends, and I don't know what's going to happen, Mom . . ." I trail off, my anger dwindling into sadness. I silently beg her to understand. To say anything that shows she understands this fear in me, and for my future, and for my friends.

She's just been waiting for me to stop talking. She jabs her barely smoked cigarette into the ashtray. "Were you laughing at me when I told you to make sure you stayed focused? Because that's what it sounds like."

"I *was* focused, Mom, I have never lost focus—"

"Well, you're coming back this summer, and you're going to get a real job. How's that?" Before I can respond, she shakes her head. "Go to sleep, Adeleina. I'm exhausted."

And she's gone. She's not surprised I made a mess of things. It always feels awful to know I've disappointed her, that rock in my stomach. It feels worse to be so furious at her. For not listening. For not understanding. Furious with myself for thinking she might. Or that she could.

Nevaeh finds me with my forehead on the desk. Katherine brings the candy.

"There's nothing we can do right this second," she says, and hands me the bag.

"No," I agree.

"So tonight, we Twizzler."

One thing first, though.

"Do you regret it?" I ask them.

"We knew it was risky," Nevaeh says. "We knew we could be caught."

"I really did think it would just be demerits and detention," Katherine says.

"Immoral conduct, fuck." Nevaeh shakes her head. "Unbelievable."

"Whatever happens, I believe we'll be okay," Katherine says softly. "I really believe that. I believe we don't have to be locked into one idea of the future."

"We'll find a new way," Nevaeh says. "We'll make new goals. We will be *amazing*."

"It's not that easy to stop us," I say. My heart shouldn't fit in my chest. "I love you so much. Do you know that? I should say that more."

"No regrets," Nevaeh says. Katherine nods.

"None," she says. "Don't cry!" she says.

"Fine, fine, let's bust out the capybaras, then," I say, sniffling and settling back, all of us crammed in my bunk. Resting up for tomorrow. We'll be ready for them.

23

What I'm not ready for is people staring. Or at least that's what it feels like as I make my way over to the studio. We're news, even to kids in the academic-track classes, because this is a small school, and I guess that I'm pretty easy to spot as the fat dancer who put on a sex show.

The locker room goes silent when I walk in. The door of the locker too loud when I swing it shut.

"Is it true?" Ellory says, taking a spot at the barre next to me.

She knows the basics—she's on the honor board. But does she really think it was a sex show?

"Of course not," I snap.

"Not judging," she says. "Curious."

Right. Sure.

"Well, thanks for asking," I say.

She lifts her eyebrows at my tone.

"I mean, I'm sorry. I'm on edge." I shouldn't piss her off, right?

She shrugs. "See you later," she says, moving back to her regular spot at the barre.

I keep my head down for the rest of the day, not wanting to

catch anyone's eye, assuming they're judging me too. I can't have any more of those conversations.

Nevaeh and Katherine are dealing with the same shit, they each say, texting the group.

I type, *here's our new future plan: run away and join the circus the circus is unethical and abusive to animals*, Katherine writes.

ok fine let's just run away, I type. I'm only half joking.

I'm late to history class, rushing through the door and taking the last open seat, directly in front of Jack.

"Hi," he whispers from behind me, but I don't turn around, because Mr. Hoffman is glaring at me.

When class is over, I have to make myself turn around. I look at his socks first. Stars and moons. His sock drawer is bottomless.

"Hi," I say, as Mr. Hoffman and the other students file out, talking low, glancing back at us. My shoulders start to creep up, but I catch myself, straighten. Jack's watching me with his head tilted to the side. He glances around the room, then back at me.

"Are you okay?" he asks.

I spent most of the class trying to figure out what I wanted to say to him. What I had to say. I still have nothing, but I can answer his question.

"No," I tell him. "We have an honor board hearing to get ready for, don't we?"

"I'm so sorry," he says. "That's so unfair."

It takes me just a moment to catch up.

"What do you mean? You're going to be there, right? You're as immoral as we are."

He smiles at that, but he's shaking his head. "They're giving me demerits for the curfew violation."

I pause. "That's it?"

He's looking at me strangely. "Yes."

"No. Are you kidding me?" The surprise of it. The disbelief that's making it hard to think straight.

"No, Addie, of course not. I don't understand—"

I'm shaking my head, and I can't listen to him. He doesn't understand why I'm getting upset. Which is even more upsetting.

It all spills out in a rush. "You weren't just *there*," I say. "You were *involved* in the show. You were onstage. You were performing. We were all performing in a burlesque show. All four of us. But only three of us—Katherine and Nevaeh and me—are getting hit with an immoral-conduct charge."

"Well, yes—"

"You don't think it's unfair? You don't see the discrepancy here?"

"I know I was performing, technically. And they're not charging me, but I mean, I can see what they're saying—"

My brain shrieks to a halt.

"Technically!"

"Well, yeah—"

"And you can see what they're saying?"

He's shaking his head at me.

"Addie—"

I jump up and push the classroom door shut, maybe a little too firmly, because I am afraid I'm going to raise my voice.

I stand against it. His hair is all riled up, and he's wearing his glasses, and he looks like he has no idea what I want from him, and I feel like I'm made of tissue paper and I just need a match.

"What is it, Addie?" he says. "Are you okay?"

"You asked me that already," I tell him. "I'm definitely not okay."

He looks horribly uncomfortable, but also really sincere. "If this is about last week, I'm so—"

"Last week?"

"In my room," he says. "When I—"

In his room? I cut him short again.

"That has *nothing* to do with why I am upset right now, but while we're at it, yes! Yes, I'm still pretty pissed about last week, now that you mention it."

He flinches at that. He really doesn't understand, and I want to cry. Why is he bringing this up now? I can't think about it on top of everything! I've never come up with a good reason why he would have run away from me that night, and I've never gotten brave enough to ask him. And now I've put it off too long, and I can't do anything about that. But he's still looking at me like he has no idea what's wrong. And he *really* just said, *I can see what they're saying*!

Deep breath. Another one.

"Okay. Look. Please. One thing at a time. Please."

He reaches out his hand, but he drops it again.

"We're getting an immoral-conduct hearing," I say. "Me, and Nevaeh, and Katherine. We are being charged with immoral conduct. For the burlesque show. That you performed in."

He pauses. "I wasn't performing like that, though."

"Like that? You were onstage with us! You had a microphone! You rehearsed! You rehearsed with us, and you put on two shows with us, and all you get is a slap on the wrist?"

"I wasn't naked!" he snaps.

My head rockets back like he's slapped me, and I stare at him. I don't want him to have said that. I want to pretend those words didn't come out of his mouth. He doesn't get it.

"We weren't naked, either, Jack," I say, my voice surprisingly calm. "None of us were naked. Nothing about our bodies is lewd, or dirty, or any of the things they're implying they are. Immoral, Jack. That's what they're saying. The thing that's immoral, about this whole show, is our skin. And we're going to get expelled for it."

"It is *terrible* that they might expel you," he says, and he reaches out again, but I step back.

"But you don't see the double standard here."

"Of course it's a double standard—"

"But what you're saying is that the double standard makes sense. Because they think we got naked and we shouldn't have."

"Of course not! I don't care if you get naked, Addie—" And he stops when I laugh.

The shock of it. The hurt, burning bright. Irony.

"Well, that explains why you ran away when I pulled off my shirt, then, right?"

Ringing silence. I had not realized I was going to say it. I hadn't meant to say it. His entire face has flashed red.

He picks up his bag, swings the door open, and leaves.

At least I have all my clothes on this time.

———

And then dinner. Nevaeh hands me her phone. Messages from anonymous accounts.

She is *insert racist slur*. We are all *insert misogynistic slur*. She is *racist misogynistic slur*. I am a *fat misogynistic slur*. We are all disgusting, and we are pathetic attention seekers, and why would anyone pay money to see these nasty girls? We have been sleeping with a lot of dudes, and not always for money.

"You see this?" Nevaeh says to us, snatching the phone from me, slamming it back in her purse. "I deal with this literally every goddamn day. I am *so tired* of these people. And now there's *more* of them, shrieking at us because the school has slapped an immoral-conduct charge on our foreheads." Her phone whistles a notification from her bag. "Fuck these people. I have a paper due tomorrow."

Nevaeh lets Katherine and me go through all the messages and comments to delete them, then posts that she's putting her account on hiatus. She doesn't open up the comments on that one.

Most of the messages—at least all the ones that are referring to the show—have to be from people from school. Who else would know what was happening on campus? We spend all day wondering who our real friends are, what else they could be saying.

On Friday, I find a photo of me posted on the bulletin board in our dorm lobby—a still from our Spring Dance performance last year. My costume is a sheer skirt, dance briefs, a bandeau. I'm smiling, in that costume the dance department issued us. The words *FAT SLUT* are written across the print in black marker.

I tear the photo down.

I am frozen all the way through now, staring at this photo in my hands, and I know there are probably people standing behind me, laughing at my reaction. Maybe filming it on their phones. I don't care. I crush the paper in my fists, into a tiny ball.

I'm glad I go to rehearsal anyway, because Zoe is sitting in front of my locker. She jumps up when she sees me, throws her arms around me.

"My mom called and made me promise I wouldn't talk to you, but that is ridiculous, of course. The first thing I was going to do was come find you and make sure you were okay."

"I'm okay, Zoe-bear," I say, smoothing her pale hair, which

is falling out of a sloppy bun, out of her face. "This is not regulation hair."

Zoe scoffs. "I am boycotting recital today. So are Bisma and Kaitlyn and Riley and Logan and Leslie."

All my mentees. My heart hurts.

"It is not fair that they're treating you so bad and acting like you've done something wrong or immoral or nasty," she says. "It is so *ridiculous*."

"Don't get suspended because of me, Zoe, please," I say. "You don't have to boycott—"

"It's not just you!" she bursts out. "Do you know I got a demerit yesterday because I was showing my shoulders in class?" She's building up steam. "Mr. Elliot sent me back to the dorm to change, but I refused and I told him, 'You care more about boys getting an education than you do about girls,' which is *true*, and he gave me *another demerit*, and it's all bullshit, Addie; it's not right." She grabs my hands, and she looks so distressed. "Like, you can't just not say anything about how hypocritical they are. We are so mad, Addie. I don't care what my mother says. You don't have to mentor me anymore if you don't want to, but I am on your side, all the way, and I am telling everyone that, and also you are my friend."

I look at her pale, angry face, her fierceness. And I think about how the boys' soccer team stripped naked last semester and ran across the entire campus, screaming and waving their jerseys above their heads, their dicks bouncing in the late fall sunshine, and you could see *everything*, and how everyone just said, *boys will be boys!* Did they even get detention? Or just congratulated for winning their match?

And I realize I haven't really gotten mad yet, not about the right thing. I pull Zoe into a tight, swift squeeze.

"You're amazing, kid," I say to her, and she ducks her head.

"Well, it's just all true, and that's the important part, right?" she says. "It's the worst thing, what they're saying about you, and it's such bull crap, and they can't do this to you."

"They can," I say. "And they will. But it'll be okay," I promise her. And now that means I have to make sure it is.

The fourth-floor common room after dinner, the ugly brown couches, the place we decided we were going to do something amazing—not that long ago. Just a few weeks ago. And it looks just the same, but how ridiculous is it to think anything would be different? No matter how different I feel. I want to draw a map from that moment to right now as Taylor smooths the crumpled photo out flat on the floor with his palms. Map out all the changes. How we got here. This was not what I expected. We all stare at it.

"So, what do you think they're trying to get across?" I say. "I can't really tell."

"It's so subtle," Taylor agrees.

"I think the dean agrees with them, that I'm a fat slut," I say.

"What the fuck?" Nevaeh says.

And I tell them—Katherine, Nevaeh, and Taylor—how I marched to the dean's office after my encounter with Zoe, the ball of paper wadded up in my fist. Ms. Flores was there, telling me to wait, that she didn't know how long it would be, that perhaps I could come back later. I sat, folding and refolding the paper on my knees. Thinking about Zoe and my mentees and ignoring the rapid beating of my heart, the urge to say yes, okay, I'll come back another time.

"No," I said. "I have something to show him."

He looked irritated when I entered his office. I put the folded paper on his desk.

He picked it up, held it between his fingertips like it was distasteful.

"I found it on the bulletin board in the lobby of my dorm," I said.

He glanced at it for just a moment and shook his head, dismissing me.

"Sir—"

"What do you expect?" he said. He slapped his hand on the desk. "Are you truly surprised?"

"That someone would call me a fat slut?" It was rage, I thought, the reason I was trembling. This man who was waving me away, the look on his face completely disdainful. A little disgusted. The dean of my school. I waited for him to answer.

"I don't have time for this," he said. "Say what you need to say at your hearing. Stop bothering me with this nonsense. And keep your clothes on if you expect to be treated with respect."

"Or expect to be called a fat slut," I persisted.

"As you say, Ms. Grant."

I snatched the paper off his desk, was shaking when I left. There's a hollow in my chest, still.

"I'm going to kill him slowly, Adeleina," Nevaeh says.

Taylor is muttering, not joking, and Katherine has snatched the paper, tearing it in half and in half again.

They're here with me. I am here with them. And I'm not bulletproof anymore, I remind myself. It's not a shell; it's a confidence that's burning at my core. I'm a star, a nuclear furnace, solar flares and all, and I will go supernova.

"We can shred him at the hearing, to start," I say.

We've been talking about that for the past two days, and what we need to tell them. What I'm going to stand up and say. Adding things to the bonfire. We were supposed to just be working on that, not getting worked up about the photo, the dean. Because screw that.

"I need a pen," I say.

We're here until it starts nearing freshman curfew, and as Taylor gets ready to leave, Nevaeh yanks him onto the couch next to the three of us. It takes a moment to get it right, but finally, in the photo, you can see how her arm is stretched up high to fit all of us in the frame, her eyes bright, and I've got my arms around her waist, laughing so hard my face is scrunched up, and Taylor's smacking a kiss on Katherine's cheek.

Looking at the photo on her screen, I don't know what's going to happen to us. But this is a good place to start from. We are going to be okay, no matter what happens. Despite the cruel people and the vicious people. The people with Sharpies and too much time on their hands. I refuse to believe that they'll win in the end.

And then I have an idea. And I tell them.

"Oh, fuck yes," Nevaeh says when I finish.

"I'm in," Katherine says.

"Full-speed ahead," Taylor says. "To Dirty Little Secret," he says with a grin, the imaginary champagne glass. "Who knew they'd take that so literally?"

We lift our glasses to that.

The alchemy of love, turning all my fear into fierceness. And this brilliant idea.

24

Afterward I keep writing and deleting texts to Jack. *Listen, I'm still mad at you but I need to ask you a really, really big favor because it's really, really important. Listen, I don't want to make up, but I do want your help. Hey, let's pretend everything is okay so I can ask you to please do something for me.*

It's impossible. I'm awful at explaining myself in text. I can't find the words. And I realize I need to see his face when I ask him. I need him to see me and tell me he understands, that he's thought everything through. I want to stop having angry imaginary conversations in my head with him where I win and he apologizes when he realizes why he's wrong. We need to talk. I need to explain why I was so upset. God, I hope he gets it, because I want this distance between us to be fixed.

So I hurry to his studio, the time of evening when the quad is filled up with students rushing between buildings, from spotlight to spotlight, to make the most of the time before final curfew.

The only light in the studio is the lamp above Jack's table at the back. And he's here, bent over papers in front of him, humming absently to the music playing on his laptop, swinging his hips but not to the beat. He always works Friday nights because he gets the whole room to himself, and I guess he gets to dance terribly without anyone seeing him.

He doesn't hear me making my way around the clutter on the floor, I guess, because he doesn't look up, and then he jumps and yells a little bit when I say his name, clutches his chest, his eyes huge and his hair, still too short, a complete mess. And then his face is like the first time you plug in your Christmas tree when he says, "Addie!"

He drags a stool up for me to sit on, and I do, even though I feel like I should stand to maintain my dignity. To stay on task. Because he's smiling at me, a little hesitantly, and I want to smile back, because it would be so easy to let it go, but it's not something I can let go.

"I'm working on my light trail project," he says, then adds, "It's Friday."

"I know," I say.

"I'm sorry it's such a mess," he says. "The studio, I mean." He stands up, sweeps together the photos and papers scattered across his table. His hands are covered in Sharpie notes to himself.

"I'm sorry," I say. "I didn't mean to barge in—"

"No, it's okay," he rushes to say. "I'm so glad you're here, Addie. I have to tell you something." He frowns. "No, you came here to talk about something."

"You go first," I say. Hopeful despite myself.

"Right. Okay." He sweeps his hand through his hair. Shakes his head. "Right. I went to the dean's office," he says. I sit very still and wait, afraid to think anything at all. "After we talked." He shakes his head. "Because of course you're right."

A deep breath in. I'm not sure what to say, not yet. He goes on.

"I wanted to text you. And tell you about it. Before I went in. While I was waiting. After. But I wasn't doing it for brownie points. I didn't want you to think that I was."

He hurt me, when he acted like my anger was unfounded. I want to forgive him. I want to believe he understands.

"What happened?" I ask.

"Among other things, I believe I accidentally accused the dean of being an ignorant misogynist. And now it seems I get my own hearing."

"What." I stare at him. I did not expect that.

"Yeah. I got detention too." He looks thoughtful. "I am not sure I've ever gotten detention before."

"Well," I say. "Make sure you have lots to read."

He smiles at that.

He's not finished, and I'm still afraid of forgiving him too fast, of saying sure, I believe you, everything is okay, but I want to, so much. I clasp my hands tight.

"So," he says, "this whole situation. This is the kind of situation in which you're very aware you screwed up. And you know you need to make amends."

Deep breath. Leap of faith.

"It's—a good start," I say.

"I really like you, Addie," he says. "I am so very sorry I screwed so many things up, so well."

I close my eyes, the lamplight bright against my lids. I have been putting off this question, and putting him off, for days now, because I don't want to hear the answer. But that's unfair to both of us.

"You ran away," I say. He's just a silhouette when I open my eyes again. "You ran away from me, from your own room, that night. Do you know what I thought?" I spread my hands out. "That I was sitting there, with my shirt off, and your reaction was to get away as fast as possible. As if you had seen me and realized you couldn't go through with it. That it turned out you were a fatphobe."

"Oh, fuck," he says. "Oh, Addie, no. I looked at you, and you were so beautiful, and you were smiling at me. And I panicked. I panicked. Because I've never been with anyone before." He clears his throat, pauses. "I have never felt attracted to anyone before," he says. "I spent a long time thinking there was something wrong with me, that I never wanted anyone like that." He smiles. "And then I met you. And I thought—I wanted you to notice me, in class. If you couldn't tell."

"You were kind of an ass about it."

"You weren't blown away by my truly comprehensive historical knowledge?"

"I figured you thought I wasn't smart enough for you."

"Aw, shit," he says.

"Yeah."

"Well. Thank god for Katherine," he says. "Accidentally matchmaking. Because I got to know you." His voice is low. "You are funny. And smart. And fun. And so alive and so focused and ambitious and brilliant and talented. And beautiful." He swallows.

"Go on," I say.

"Addie," he says. "I am trying to be very serious here."

"Continue," I say, gesturing grandly. He reaches for my hand, and I let him take it.

"Addie, I wanted you so much. I didn't know what to do with that."

My heart's a hummingbird.

"And that night—you were just—in my arms, and we were kissing, and I couldn't believe I was there. I looked at you and I was so overwhelmed. By how much I wanted you and how badly I could screw everything up." I laugh at that, and he smiles. "Yes, and then I made an extremely poor choice, and I panicked, and I screwed everything up."

A long, long silence.

His voice is careful, when he continues. "It's this," he says. I look up because his voice is so serious, and so are his eyes. "I've figured out that I'm not attracted to someone unless I care about them. And I don't want to have sex with anyone unless I like them very much. I knew that in theory. But when I realized how much I liked you—" He swallows. "How much I wanted to be with you. I was overwhelmed."

My hummingbird heart is in my throat, and I try to swallow it down.

"I wish you had *just said that*," I say in a croaky voice. "At the *start*. Before we *got naked*." I wave the hand he's not holding. "Anytime before! Especially if this is all new for you! I want to know that! I need to know that!"

"I didn't know what to say," he says.

"Anything! You should have said anything! You could have tried. You could have drawn me a picture. Or brought me a library book. Or written it on a cake! Because listen, Jack, *that* happened instead, and I spent a lot of time trying to remember I didn't care about other people's opinions about my body, thinking you were horrified by it. And I didn't want to talk to you and hear you say yep, that's exactly what it is, sorry about that. And it sucked."

He's shaking his head. "Oh no. Oh no, no, Addie. You are so gorgeous. And so sexy. And so confident. Have I said that? I want to keep telling you that. And you're so not horrifying."

"I know," I say.

He laughs at that, pleased, and I am smiling back at him.

"Thank you for telling me," I say. "I'm sorry it was hard to tell me sooner. I do get it."

"I know," he says. He moves like he's going to reach for my other hand, but pulls back. "You had a favor to ask me," he guesses. "And I want to say yes."

"Can I still kiss you?" I blurt. Because his hair is rumpled and his face is all relief that we finally talked, and because I was sad when he pulled back just now. Because I want to. Because I like him. "That's not the favor, though," I add hastily, when his eyes get big.

"Please," he says, and I don't even think he heard my joke, so I slip my arms around his neck, laugh against his mouth when he pulls me hard against him, almost frantic as he kisses me, and I kiss him back.

"Is it okay that I like you a lot?" he says, and I nod. "Is it okay if this is slow?"

"Of course," I say, and I shiver when he kisses my neck.

"Is it okay if I tell you all the things I like about your body?"

"As long as you don't tell me I look like a Renaissance painting of a naked lady you once saw in a museum," I whisper back, and we dissolve into giggles.

———————

He's the one that remembers the favor, when the senior curfew warning chimes.

"It's a big project," I tell him. "We need to get it done over the weekend." He's nodding. I take a deep breath. "And it's a message."

"I'm definitely listening," Jack says.

We work all weekend, my friends and Jack and me. And Sunday night, the night before the hearing, we're done.

Jack's been staring at the monitor for hours, tweaking the photos we've been taking. It's late when he turns to me. "Are you absolutely sure you want to do this?" He puts his arms around my waist. "I love them. But I want to make sure you're sure. Absolutely positively."

I look over his shoulder at the picture he's just finished adjusting, the light and shadow stark, unforgiving, beautiful.

"Yeah," I say. "I'm not ashamed. And I won't let them make me ashamed."

"Printing is go," he says, spinning around.

It's done, I message the group.

I stack the flyers as they print, dozens of each photo. Just a handful of hours from now, Monday morning, we'll slip out of the dorms as early as we're allowed, before almost anyone is up, and plaster them all over campus, in every building, on every building, on every lamppost, to greet the whole school when they wake.

I barely sleep.

As planned, we meet, most of us sleepy-eyed, in front of the girls' dorm. I distribute coffee, flyers, duct tape, and it takes only a couple of hours before we're done, meeting back up in front of the administration building. We've plastered the double doors. Wallpapered them with my body.

That photo of me on the bulletin board started it. I'll finish it.

My stomach, soft, stretch marked, over strong muscles. Skin pale and dimpled. No Photoshop. In big red block letters, though, the word *SLUT* slashes across my skin, my hands framing it.

As you say.

Jack spent hours on Saturday photographing the three of us. Close-ups of all the parts that we hate, always want to hide. Our skin and our fat and our muscles and bones, naked and on display, unretouched. Thighs, backs, hips, collarbones, foreheads, feet, arms. The words carefully spelled out in red lipstick: *PROUD, BEAUTIFUL, FIERCE, ANGRY, LOUD, BRAVE, POWERFUL, STRONG, FORMIDABLE.* The words *SLUT, WHORE, BRAZEN, IMMORAL, DEPRAVED, PORNOGRAPHIC, DISTRACTING, OBSCENE, LEWD, SHAMEFUL.*

The photos are beautiful. And soon we'll all be inside this building, saying these words to the honor board. Defending our bodies and our choices and demanding they apologize.

If I say my skin is vibrating off my muscles, which are bursting off clattering bones, that's exactly what it feels like, with the fear that they just won't hear us, and I've got to get it together. I want to yell in their faces.

I'm going to yell in their faces.

"I would like to go back inside now. I want to be warm and filled with coffee when everyone wakes up and the shit hits the fan," Taylor says.

"This day we fight! By all that you hold dear on this good earth, et cetera," Nevaeh says.

We gather up our stuff. I take Nevaeh's hand to help her down the icy stairs. Katherine plucks my mittens out of my pocket and hands them to me. The hearing is a few hours away, but right now the sun is rising, bright and sure, and on the sidewalk in front of us, our long shadows merge.

25

I keep calling it a trial room in my head, instead of a hearing room, which is maybe why the hearing room looks nothing like I pictured it. The floor isn't marble, and the ceilings aren't high overhead, no long velvet curtains, no judge in black robes. Instead, Ms. Flores shows us into a conference room down the hall from the dean's office. It looks nothing like the rest of the building, with dull white walls and flat gray carpet, mini blinds pulled shut on each of the three windows lining the wall. A long conference table and black rolling chairs. Too ordinary, for the ragged block of ice cutting up my gut, the way my heart feels like it's beating around the spike slammed directly through it.

"There," Ms. Flores tells us, holding the door wide and waiting for us to move to the seats she's pointing to, across from the honor board. The group isn't large—two teachers, Mr. Banerjee and Ms. Warren, Nevaeh's Shakespeare teacher. Three student council members—two I don't know very well, though I bet Katherine knows them, and Ellory. She nods when she looks up from the laptop in front of her. I take a rough breath. I can feel Katherine trembling at my side. She and Nevaeh are hand in hand, and Katherine reaches for mine too. It's shaking.

"We're okay," I tell her, my voice soft. We make our case or we go home, try to reassemble lives from whatever they leave us. We make our case or they take away Tisch, Juilliard, Angles.

They've torn us apart. They've demanded that we explain ourselves. We've come to fight. I have never felt this light-headedly frightened in my life.

"Your coats?" Ms. Flores says. I shake my head at her, and she looks me over with a raised eyebrow, taking in my ragged winter coat, and glances at my friends, still in their parkas. She leaves us there to take a seat on the other side of the table.

The dean isn't here, but we haven't heard the clock tower strike nine.

Katherine swallows and squeezes my hand before she drops it. We pull the chairs in front of us out, but push them aside, so that we can step up to stand at the table and wait for the tower to chime. All five members of the honor board stare at the three of us, but none of us says anything for the longest thirty seconds ever, before the clock tolls.

There it is, and there he is, coming through the door at the far end of the room, a dark leather folder under his arm, the door snapping shut behind him. Katherine flinches. My breath stops. Nevaeh catches my eye. I hear her say it—*by all that you hold dear on this good earth, et cetera.*

Guess what I hold dear on this good earth, Dean Pembrooke?

He strides down the length of the table, flicks open the button of his suit coat, and shakes out his sleeves as he takes the empty chair next to Ms. Flores. He looks us over, still standing there in our coats.

"Now, then," he says, his forehead wrinkling as he takes us all in. "Would you like to take off your coats and join us, Ms. Grant, Ms. James, Ms. Thompson?"

"We had hoped to keep them on for now," Katherine says politely. Her voice is rock steady, her chin up.

"Take them off," the dean orders. "And sit down."

A beat. A collective indrawn breath. As if we're onstage, a troupe with flawless precision and timing, we each unzip our coats and let them slip off our shoulders to crumple to the floor at our feet. Several people gasp, and the dean is saying something loudly, and Mr. Banerjee is answering him, and I am just trying to stay upright.

They see us with our hair pulled up high off our necks, wearing our costumes for the dance-program performance. Spaghetti strap leotards that almost but not quite match Katherine's and my winter-pale skin tones and don't match Nevaeh's very dark skin at all. They're cut low at the neck and high at the hips, and they're aggressively rhinestoned.

When we got them, I joked that they were trying to make us—well, those of us with pale skin—look like we were dipped naked in sugar. Ellory's got a tiny smile on her face now, and she has her phone out. Is she recording this? I hope she is. I lift my chin. I'm trying to remember the names of the other two students. Katherine would know. They're scribbling notes to each other on a legal pad between them.

"Do you think you're being funny?" the dean says. The look on his face is pure ice. Mr. Banerjee leans over to say something in a low voice to Ms. Warren.

"Absolutely not," Nevaeh says.

"Because this is absolutely disrespectful," he goes on like he didn't hear her. "Are you mocking the honor board?"

Before any of us can answer, the noise of doors squeaking open comes from behind us, and I turn.

Taylor is standing in the wide doorway, and behind him, the lobby is crowded with students I recognize—ones who bought tickets to Dirty Little Secret, dancers from my classes . . . I think I hear Zoe's voice.

"Why are those doors open?" the dean says. "Close the doors! Ms. Flores—"

I interrupt him before I can lose my courage.

"Sir!" I say, and his gaze snaps to mine. "We do not intend to be disrespectful."

"Is that right, Ms. Grant? Ms. Flores," he says impatiently. She hurries around the table. Behind us, Taylor is arguing with her. The crowd of students is less quiet.

"We intend to make a point, sir. Are you aware that this is what we will be wearing in our recital this year?" I ask him politely.

He blinks at me and then takes his glasses off, drops them on the folder in front of him. "I am sorry, Ms. Grant, but I fail to see what that has to do with anything."

"These are the costumes all the senior dance students will be wearing for the second piece in this year's showcase. Sir. All the female students. These costumes were chosen for us by our costume designer and our director." The noise from the hallway is growing, and I refuse to look over. Nevaeh mutters something next to me. Ellory's still got a small smile on her face. "They're school sanctioned, in other words."

"These outfits?" he says. He is absolutely doubting us.

I spread my hands wide. "These outfits," I say.

"In the third piece, the modern dance students will be wearing nude bodysuits," Katherine says. "They look naked," she adds helpfully.

"I don't appreciate this distraction," the dean says. "What is the point of all this?"

"The point?" Nevaeh says. "Here's the point. Do you think these are too revealing?"

"Watch your tone with me," he snaps. "You're trying to confuse the issue."

"We would appreciate an answer," Katherine says, her voice icy.

"I don't mean to put words into your mouth, sir," I say. "But I think you might find these costumes obscene. If you object to our burlesque-show costumes."

"You came to the show last year," Nevaeh says. "Did you have anything to say about our costumes last year?"

He blurts out, "Well, they certainly weren't this—"

"Yes, they really were," Ellory says, her voice cutting through the room.

We trade smiles.

"Miss Lang, when I want your opinion, I'll ask for it." The dean is starting to boil, losing his temper but still grasping to keep this under control.

"You might even recall that photograph of me in the costume, Dean Pembroke," I say, calling his attention back to me. He stares at me. "The one I brought in to show you," I clarify. "You seemed to think the costume was pretty revealing."

"Your point," he says stiffly. I leave it, but just for now.

"You keep telling us that showing our skin is sexual, and it's wrong too," Katherine says. "And you also dress us like this, year after year."

Mr. Banerjee winces. Ms. Warren has started to smile.

Katherine squeezes my hand, and Nevaeh nods at me. I push forward. My voice is steady and clear. I'm on.

"Every time you throw us out of an academic class for showing our shoulders or our collarbones, you tell us being modest is more important than our education," I say. "Every time you claim our skin is distracting, you turn a bunch of teenage girls into sexual objects. And then you *shame* us. That's the reason we're here, isn't it, sir?"

Silence in the room. The dean's face is pure fury. Ellory is nodding, and her phone is still pointed at us.

"And then you're horrified when we take control of our own bodies," I say. "You're horrified when we tell you that you don't get to decide how and when and where and why we show our skin—*we* do. You're horrified when we own our beauty and our sexuality.

"We are talented. We are creative. We put on a beautiful show, and we were *powerful*," I tell them. "And strong," I say. "And fierce." I put my hands on the table and lean forward. "And *you* want to turn that into something ugly, and that is what is immoral, and you are the ones degrading us.

"We snuck out after curfew," I admit. "And that was a really, really bad choice, and that deserves punishment.

"But," I say formally, "as for the charge of 'immoral conduct' that has brought us here to the honor board, we refuse to accept it."

A burst of cheers erupts from the lobby outside, startling me, and the noise is growing.

"Ms. Grant—" the dean says loudly.

"We refuse to accept it," I say again, as loudly and more firmly, over the crowd. "I don't have to ask you to imagine what you'd think if the gender roles were reversed—there's a reason Jack wasn't called here today. Jack was onstage with us, performing next to us, a part of our burlesque club. Is there a reason he's not standing next to us?"

The dean glances at the door, and Jack, standing next to Taylor, gives him a thumbs-up. Behind them, kids I recognize—Zoe and Grace and Halim and Max, with photos in their hands. The ones we've posted all over campus. Taylor gives me finger guns, and I have to cough instead of laugh, and it takes me a second to go on.

"Maybe you remember when the soccer team won their match and ran naked across the quad?" I continue. "And none of them, I believe, received serious punishment. Or an immoral-conduct charge. Because boys will be boys, right?"

I stop for a second, and Nevaeh squeezes my hand.

"If for no other reason, the discrepancy in the severity of the punishment is clear and should be enough to make this all moot," I say. My voice has gotten loud. After I finish, for a moment there is only silence.

"Is that all?" the dean says sarcastically.

"No, sir," I say.

"How long do you expect me to sit here and—" he starts.

"Dean Pembrooke," Mr. Banerjee says, "I'd like to hear the rest of what they have to say."

"Fine!" the dean says. "Let them keep running their mouths." He settles back in his chair with his arms crossed over his chest.

I look at Nevaeh and Katherine, standing hand in hand next to me, faces composed and serious and angry. They nod at me.

"Just one more small thing, sir." I pause and look at him, remember his face when he was looking at that crumpled photo on the desk. That dismissive snort.

"When I came to you about the photo on the bulletin board—of me, in a costume chosen for me, for a dance performance, the words FAT SLUT written across it, what did you say?"

He is glaring daggers at me. He refuses to answer.

I clear my throat. I'm shaking so hard I'm afraid my voice will be torn from my throat, but I go on. I don't look away from his glare.

"I believe you suggested that there was a reason someone would post this flyer, would write those words across that picture of me. I believe you suggested, perhaps, that if I wanted to be respected, I should not be wearing the costume the dance department chose for me. I believe you agreed, when I asked you if the words *fat slut* applied to me."

I hear noise in the lobby. Katherine moves closer to me.

"Dean Pembrooke, is this true?" Ms. Warren bursts out.

"Absolutely not," the dean says.

I clear my throat.

"I am fat, Dean Pembrooke. You seem to find that particularly contemptible. I don't find that word to be the insult you want it to be. I don't find the word *slut* insulting either. How dare you suggest that I should be ashamed? That I am asking to be shamed? That it's understandable that someone would be so vicious?

"How dare you police my body? Our bodies. I'm not going to hide because you find my ordinary body offensive. I'm not going to apologize for being fat but not hiding it, not finding it the insult you think it is. You need to figure out why you find any of our bodies offensive, because that's not okay.

"And I refuse to be a part of that conversation. I'm not going to argue anymore that I deserve to live as a fat person and be visible as a fat person and be respected as a fat person. I'm going to be a fat person, and you're going to deal with it.

"And we are not going to live as girls—as women—hiding, ashamed of our bodies, allowing you to make us feel small."

I take a deep breath. Everyone, it feels like, takes a deep breath.

Silence, and shuffling papers, and Ms. Warren leaning over to say something to Ellory.

"In *conclusion*," I say into the loudest silence I've ever heard, "we accept that we broke school rules and made bad judgment calls. But we refuse to accept your disgust for our bare skin. We refuse to accept the idea that you find our skin offensive, we refuse to accept your judgment of our bodies, and we reject your claim of ownership."

I clear my throat.

"Thank you. The end."

There is absolute silence.

We pick up our coats, turn, and the three of us walk out the door and into absolute chaos.

26

I'm going to be sick," I say, lowering myself to the cold concrete steps outside the admin building. We've slipped away from the crowd, that roaring group of students who gathered around us in the lobby, hugged us, cheered us. They all had found the pictures on their dorm bulletin boards and elevator doors and lampposts, and word had spread about the honor-board hearing, and now they're all buzzing with the excitement of it and with their own thoughts and stories and opinions.

Even out here in the relative quiet, I still can't think straight.

"You were amazing," Katherine says again. She's been saying it a lot, thinks we must have made a difference, that we must have changed their minds. Nevaeh is at the bottom of the steps, talking to someone she knows.

"You need to eat something," Jack says to me, rummaging around in his bag. "I have peanut butter cups."

"Aw," Taylor says.

"No, I will die if I eat something," I say, squinting into the sun, and then I hear my name.

Ellory, rushing out of the building, a bit out of breath, looking at all of us, holding out her phone.

"Can I post this?" she asks. "I recorded it. It was—it was pretty perfect." She pauses, then adds, "I hate our costumes this year. I hated them last year too."

"Send it to me?" Nevaeh calls to Ellory, then asks me, "Can I post it?" They're both looking at me. Katherine and Jack are staring at me too.

"Yes," I say. "Everyone can post it everywhere. Let's print out stills and post them all over school too," I joke.

"For real?" Jack asks, looking a little exhausted at the thought.

"No," I say, nudging him. "Not for real."

"I knew those were your photos," Ellory says to him. "They were awesome."

"How long will it take for the honor board to make its decision?" I ask her.

She shakes her head, looking at her phone. "We're meeting to talk after classes tonight."

"Well, this is going to be the longest day in the history of space and time," Taylor says. And then he stiffens.

I turn to see Christopher jogging up the steps. Nevaeh right behind him, looking grim. He stops at the one below me and leans down into my face. I lean away, take Katherine's hand, and stand up.

"You want to sign this for me before you get kicked out?" Christopher says, thrusting one of Jack's photos in front of my face. The length of my thigh, the word *WHORE*.

I snatch it from him and he laughs.

"Only if we get a signed pic of your dick," Taylor says.

"Did you save them?" Christopher says. "Or did you need me to send more?"

"Oh, so that really was you in those shots?" Ellory says. She's holding up her phone.

"Are you filming me?" Christopher says.

"Did you just admit you harassed us?" Nevaeh says.

"I got him admitting to it," Ellory says.

"Did you turn us in?" Katherine says. "I think it was you."

"'Sorry not sorry,'" I say to him. "That was classy."

"Dude," Jack says. "Not cool."

Christopher ignores him. "You'd love to know," he says to me, a little red now.

"Actually, we don't really care about that," I say. "But I do love that we have receipts. I wonder if admitting you sent dick pics is an immoral-conduct thing."

"Back off," Katherine says when he takes a step toward me, and he laughs and shakes his head, rolls his shoulders like he's throwing off his anger.

"Fuck-all is going to happen," he says, and then adds, "Be sure to say goodbye before you're kicked off campus, Addie." With that, he saunters down the steps.

"That dickhead," Jack mutters under his breath, and I squelch a laugh.

"I'm just going to go ahead and share this video with the honor board," Ellory says, her thumbs moving fast across the screen. "See what they say about his college acceptances."

Nevaeh high-fives her.

"Ms. Warren wants to talk to you," Ellory says to me. "About what the dean said to you." She hesitates, then touches my arm. "I'm sorry."

"She wants to talk to me?" I say. "I didn't expect anyone to care."

"Just wait," Ellory says. "I'm pretty sure he's going to get into a fuckton of trouble."

"Good," I say.

"I'll let you know as soon as I hear anything," she says as she returns inside.

"I hate waiting," Taylor says. "It's all been waiting. I want now."

Jack kisses me sweetly, tells me he'll help any way he can, and I close my eyes when he hugs me.

When we break apart, he leaves for the studio, and Taylor, Katherine, Nevaeh, and I head back to the dorms to change, get our books, and pretend the day is normal and that I didn't just peel open my chest and give the whole room a good look at my heart.

"I don't think I've ever said so many words in a row like that," I say. Why am I still so wobbly? "Do you think they heard us? What's going to happen to us?" Asking that out loud is scary.

"Here's what I know," Nevaeh says, taking my hand. "We do have genius, marketable skills. And there is no way they're going to steal our futures from us."

I start to smile. But I'm still scared. I'm still shaken. I still want to believe that there's something like justice. I don't want them to lose the spots they worked so hard for. It's impossible to even consider.

"We'll do something wonderful," Katherine says. "You know that."

"I'm not scared," Nevaeh says to me. "And I still have zero regrets."

Katherine seizes me in a hug.

"I still hate waiting," Taylor says.

I don't know if I can be as brave as Katherine and Nevaeh are, but the relief is real, all of us here together at the end of this ridiculous dare we took. We said yes, let's do this. It'll be the best adventure ever.

"I'm going to wear this costume to all my classes today," I announce. "Because, you know, I can't pretend this is a normal day. There's nothing normal about it."

"Not a thing to lose," Katherine says.

There's nothing like putting your money where your mouth is.

27

Mr. Acevedo glowers at me as I sit sparkling in my seat in Spanish, my shoulders bare, shivering but sitting up straight. He opens his mouth and then snaps it shut and doesn't look my way for the rest of the class. It happens again in English with Ms. Robbins, and Ms. Sebold in ecology. I sit there shivering but upright, every time. Delighted by this feeling, which is part powerful, part giddy, and crashing through my stomach.

Thumbs-up from classmates, *Fuck yes* and *god that looks itchy* and *wow, you look amazing* and *I'm wearing a halter top tomorrow.*

At dinnertime, everyone—even kids who've never said a word to me before—keeps stopping by our table to say *hey!* and *hi!* and *oh my god, you're awesome* and give me high fives until my palm is red. I mean, I know that rumors spread fast, but these are waves of kindness that keep knocking me off my feet.

"Viral," Nevaeh says, slipping into her seat next to Katherine. "The video of the hearing is all over campus. And someone posted it on the school forums, but they took it down."

Taylor's right behind her, and he's bursting with news. "They're showing up at the admin office!" he says excitedly.

"Who?" Nevaeh, Katherine, and I say at the exact same time.

"Students!" Taylor says. "Showing up and saying that they were at the show and demanding that they be expelled if you three are going to be. But get this!" He pauses for dramatic effect. "They weren't even all at the show, from what I hear. And they're confessing anyway!"

"No!" Katherine says delightedly.

"You love to see it," Nevaeh says.

"Yes!" Taylor says.

"Jack said that the honor board was completely quiet during his hearing," I tell them, remembering. "He had no idea what they were thinking. Maybe they're realizing how big this is getting. They've got to see that now." I flatten my hands on the table. "I love this. I didn't know any of this would happen." It started as a way to make money for tuition, and now it's becoming a movement for change. There's a confetti feeling in my stomach. Angles is my dream—I'm not going to say *was*. But if we had to get caught, this is the best thing that could have happened.

"Just look what we've started," Katherine says to Nevaeh.

"I wish I could believe it'll lead somewhere real," Nevaeh says. "We'll see."

She's right, though—there's a lot to do to go from "this sucks and it's wrong" to fixing school policy. But this part, before it all happens, is the exciting bit. All the potential for change exploding like fireworks around us.

Jack drops into the chair on my other side and pushes a basket of fries in front of me. "Everyone's saying the whole school is demanding to be expelled," he tells us.

"We know," we say.

"Gavin's coming to tell us the same thing," Taylor says, nodding over at Gavin and Ellory weaving through the tables toward us. "We know," Taylor tells them when they reach us.

Ellory says, "I'll be honest—I don't know how it's going to go tonight."

"Well, that's comforting," Taylor says.

"I'm going to argue for you," she says. "Obviously."

"I told them to suspend me too," Gavin announces proudly.

"Thank you, Gavin," I say. A squeeze of affection for him. I forgive him, I think. He was a bonehead last summer and behaved badly, and he hurt me. But that hour in his room, the talk we had—I can let go of that shame, which I wish I hadn't let consume me. It is a reminder that I'm whole on my own, and his reassurances were just a gift with purchase.

"Good job, Gavin," Nevaeh says.

"You're a hero, Gavin," Taylor says.

"You're the best, Gavin," Katherine says.

"I think you're being sarcastic," Gavin says.

"I'll text you when I know something," Ellory says to Nevaeh, and leads Gavin away by the elbow.

"Are they back together?" Nevaeh says. "I thought she had that boy's number."

"Maybe that's why they're back together. He's easy," Taylor says.

We settle into gossip and french fries, trying to cut through that tension in our shoulders. I want to wish the hours away, leap forward past all this waiting.

But this is a good way to wait. The best. Friends around the table and french fries, even though Jack insists on dipping them in barbecue sauce like a barbarian. The feeling that we've had a good day despite everything, even though our costumes are itchy. Knowing that we're going to be okay, because look at us. We're together.

———————

Late in the evening, Jack texts us—he's getting Saturday detentions and probation. He sounds happy. Taylor confirms that they high-fived when he got the news, hanging out together in the common room.

Ellory stops by Katherine and Nevaeh's to tell us they haven't decided yet on our fate. She can't give us details, but apparently there's intense debate happening. All about us.

I crawl into bed, hold Rachel close, and leave my mother a message because she doesn't pick up.

"I think you'd be proud of me," I say, staring at the dim star stickers on the ceiling. "I think it went really well. I sent you a copy of the video a friend took. For you to watch. I want to show you." I close my eyes. I don't know what I want to show her. "I wanted to explain. I hope this explains."

I wake up on Tuesday morning to hear that the students who "confessed" to being in the audience are getting detention and probation too.

The video of the hearing keeps circulating, posted on our class forums over and over again, every time they're taken down. The photos that Jack did of us—the ones students brought with them to the hearing—keep showing up around campus, posted so relentlessly that the school eventually announces a ban on students posting flyers. But it doesn't stop.

And then in pre-calc on Wednesday, I get an email from someone at BuzzFeed. I'm frozen there, leaning over my messenger bag, looking at my phone's notification screen, which flickers black again. I was just getting a pen, and now I'm waiting to write Buzzfeed back when class is over.

That would be something else to leave my mother a message about. She'd tell me I was getting a little famous, I think. She might care about that. I wonder if she's gotten an email about the quiz I near-flunked on Tuesday.

They want to interview me for a story, the email says. They've heard about our situation.

"our situation" I type to the group. *we have a situation*

we have made a situation, Nevaeh says. Firecracker emoji from Katherine. I am still laughing at that when Taylor types, *have you emailed them back yet? email them back.*

There's a video of me circulating the internet. My furious speech. The idea of it being so far out of my control makes me nauseated, but I am fiercely glad that it's out there. That it caught the attention of a reporter, because enough people are talking about it. I want more people to watch, to understand my anger, to get angry not just on our behalf, but the whole shitty situation, from dress codes to slut shaming and all the lousiness in between.

I email BuzzFeed back. We haven't heard from the school, I type to Jessica at BuzzFeed, who tells me to call her when we find out. As if I am going to use my phone to call someone.

ridiculous, Nevaeh agrees.

At dinner, we all get the email at the same time. We'll hear the honor board's verdict on Friday morning.

Good luck! Jessica at BuzzFeed emails. *We're rooting for you. We hope you win!*

Same, Jessica at BuzzFeed. Same.

28

We don't wear our ensemble costumes the next time we go to the dean's office, though the temptation is strong.

Snow is falling again, the tiny flakes that look like diamonds, that land in your hair and immediately melt, if you've forgotten your hat again. Katherine pulls my mittens out of my pocket for me, and we crunch across the salted paths, the sky gray and hanging just inches above our heads. Nevaeh has hooked her arm through Taylor's, and all of us are feeling a loud kind of quiet, our hearts humming. Wishing we could be optimistic. Knowing we should be realistic, at the very least. Hope feels good, but that's why it hurts so much when you lose it.

Ms. Flores seems surprised that we're smiling when we arrive at the office. She's probably also surprised when we take off our coats and are fully clothed underneath.

Butterflies are in hot pursuit of one another in my stomach when I see the dean isn't in the conference room yet. I manage a smile at Ellory, who nods at me.

I wonder if he'll be angry about everything we've set in

motion—about the protests and the exposing of the conversation we had about my photo. The pushback against this whole ridiculous charge. When your opponent gets angry at you, it seems to me like you're on the right track.

When he walks in, the look on his face makes me think, *Oh yes, we are indeed on the right track.*

He asks us to stand. The members of the honor board remain seated.

"I don't need to tell you what grave mistakes you three have made," the dean says. And then he pauses, for an interminable moment. He's angry, yes, but now I also see that he's tired. "However, we have taken your words into account."

I hold my breath.

He looks at each of us in turn. "After a great deal of discussion," he says, "the immoral-conduct charge has been dropped. Until the end of the year, each of you will be on probation. And Saturday detention for the duration."

It's a lot. It's the rest of our school year. But they're safe. Katherine's and Nevaeh's acceptances are safe. I collapse back into my chair and put my forehead on the table. They're safe, and they're going to Tisch and Juilliard, and they're going to launch their careers, and that is the most important thing. They risked it all for me, and we are safe and that's what matters.

I lift my head and scrub the tears out of my eyes. Nevaeh is glowing, and Katherine looks so happy she's going to cry. I'll find a way to get the rest of the money for Angles. I have enough for the deposit. I have to talk to Carly—we have to make sure I still have my Angles spot, despite getting into this trouble. I have to still have my spot. I press my palm against my chest like I can stop it from breaking through my rib cage.

"Thank you, Dean Pembrooke," I say. "We are—"

"I'm not done," he says.

"What?" And then my heart stops, midpound.

"You'll forfeit the money you collected from your illicit endeavor." He smiles a dry little smile. "I'm sure you understand why it would be improper and frankly unethical for you to keep any of those funds."

I hear Katherine gasp. Nevaeh's hand grips mine. "Dean—" she says.

"You're dismissed," he says. He stands up, and he's gone from the room.

I don't move. They are safe, but . . .

It was all for nothing.

Ms. Warren smiles at me sympathetically, and Mr. Banerjee is frowning as he wraps his wide scarf around his neck. Ellory pauses by our chairs but doesn't say anything to me, though I hear Katherine say something to her, to the other two students on the honor board.

I can't move. Katherine puts her hand on my shoulder, shakes it a tiny bit. Nevaeh says, "Hon?"

"I'm fine," I say. "We did it."

Should this feel so terrible? We won. I know there's more in life than Angles, right? I know it was all worth it. It wasn't all for nothing. I shake myself, follow them out.

Outside, Katherine rushes to hug me. "I'm sorry," she says, and Nevaeh puts her face in my hair, her arms around me.

Jack and Taylor look at each other.

"No," Taylor says. "Do not say he charged you—"

"We won," I say. I'll keep saying it. "We won."

"Then what is it?" Jack asks.

"Maybe it's just not meant to be," I say, shrug, smile. "Angles," I explain. "The money's gone." We earned it, every dollar. We watched the balance grow, every single day, because we were putting on a hell of a show, and people wanted to see us. We worked hard and we were amazing.

Jack's face changes and he puts his arms around me, and I press my face into his shoulder for just a second, let myself wallow deep in self-pity. Then I push away.

"It's fine," I say. I'll keep saying that too. We won; it's fine.

My mother texts me, instead of calling back, and I look at it for a long time. Just one line.

are you coming home in May

yes, I tell her, typing out every letter slowly. She's calling it home again, I notice. I'm going home.

It takes her an hour to respond, but finally she sends, *ok*.

29

This story, our story, goes everywhere, and in between catching up on my homework and rehearsal and talking through my new future with Carly, I think about Angles. Carly got a note from the Angles program director—I am still heartily welcomed to join them for the summer in Milan. But, of course, that's not the issue. The money is. Once again. Most of the time I'm okay. Most of the time I'm happy to brainstorm with Carly about what's next. But I still haven't taken that photo of Madame Rabei off my bulletin board. It still hurts to have wanted something for so long, to have been so close but never close enough, despite everything we went through. How hard we tried.

I learn how to not totally freak out on the phone with all the nice people from the sites who have seen our video on the internet, who want to talk to us. The *New York Times* asks what it feels like to have been thrust into such an intense but incredibly relevant debate; the reporter at Slate asks what's next for us. What's next, most immediately, are school-wide assemblies to address the issue, in-class discussions, and an official movement to revise the dress code. The *Daily Mail* asks if we thought it was a witch hunt and if we could maybe send them lots of pictures of us in our burlesque costumes.

We say no, and their headline isn't very flattering.

We get a lot of emails, and some of them are terrible, and some of them are the familiar kinds of photos we could wallpaper a whole building with, but most of them we can read together on Thursday Twizzler night and high-five one another.

"Do you think I've peaked?" I ask my friends.

Katherine hits me on the head with a pillow.

Finally, Friday night.

We can't go out and celebrate not getting expelled, so we're taking over the common room, fourth floor, site of historical shenanigans and now a girls' dorm dance party. I'll start decorating as soon as I finish this text, but Jack is making it difficult.

He puts his arms around me and kisses the side of my neck and I smile, leaning into it, but I keep typing on my phone.

"I mean, not to nag—"

"Nagging a little bit," I say, my thumbs flying.

"Nagging a lot. Nagging obnoxiously. Nagging you with kisses." Behind my ear, the line of my jaw, tickling a little bit, so I shrug, laughing.

"I'm messaging Carly. Just one more second. Two more seconds." Another kiss on the side of my neck, softer, and I close my eyes, tilt my head. "You're the worst. Okay. Brief break." I turn and put my arms around his neck and I kiss his smile, and kiss him a lot, and his arms around my waist are so good.

Downstairs, apparently, there's a line of guys being signed in to come join us. Up here, Nevaeh is standing on a chair and

Taylor's got her calves, steadying her, saying something ridiculous, as she slaps Velcro tape on the walls, to drape them with the fabrics we used for our burlesque show. We have boxes and boxes of shimmering, shining decorations, and slowly the room is getting transformed. A little bit of nostalgia, already. Is it too soon? Happiness, then. I have to finish writing my message and help them.

I break the kiss, murmur, "Just one second, I promise," against his lips, and slap his butt as he goes to set up the Bluetooth speaker. Elsie is pushing couches to the walls, and people are pushing through the doors.

Thank you Carly, I type. *I really want to talk to you too. Been doing more research.* I've been reading about the Brooklyn Studio of Dance, and about Gibney in Manhattan. Classes, contacts. Maybe a way in.

She'll pour me tea on Sunday, and I'll explain that, yes, I really am still okay, and we'll brainstorm some more.

"Ready?" Jack says.

"Half a second, I swear," I say, as the music kicks on, and I laugh at Jack as he starts to very earnestly, but with great abandon, dance completely off-tempo.

I turn to find my bag, and the screen flashes again.

Joffrey San Francisco—*would like to extend an invitation to join our summer intensive in* . . . and I see the word *scholarship.*

The lights in the room go out, and the music is suddenly blasting, and my screen is so bright.

"You for-real ready?" Nevaeh says.

"Come on!" Katherine shouts.

"Put your phone away!" Taylor says in my ear. He holds out his hand, I slap it in his palm, and he slips it into his back pocket. And then the bass goes *boom*, and he grins at me, grabs my hand, and yanks me through the crowd that's already gathered, more people slipping through the doors every minute. Someone pulls up the window, and Zoe's arms are around my waist, her hug fierce, the music not stopping.

"Oh my god, no, I am not going to do a striptease," I say to Ellory, who grins at me and says, "I wish I could have seen you all," and I don't hug her but I want to. We smile big at each other.

Jack's shimmy around me, hands in the air, is the worst, and my stomach hurts from laughing. "You're a terrible dancer," I yell in his ear, and he yells back, "Isn't it great?"

Katherine is explaining her Hula-Hoop tricks to a group of students, and Nevaeh is almost not joking about getting her fedora. Taylor says, "My act would have *killed*."

He might come back in an hour wearing his costume. Katherine might go get her Hula-Hoop. I could change into my tutu, if the mood strikes me. It's still hanging on the back of the door. I hope Nevaeh comes swaggering back in the suit.

We're all going to be here dancing until the first curfew bell, maybe until the warning, maybe until the RA comes and turns the lights on, but she's over near the couches, waving her hands, telling a story to Grace and Shima and half our audience from the second show.

The urge to get my phone from Taylor is mighty—could I do Joffrey San Francisco and then head to New York? Could I do anything? I could do anything.

I thought Angles was my only way into the modern dance world that isn't enthusiastic about a body like mine. But Mohadesa Rabei didn't go to Angles—she became the director of the program, the lead dancer. And I'm going to meet her one day.

"I've learned the shopping cart!" Jack yells, slipping through the crowd to where Nevaeh, Katherine, and I are dancing.

"Don't you dare," I yell.

"I swear I had nothing to do with this," Taylor shouts.

My stomach hurts so much from laughing. And we don't stop dancing for hours.

30

G uess what!" I tell Carly, flinging her door open on Sunday, dancing through it, throwing myself on the sofa, and kicking up my feet. "You'll never guess!"

"I thought I'd be the only one with news," she says. She looks delighted.

I've been holding on to the Joffrey offer since Friday because I wanted to see her face, and it's the best when I tell her.

"Oh, Addie!" she says. She actually throws her arms around me and squeezes me, rubs my back, smiles at me with tears in her eyes, then squeezes me hard again.

"Carly!" I say. "Oh my gosh, Carly."

"Oh, honey, I'm so proud of you."

"Obviously." I squeeze her back hard, and we're both laughing a little breathlessly, halfway to crying.

"You are just—" She shakes her head and pats me on the shoulder again.

"I know, right?"

She shakes her head again. "So this is going to be the best day ever. And we are going to have a lot to talk about."

The grin on her face is so big.

And then she tells me.

Bisma and Kaitlyn and Riley and Logan and Leslie and Zoe have started a Kickstarter campaign. A campaign to fund my summer at Angles.

"They told me they were going to do it," she says. "I didn't say no. The goal is eight thousand dollars. And Addie? It's already a third of the way there."

Carly is still smiling so wide. And . . . I don't know what to say. It's amazing and thoughtful and kind, of course, but a hollow sense of wrongness has opened up inside me. So many people needing so many things in this world, and we're asking for money for this? It's why I never wanted to do it in the beginning. I want to earn my way.

"Well?" Carly says, maybe sensing my ambivalence. "What do you think?"

"They are the best, those kids," I say truthfully. "I just . . . I don't know."

Carly nods. "I understand. Think about it. Look at the site."

Before I leave, she gives me the biggest hug, one that says she's proud of me no matter what I decide and where I end up.

Later, sitting outside in the roofless gazebo where we first started hatching the plan for Dirty Little Secret, I take out my phone and force myself to look at the site, even though it gives me that strange, hollow feeling in my stomach. The feeling worsens when I see how much money is in there. So many donors! From the looks of it, the donations are all small, five and ten dollars, mostly.

Then I start reading the comments, and the feeling in my stomach begins to shift.

Heard about you while waiting in line for coffee, you're an inspiration . . . you can have my coffee money today.

I'm also a fat dancer. Saw your IG feed. You can MOVE. Good luck in Milan!

I got suspension for wearing an off the shoulder shirt & the soccer team practices with no shirt at all. Thx for calling this kind of thing out.

The comments go on and on.

"Holy crap," I say.

This is my future I'm looking at. *All* of our futures. This is the kind of world we live in, where sometimes magical things happen and good wins because evil is bad, and I am pretty sure I am going to fall over and die in just a second here, reading all these wonderful things. Knowing that there are people out there who understand, who share what they have because that's what communities do—communities of artists, of dancers, of people who get it and want to give back.

I want to make a difference as a fat dancer. And I want to put my mark on the art as someone extraordinary, and talented, and wildly creative and innovative and new. But here is proof that we've already made a difference to people in another sort of way. And that is so much bigger than any other part of this.

———

By Wednesday it's funded; by Thursday I say, "What am I supposed to do with all this money?" On Friday there's a plan.

31

There's a row of rainbow-frosted cupcakes in the middle of the table, each one of them has a match in it, and Taylor and Katherine are racing to get them all lit before the other ones go out so that Nevaeh can take a snapshot. And since I've already burned my fingers twice on the last set of matches, I have been banned from helping, and Nevaeh threatens to send me across the coffee shop to a table in the corner if I don't stop laughing because I keep blowing them out.

"Yes!" Katherine yells, and I clap when Taylor gets the last one lit. Nevaeh is fast on the photo button, capturing the flames before they flicker out, the happiness on my face, the photo we've been dying to upload with the caption we've been waiting to use, hashtag met the Kickstarter goal, hashtag blew the goal out of the water, hashtag wait until you see what we're going to do next. Nevaeh rejects all my ideas for hashtags because she has much better ones, because she's the internet genius, the marketing genius, the make-it-viral person.

"Hashtag where the hell is Jack?" Nevaeh says, typing on her phone.

"On his way," I tell her, and he's coming with his laptop under his arm. He wanted to show it to us in person. Taylor doesn't want to wait until he arrives to start eating the cupcakes, but I save mine for him and slide over in the booth when he arrives, smelling like snow and cold air, his cheeks red and his eyes glitteringly happy as he wiggles out of all his gear.

Nevaeh makes grabby hands at the laptop. "Show it, show it, give it," she says.

"Hello, it's so nice to see you," he says. To me, he says, "Have you had anything to eat? How's your day been?"

"Show it to us before I whack you with this cupcake," I tell him.

He stands and reaches into his backpack, turns to all of us. Nevaeh reaches across the table and takes my hand. He opens the laptop and spins it around.

My picture. I'm leaping through the air, looking like I can fly. Like I'm flying. And underneath, the quote, bold and strong.

Don't shape yourself to fit the world. Make the world shape itself to fit you.

The Adeleina Elizabeth Grant Dance Scholarship Fund

He's finished the website.

We're putting the money back into the world, giving the money to the dancers who deserve the kind of financial support I was so desperate for.

My mother brags to her friends that we're doing important things, the four of us, she tells me.

I want to do important things.

"Here's to the scholarship!" Nevaeh says, toasting with her mocha.

"And to leveling the playing field a little bit," Katherine says. "For girls who are fighting the odds."

"And who are playing to win," Taylor says.

"To Addie," Jack says, snugging up against me.

"To all of you jerks who keep making me cry," I say. "I'm eating the last cupcake."

EPILOGUE

I'm sweating in my graduation gown. I'm sweating because it's gloriously hot, but also because I'm standing up onstage in front of everyone—teachers and administrator-type people and a whole sea of graduates, like me. My whole class. The kids who supported us and the kids who laughed at us and the kids who had no idea what was going on, because their own lives come fast and furious too.

Katherine and Nevaeh and Taylor and Jack are all out there somewhere, seated at the whims of the alphabet, and my voice is hoarse from screaming for them when their names were called, when they walked across the stage. I'm sure I heard my mother's own hooting and hollering from the back, where all the parents are sitting, fanning themselves with their programs and checking their phones and looking bored.

I walked, too, got my diploma, and then I was surprised when Grace—our valedictorian and the only other full-scholarship student—called me back up onstage.

"You might have heard the story of the underground burlesque club here at Lakeshore," Grace says now, and the audience laughs.

I cover my mouth with my hand, but I'm grinning. "And how three senior dancers started a conversation on campus. Made a lot of us wish we could be as cool."

She grins at me, and I am flushed sunburn red—I can feel it across my face and down my neck. The audience cheers, and I clap my hands over my cheeks, grinning, shaking my head. This is so weird, and so wonderful.

"We thought it was only appropriate," Grace says, turning to me, "that you be the one to lead us in the removal and tossing of these unflattering hats."

There's a ripple of laughter.

"No!" I say, laughing too.

"Yes!" she says, and urges me to the podium. "Just ask them to 'Please stand and applaud for the graduating class,'" she tells me, low.

"Okay," I say into the microphone. "Let's do this." Cheers break out. "On the count of three: Please stand and applaud for the graduating class!"

The hats fly into the air. And then my choked gasp is caught and magnified over the sound of the microphone as, in a single coordinated movement, half the class—more?—have reached down and whipped off their gowns, all of them throwing them in the air, all of them in bikinis and bathing suits and all kinds of clothes that violate all the dress codes, and then there is a roar that blows the top of my head off, and a thundering cheer that feels like every beat of my heart.

All of us, in every type of body, brave and mostly naked and cheering under the sun, hugging, happy to be out of the sweaty black robes and beautiful, all of them. I had no idea this was going to happen.

"Oh my god!" I shout into the microphone. "To the greatest senior class that ever was!" And they all erupt and swarm their friends and family sitting behind them, onto the lawn, down to the lake, the cheers and laughter as bright as today.

I unzip my own gown—I've got a dress underneath, unlike almost everyone else—and push my way through the crowd to find my mother, who throws her arms around me and gives me a huge bouquet of red roses. Her new boyfriend, whose name I can't remember, smiles kindly and tells me that I was good up there, and I kind of like him.

"We'll meet you at the restaurant, honey," my mother says, putting her arms around me. "Oh, you look so slim in this dress."

"Thanks, Mom," I tell her.

"Benny's paying!" she whispers too loudly in my ear. "So the place is fancy."

"Thank you, Benny!" I say, and he actually blushes, puts his arm around my mother, and squishes her tight.

"Bring your friends!" my mother says, and I spin around to see the three of them converging on us, and we're crying and babbling and laughing and big messes, because we've graduated. We've graduated!

We made it and it's wonderful and it's the end of everything.

"You didn't tell me about the whole surprise," I say to Katherine.

"It would not have been a surprise, Addie," she says.

"How the hell am I supposed to do this without you?" I say, pushing my face into Nevaeh's neck.

"You won't ever have to," Katherine says. "We're in this for life."

"We'll strip at your wedding," Taylor says.

"If you don't outlive me, I'll strip at your funerals," I tell them.

"I will follow you to the end, my siblings, my co-captains—" Nevaeh sings out.

"Come on, come on, come on," I say, taking their hands, dragging them to dance in circles in the sunshine like goofy new graduates who know they have absolutely everything in front of them. "Let's all go get famous!"

THE END

ACKNOWLEDGMENTS

First: Thank you to all the powerful, fierce fat girls and femmes who are taking the world by storm. Addie is the person I wish I could have been as a fat teenager.

It's not your job and never should have been, but you are the kids who are changing the world, and we don't deserve you.

Thank you always to the wonderful Marianna Baer and Lynn Weingarten, for making this book everything it was meant to be.

The bits of this book I managed could not have been written without Shyamala Parthasarathy, Loren Taylor, and Meagan Black. Thank you for the yelling, the brainstorming, the writing sessions, for being on my side. I love your brilliant amazing bonkers brains and you.

Thank you to Kate Farrell at Holt, who loves Addie as much as I do, and whose insight made this a better book in every way.

Thank you to Cheryl Pientka for always having my back.

Thank you to all the folks at Holt who helped make the final product perfect: Sarah Chassé, Lelia Mander, and Jie Yang. Any mistakes in the book are mine.

Thank you to Liz Dresner, Mallory Grigg, and to the amazingly talented Prashanti Aswani for the stunning cover that made me cry.

Thank you to the talented writers and friends who inspire me, give me space to write and space to complain and space to be myself, including Tania de Rozario, Rachel Hartman, Karen Meisner, Monique van den Berg, and Yilin Wang; to grad school friends both silver and gold; and to all my imaginary internet friends, from the OLJ crowd to the newest of palm-top computer friends. Thank you for being hilarious, for being the kind of people I look up to, for cheering me on even when I've felt like I didn't deserve it, and for keeping me sane in a world that is less so.

And finally, thank you to brilliant, extraordinary Kelsey, who makes it all worthwhile and tells the worst jokes. I love you always.

I made it! And I believe in you too.